CHRISTO

THE CASE OF THE BENEVOLENT BOOKIE

CHRISTOPHER BUSH was born Charlie Christmas Bush in Norfolk in 1885. His father was a farm labourer and his mother a milliner. In the early years of his childhood he lived with his aunt and uncle in London before returning to Norfolk aged seven, later winning a scholarship to Thetford Grammar School.

As an adult, Bush worked as a schoolmaster for 27 years, pausing only to fight in World War One, until retiring aged 46 in 1931 to be a full-time novelist. His first novel featuring the eccentric Ludovic Travers was published in 1926, and was followed by 62 additional Travers mysteries. These are all to be republished by Dean Street Press.

Christopher Bush fought again in World War Two, and was elected a member of the prestigious Detection Club. He died in 1973.

CHRISTOPHER BUSH

THE CASE OF THE BENEVOLENT BOOKIE

With an introduction
by Curtis Evans

DEAN STREET PRESS

INTRODUCTION

RING OUT THE OLD, RING IN THE NEW
CHRISTOPHER BUSH AND MYSTERY FICTION IN THE FIFTIES

"Mr. Bush has an urbane and intelligent way of dealing with mystery which makes his work much more attractive than the stampeding sensationalism of some of his rivals."
—Rupert Crofts-Cooke (acclaimed author of the Leo Bruce detective novels)

NEW fashions in mystery fiction were decidedly afoot in the 1950s, as authors increasingly turned to sensationalistic tales of international espionage, hard-boiled sex and violence, and psychological suspense. Yet there indubitably remained, seemingly imperishable and eternal, what Anthony Boucher, dean of American mystery reviewers, dubbed the "conventional type of British detective story." This more modestly decorous but still intriguing and enticing mystery fare was most famously and lucratively embodied by Crime Queen Agatha Christie, who rang in the new decade and her Golden Jubilee as a published author with the classic detective novel that was promoted as her fiftieth mystery: *A Murder Is Announced* (although this was in fact a misleading claim, as this tally also included her short story collections). Also representing the traditional British detective story during the 1950s were such crime fiction stalwarts (all of them Christie contemporaries and, like the Queen of Crime, longtime members of the Detection Club) as Edith Caroline Rivett (E.C.R Lorac and Carol Carnac), E.R. Punshon, Cecil John Charles Street (John Rhode and Miles Burton) and Christopher Bush. Punshon and Rivett passed away in the Fifties, pens still brandished in their hands, if you will, but Street and Bush, apparently indefatigable, kept at crime throughout the decade, typically publishing in both the United Kingdom and the United States two books a year (Street with both of his pseudonyms).

Not to be outdone even by Agatha Christie, Bush would celebrate his own Golden Jubilee with his fiftieth mystery, *The Case of the Russian Cross*, in 1957—and this was done, in contrast with Christie, without his publishers having to resort to any creative accounting. *Cross* is the fiftieth Christopher Bush Ludovic Travers detective novel reprinted by Dean Street Press in this, the Spring of 2020, the hundredth anniversary of the dawning of the Golden Age of detective fiction, following, in this latest installment, *The Case of the Counterfeit Colonel* (1952), *The Case of the Burnt Bohemian* (1953), *The Case of The Silken Petticoat* (1953), *The Case of the Red Brunette* (1954), *The Case of the Three Lost Letters* (1954), *The Case of the Benevolent Bookie* (1955), *The Case of the Amateur Actor* (1955), *The Case of the Extra Man* (1956) and *The Case of the Flowery Corpse* (1956).

Not surprisingly, given its being the occasion of Christopher Bush's Golden Jubilee, *The Case of the Russian Cross* met with a favorable reception from reviewers, who found the author's wry dedication especially ingratiating: "The author, having discovered that this is his fiftieth novel of detection, dedicates it in sheer astonishment to HIMSELF." Writing as Francis Iles, the name under which he reviewed crime fiction, Bush's Detection Club colleague Anthony Berkeley, himself one of the great Golden Age innovators in the genre, commented, "I share Mr. Bush's own surprise that *The Case of the Russian Cross* should be his fiftieth book; not so much at the fact itself as at the freshness both of plot and writing which is still as notable with fifty up as it was in in his opening overs. There must be many readers who still enjoy a straightforward, honest-to-goodness puzzle, and here it is." The late crime writer Anthony Lejeune, who would be admitted to the Detection Club in 1963, for his part cheered, "Hats off to Christopher Bush....[L]ike his detective, [he] is unostentatious but always absolutely reliable." Alan Hunter, who recently had published his first George Gently mystery and at the time was being lauded as the "British Simenon," offered similarly praiseful words, pronouncing of *The*

Case of the Russian Cross that Bush's sleuth Ludovic Travers "continues to be a wholly satisfying creation, the characters are intriguing and the plot full of virility. . . . the only trace of long-service lies in the maturity of the treatment."

The high praise for Bush's fiftieth detective novel only confirmed (if resoundingly) what had become clear from reviews of earlier novels from the decade: that in Britain Christopher Bush, who had turned sixty-five in 1950, had become a Grand Old Man of Mystery, an Elder Statesman of Murder. Bush's *The Case of the Three Lost Letters*, for example, was praised by Anthony Berkeley as "a model detective story on classical lines: an original central idea, with a complicated plot to clothe it, plenty of sound, straightforward detection by a mellowed Ludovic Travers and never a word that is not strictly relevant to the story"; while reviewer "Christopher Pym" (English journalist and author Cyril Rotenberg) found the same novel a "beautifully quiet, close-knit problem in deduction very fairly presented and impeccably solved." Berkeley also highly praised Bush's *The Case of the Burnt Bohemian*, pronouncing it "yet another sound piece of work . . . in that, alas!, almost extinct genre, the real detective story, with Ludovic Travers in his very best form."

In the United States Bush was especially praised in smaller newspapers across the country, where, one suspects, traditional detection most strongly still held sway. "Bush is one of the soundest of the English craftsmen in this field," declared Ben B. Johnston, an editor at the *Richmond Times Dispatch*, in his review of *The Case of the Burnt Bohemian*, while Lucy Templeton, doyenne of the *Knoxville Sentinel* (the first female staffer at that Tennessee newspaper, Templeton, a freshly minted graduate of the University of Tennessee, had been hired as a proofreader back in 1904), enthusiastically avowed, in her review of *The Case of the Flowery Corpse*, that the novel was "the best mystery novel I have read in the last six months." Bush "has always told a good story with interesting backgrounds and rich characterization," she added admiringly. Another southern reviewer, one "M." of the *Montgomery Advertiser*, deemed *The Case of the Amateur Actor* "another Travers mystery to delight the most critical of a reader audience," concluding in inimitable American lingo, "it's a swell story." Even Anthony Boucher, who in the Fifties hardly could be termed an unalloyed admirer of conventional British detection, from his prestigious post at the *New York Times Books Review* afforded words of praise to a number of Christopher Bush mysteries from the decade, including the cases of the *Benevolent Bookie* ("a provocative puzzle"), the *Amateur Actor* ("solid detective interest"), the *Flowery Corpse* ("many small ingenuities of detection") and, but naturally, the *Russian Cross* ("a pretty puzzle"). In his own self-effacing fashion, it seems that Ludovic Travers had entered the pantheon of Great Detectives, as another American commentator suggested in a review of Bush's *The Case of The Silken Petticoat*:

> Although Ludovic Travers does not possess the esoteric learning of Van Dine's Philo Vance, the rough and ready punch of Mickey Spillane's Mike Hammer, the Parisian [sic!] touch of Agatha Christie's Hercule Poirot, the appetite and orchids of Rex Stout's Nero Wolfe, the suave coolness of The Falcon or the eerie laugh and invisibility of The Shadow, he does have good qualities—especially the ability to note and interpret clues and a dogged persistence in remembering and following up an episode he could not understand. These paid off in his solution of *The Case of The Silken Petticoat*.

In some ways Christopher Bush, his traditionalism notwithstanding, attempted with his Fifties Ludovic Travers mysteries to keep up with the tenor of rapidly changing times. As owner of the controlling interest in the Broad Street Detective Agency, Ludovic Travers increasingly comes to resemble an American private investigator rather than the gentleman amateur detective he had been in the 1930s; and the novels in which he appears reflect some of the jaded cynicism of post-World War Two American hard-boiled crime fiction. *The Case of the Red Brunette*, one of my favorite examples from this batch of Bushes, looks at civic corruption in provincial England in a case concerning a town counsellor who dies in an apparent "badger game" or "honey trap" gone fatally wrong ("a web of mystery skillfully spun" noted Pat McDermott of Iowa's *Quad City Times*), while in *The Case of the Three Lost Letters*, Travers finds himself having to explain to his phlegmatic wife Bernice the pink lipstick strains on his collar (incurred strictly in the line of duty, of course). Travers also pays homage to the popular, genre altering Inspector Maigret novels of Georges Simenon in *The Case of Red Brunette*, when he decides that he will "try to get a feel of the city [of Mainford]: make a Maigret-like tour and achieve some kind of background. . . ."

Christopher Bush finally decided that Travers could manage entirely without his longtime partner in crime solving, the wily and calculatingly avuncular Chief Superintendent George Wharton, whom at times Travers, in the tradition of American hard-boiled crime fiction, appears positively to dislike. "I generally admire and respect Wharton, but there are times when he annoys me almost beyond measure," Travers confides in *The Case of the Amateur Actor*. "There are even moments, as when he assumes that cheap and leering superiority, when I can suddenly hate him." George Wharton appropriately makes his final, brief appearance in the Bush oeuvre in *The Case of the Russian Cross*, where Travers allows that despite their differences, the "Old General" is "the man who'd become in most ways my oldest friend."

"Ring out the old, ring in the new" may have been the motto of many when it came to mid-century mystery fiction, but as another saying goes, what once was old eventually becomes sparklingly new again. The truth of the latter adage is proven by this shining new set of Christopher Bush reissues. "Just like old crimes," vintage mystery fans may sigh contentedly, as once again they peruse the pages of a Bush, pursuing murderous malefactors in the ever pleasant company of Ludovic Travers, all the while armed with the happy knowledge that a butcher's dozen of thirteen of Travers' investigations yet remains to be reissued.

Curtis Evans

PART I
THE MISSING LADY

CHAPTER I
THE EARLY CLIENT

IT WAS the February of 1953. You remember it, even if you weren't involved in actual disaster from flood and tempest. All the winter had been bad, with intermittent blizzards and plenty of fog, but just towards the middle of the month there had been a bit of a respite. A thaw had set in and roads that had been blocked soon cleared, and there was even an occasional glimmer of sun. But the sun meant fog at night and its persistence till well into the morning.

As I looked out of the window at about half-past seven I was thinking that the fog was far from thick. The early weather report had said it would clear early after a period of patchiness, and it seemed to me that I wasn't going to have any need to start earlier than usual for the office of the Broad Street Detective Agency. Norris, my general manager, was in Birmingham on an insurance job and, as usual, I was handling things till his return. And that, luckily, was to be that afternoon. Things were rather quiet except for routine work, but I liked to get in by half-past eight. You never knew what might arrive by the first post.

I'd made the early tea and Bernice had rung down for service breakfasts. I picked up the morning papers and was just about to look through them when the telephone bell rang. It was the duty man at the office.

"Sorry to disturb you, sir, but a Lord Tynworth wants to see you very urgently."

The name conveyed nothing to me. I asked him to repeat it, and I still hadn't heard it before. Or had I? Something very vague was stirring at the far back of my mind.

"Put him through," I said, "if he's still on the line."

A few seconds and I was hearing the client's voice.

It wasn't what I might unfacetiously call a noble or peer-like voice: just an ordinary workaday voice whose owner might have been anything in the lower middle-class brackets.

"Tynworth here," he said. "Sorry to be such a nuisance to you at this ungodly hour."

"No nuisance at all," I said. "My name's Travers, if you haven't been already told. I gathered you had some urgent business."

"Yes," he said. "I feel I must talk to you personally. How soon can you make it?"

"In half an hour?"

"Not earlier? You see, I'm flying to America this morning and I mayn't have all that time. The fog might mean a diversion to some other airport."

"I don't think that'll happen," I told him consolingly. "The weather report gave no hint of it."

"You're not by any chance going to your office by car?"

"No reason why I shouldn't," I said. "Why do you ask?"

"Well, I wondered if you could drive me from there to the Airport Building. I know it's an imposition, but we could have our talk on the way." I heard him click his tongue annoyedly. "The fact is, everything has to be done in such a damnable hurry. Things have happened so suddenly that I still don't know if I'm on my head or my heels."

"I've got a better idea than meeting at the office," I said. "Where are you now?"

"Liverpool Street Station."

"Right," I said. "I'll come straight there. See you outside the main entrance."

I reported to Bernice something of what had happened, grabbed hat and overcoat and gloves and made for the garage. Inside fifteen minutes I was drawing up outside the station. A man was waiting there. He was about five foot eight and looked about forty. He was wearing a brown felt hat and a heavy tweed overcoat, and a bulging portfolio case was under his arm.

"Lord Tynworth?"

"Yes," he said, and his free hand went out.

"I'm Ludovic Travers. Sit alongside me, will you?"

I opened the door and he got in. I moved the car on through the patchy fog towards Moorgate Street to avoid the traffic as far as the Bank. I didn't feel too happy about driving with one part of my mind while the other part was trying to absorb details of a probable case.

"This business of yours," I began. "Exactly what is it?"

"Something most damnably private," he said. "That's why I didn't like talking it over in a taxi. And why I as good as asked you to drive me."

"Why not?" I said. "You're in a hurry, I have this car and here we are. Very private business, you say. Let me assure you that with us it'll stay private."

"I'm sure it will. You see, it happens to concern my wife. I'd intended to spend all yesterday in town and then I was rung confidentially by my sister-in-law to say she'd gone."

"I don't get you. By *gone*, do you mean that she's left you?"

"Yes," he said. "And she did it surreptitiously. Practically in the dead of night. The night before last. She must have had her things packed unknown to anyone. I came to town in the late afternoon intending to spend all yesterday clearing up certain matters and doing some shopping, and then early yesterday morning I was rung at the hotel by my sister-in-law. I went back at once. I was scared she might have taken the boy, but she hasn't."

I slowed the car and drew up just short of the Bank.

"Before we go any farther, there's one thing I must make absolutely clear to you. If this has anything to do with divorce, then we can't handle it. That's something about which we never make an exception."

"I assure you it's nothing whatever to do with divorce," he told me earnestly. "I want her found—nothing more. Why I'm applying to you is because you were strongly recommended by a friend. A chap called Balfour. Perhaps you don't remember him. He mentioned it yesterday, but I didn't somehow like the idea of a private detective agency. No offence, I hope."

"No offence at all. But what made you change your mind?"

"Don't know," he said. "Perhaps because I realised I just damn-well had to do something besides what Balfour himself will be trying to do. I didn't really make up my mind till I was virtually at Liverpool Street. I was worrying about any scandal, and tact and so on, and then I remembered Balfour had said I needn't worry about that if I employed you people."

I'd missed one green light, but now it came on again.

"And you want us to find your wife."

"That's it exactly. Once you've found her, then you're through. But I ought to warn you that she'll have covered her tracks. It isn't going to be easy. We ourselves haven't a clue."

"Tell me some more," I said, and he began telling me more. He was worried: I'd known that from the first minute I'd clapped eyes on him. When I'd stopped the car and half swivelled round as I told him we didn't handle divorce cases I'd really been seeing him for the first time—seeing, that is, as far as the inside of a car and a devilishly dark morning permitted. He wasn't bad-looking, I'd thought, even if the face was a bit pale. In profile it was quite a good face with a rather hooked nose and what looked like a tiny mole alongside it. His hair was dark, and the desert-rat kind of moustache gave him rather a raddled or rakish look. But it wasn't a hangover look: it was the look of a man who'd had a bad twenty-four hours.

"Excuse me if I'm blunt," he said, "but there's nothing to this Lord Tynworth business. My father was a Labour peer. My only brother was killed and I came in for the title. I'm a racehorse owner and trainer, by the way, at Herndown in Essex. In a very small way. I'd have dropped the title long ago if my wife hadn't been so against it. A bit incongruous for her to have been Lady Tynworth and me just plain Tom Bolfray."

There'd been a whiff of something peculiar about that heavy tweed coat and I hadn't been able to place it. Now I knew it was just a faint scent of the stables.

"I mentioned that," he said as we began circling St. Paul's, "because the whole thing's being hushed up. No one knows except my sister-in-law and that's why enquiries can't be made openly. Even my sister-in-law mustn't on any account be told that I've consulted you, for instance."

The fog was quite thick in patches and it was hard to follow what he was saying and discern any sort of logic. There was no particular logic in my own question.

"You been married long?"

"Only three years," he said, and the shake of the head seemed to have in it a certain regret. "I'd known her for years. Used to work at a place near her home. Later on she'd been singing with a well-known band and doing quite well at it. I still can't think why she agreed to marry me."

"You don't think she's going back to this singing or crooning or whatever they call it?"

"Maybe," he said. "Or to some other man—not that that matters at the moment. That isn't why I want her found. I've had suspicions for quite a time, and if she wants another man— well, she can have him, provided I keep the boy. But that isn't the real point. The real point is that she's taken certain valuables with her to which she had no claim. She's got to be found before she disposes of them."

"Valuables?" I'd pricked my ears at that. "What sort of valuables? Mink coats and things?"

That last, as I knew afterwards, was a stupid question, but I just wasn't myself. That drive through the heart of the city in patchy fog and with slow-moving traffic was a nightmare.

"Mink coats!" The tone was bitter. "We don't run to that kind of thing. The only mink coat was her own. It was just valuables."

He took a quick look at his wrist-watch.

"But there's really no need to go into that. That'll be for Balfour to handle later."

"No use employing us if you don't trust us," I told him.

"It isn't that," he said. "I'm trusting you quite a lot. All I'm trying to do is simplify everything. The valuables are not your side of the problem. It's locating her that matters. Once she's found, we'll know where they are."

"Right," I said. "That clears that up. All we have to do is find your wife. And where do we go for enquiries?"

"Sorry again," he said, "but that's for you to work out. No one at Herndown is to be questioned. Everyone, except my sister-in-law, will think she's away staying with friends. That'll last at least till I get back from the States in about a week's time. Sorry about all that, and I do realise the difficulties for you. But I'm prepared to pay."

"It won't be cheap," I told him bluntly.

He shrugged his shoulders.

"One doesn't expect it to be. Meanwhile, what about a retaining fee? A hundred pounds be enough?"

"Ample," I said. I was crossing over at the foot of Ludgate Hill and that was all I could say till I had a clear road again. Out of the corner of my eye I saw him opening that portfolio case of his. A bus held us up, and as he closed the case I caught a glimpse of a pair of green-striped pyjamas and what looked like some documents. He had taken something out but I hadn't seen what. Then we were going round the now stationary bus, and from there on till Trafalgar Square we had the best of luck with the lights.

"And another hundred pounds to carry on with," he said, and reached across me and put two bundles of pound notes in the locker in front of me. "That be enough till I get back?"

"Plenty," I said. "What about a receipt?"

"Anything will do," he said. "Just a scribbled note. We're honourable sort of people or we shouldn't be here."

He seemed worried about the time, and as the lights turned red at the foot of Whitehall I wrote a quick receipt on a page of my notebook. He was opening that portfolio again and hunting feverishly through it. Something seemed to be lost. Then he smiled relievedly.

"Cloak-room ticket," he told me. "Thought for a moment I'd left the damn thing behind. All my stuff's parked at the Airport Building."

"You have a photograph of your wife?"

"Of course," he said. "You'll want that."

He brought out his wallet from the inside breast pocket.

"Here's one I always carry about with me. Don't think I'll want it now. It's pretty good of her."

It was an enlarged snapshot, mounted inside a stiff paper folder. I couldn't look at it till we were held up again by Victoria Station. It was tricky driving round as far as the Grosvenor Hotel, and then the fog was suddenly almost gone. I could just see the Airport Building.

"If we do find your wife, what's to be done about it?"

"Ah, that," he said, and brought out the wallet again. "You don't really do anything. You keep her under observation till you get a reply to this message which you'll have inserted in the Personal Column of *The Daily Telegraph*. This is it."

I had a look at it while the lights held us up for the last time.

HENRY—Glad to report the lost found—ALFRED.

Just enough, I thought, for one line of print. I moved the car on and asked what then.

"The morning the message appears Henry will ring you," he said. "He'll say, 'This is Henry Balfour.' That's how you'll know him. You then tell him just where my wife is and he'll take over from there. He and the solicitors will know how to handle her."

We were at the Airport Building and he was getting out of the car. I had half a dozen questions I still wanted to put to him, but now it seemed too late.

"Sorry to have had to be so mysterious," he said, "but I'm in the devil of a hurry. Also Henry's meeting me here. I rang him to say I'd taken his advice about you."

He half turned, his hand lifted as if to wave a goodbye, and then he turned back.

"I'm more than grateful to you. Put everything on the bill, including the ride. Thanks again."

A quick wave of the hand and he was gone. I was still so full of questions and hedged about with such a feeling of unreality that I hadn't even time to find the words to wish him a pleasant trip. I watched him go through the doors; and then I was suddenly fingering my glasses—a nervous trick of mine when I'm at a mental loss or faced with the unexpected. But now it was more like an involuntary attempt to get back to reality. It had been, as I said, rather like a nightmare, with moments of coherence and lucidity. Now the whole thing mightn't have happened at all, except that I was where I was, and that in the locker in front of me were two bundles of pound notes.

I pocketed the notes and moved the car on. I though I'd go to Broad Street by way of the Embankment. And then I had an idea—just a sudden burgeoning of that insatiable curiosity which with me is never really dormant. What I did was park the car in a side street and cross the road to where I could watch those doors through which Tynworth had gone. I wanted to run my eye over that Henry Balfour whose fingers seemed to be pretty deep in the Tynworth pie.

I watched for five minutes and then knew the idea was hopeless. Henry Balfour might have arrived before us. If he hadn't, then how was I to know him from the various people who were going in and out? My only hope was that Tynworth might come out with him. But I abandoned even that hope after another minute or two. At any moment the coach would be leaving for the airport, and I was late for the office. And I'd had no breakfast.

Bertha Munney, our secretary-receptionist, had some breakfast sent in, and over it I dealt with the correspondence. It was almost eleven o'clock when my desk was clear and I had a chance to sit back and think. I checked the two hundred pounds and put them in the safe. Bertha would take them to the bank in her lunch-hour, and when they went it seemed as if I would be parting with everything tangible—except a photograph—that could connect me with that nightmare interview of the earlier morning. So I tried to think back and began making notes of all that I could remember. When I'd finished there wasn't a thing into which I could really get my teeth. Just how were enquiries to begin?

I didn't for the moment know, so I tried another approach— trying to follow the course of events as far as they'd concerned Tynworth himself. Then my eye fell on the reference books in front of me and I reached out for *Who's Who* and *Debrett*. A quarter of an hour and I could digest what I'd read. I'd got just what I wanted, at least as a beginning: something of a background for Tynworth and that wife who was missing.

James Bolfray was born in 1884. He married a Margaret Waterford in 1911 and he had two sons. James Waterford Bolfray, the elder, was born in 1912 and he died in a plane crash in 1944, leaving a widow, Moira, née Finder, whom he had married two years before. There was no issue. The other son, Thomas, was born in 1914 and he married a Sarah Finder in 1949. As both Moira and Sarah were described as daughters of the late Maurice Finder and Kathleen Finder, it could be assumed that the brothers had married two sisters.

As for James Bolfray the elder, he was for a time Member of Parliament for Tynworth North. Ramsay Macdonald made him a peer and he took Tynworth as his title. His wife died in 1944 and he died two years later. Since his elder son had died in 1944, the Thomas Bolfray whom I had seen that morning became Baron Tynworth of Tynworth.

So much for that, but what I had to find out was if the first Baron had had any money and, if so, where it came from. Labour peers are of all sorts, the wealthy and the comparatively impoverished, but in this case there had been the mention of valuables. They didn't belong to the wife who'd taken them, so the question was: Where had they come from?

"My father was a Labour peer," Tynworth had told me, and the tone and context had been such as to convey the fact that he'd not been a moneyed man. As for himself, there was nothing of Eton and Balliol about him. All he had had was the assurance and fluency—both a bit nervous owing to the circumstances—of any business man or, I imagined, the owner-trainer of racehorses, which in a small way he'd admitted he was. Why he was flying to America I couldn't begin to guess—not that that mattered. What I had to try to do was to find out where the valuables in question came from. If I could get a line on them, the knowledge might possibly lead to a knowledge of the whereabouts of the vanished wife.

Luckily I had a contact, or so I hoped, on one of the big dailies, so I buzzed through to Bertha and asked her to try to get Harold Harstead, even if she had to track him down at his private address. After that I couldn't settle to what I'd thought of before—trying to look at things from Tynworth's own angle. Instead I was feeling vaguely annoyed. I was beginning to regard myself as a first-class fool for accepting a case which I'd never normally have considered. What trust, I asked myself, had I really been given? The answer was: none. What had I been given on which to work? Nothing at all, or virtually nothing. And in addition I'd been hedged about with restrictions, hush-hush and mysterious secrecies. I'd been led by the nose. I'd been left holding a mightily unpleasant baby. And since the client was now on his way to America, I couldn't get in touch and ask to be allowed to call the whole thing off.

I scowled at myself, lighted a pipe and then felt a bit more like going back to a viewing of things from Tynworth's end. He had left his place at Herndown and had come to town on the Monday afternoon. He had parked his bag at the Airport Building and had taken the portfolio case with sleeping and toilet things to an hotel, intending next day to do some private business and some shopping. But early on the Tuesday morning his sister-in-law—the Hon. Moira Bolfray—had rung about his wife. He had at once gone back home. He'd seen his solicitors later and talked with Henry Balfour—a name, by the way, that again conveyed nothing to me, even though I was supposed apparently to have known it. He'd spent the night at Herndown and I'd seen him at Liverpool Street Station, and he had looked like a man who'd been having a bad twenty-four hours.

The buzzer went. Bertha said Harstead was on the line. "That you, Harstead? Ludovic Travers here."

"Well, well, well!" The tone had an ironic heartiness. "How are you, young feller? And how's crime?"

He was pulling my leg about my occasional association with the Yard, though that's putting it far too handsomely. George Wharton—Chief Superintendent Wharton to you—had been wangling me in for years now as what they call an unofficial expert in the matter of certain murder cases.

"I'm just crawling around," I told him. "Crime's pretty dull too. I'm actually having to work for a living. But strictly between ourselves, do you happen to have heard of a Lord Tynworth? I think he's an owner-trainer of horses."

"I've heard the name," he said. "Why? What's he been up to?"

"Nothing whatever," I said. "My interest is in his father, the first Baron, but even that's strictly in confidence. Could you be a good soul and look up your morgue—he died in 1946—and send me whatever you have on him? I've gone through the reference books and they haven't got what I want. Did he have money, for instance, and where did it come from. You can do that?"

"Wait a minute," he said. "I'd better get it down."

He muttered for my convenience while he took his notes.

"You've got it," I said. "All the information there happens to be. At your own convenience, though I'd very much like it today."

He said he'd try to rush it to me that late afternoon. A few more words and I was getting back to my private ruminations. Then, before you could say knife, I had a thought that made me go hot and cold. It was the sort of thought that shows the kind of mind I have. It's one that darts hither and yon, like a tit in a tree, and seizes on something from heaven knows where and knows that it's something important. Knows, that is, till disillusionment comes.

What if Tynworth wasn't going to America at all? That was the thought, and it was sired by Precaution out of Circumstance, to put it in racing terms. Suppose he was staying in England surreptitiously to conduct his own enquiries into his wife's disappearance! Suppose no such person as Henry Balfour existed! That he, in fact, was Henry Balfour, and that all that business with me had been some kind of bluff or blind. What guarantee had I that he was flying? Anyone can walk into that Airport Building.

I buzzed through to Bertha.

"Bertha, I want you to do something urgent—the kind of thing you've done before. Take down these details."

When that was over I sat back, tried to concentrate on the little I knew and found it heavy going. Then it occurred to me that Tynworth had given me notes instead of writing a quick cheque. I found myself fingering my glasses again. Surely something was wrong? Hadn't he said that only at the last minute had he decided to use the Agency? The *last minute* meant that morning when the banks were shut. Where then had the notes come from? Why had he been carrying them? He couldn't take them to America, so what was he doing with them? It was all very puzzling and disturbing.

You'll probably be regarding it as much ado about precious little. What, you might ask, had I to worry about. I had two hundred pounds. All I had to do was to make such enquiries as I could. I might find Lady Tynworth or I might not, but when her husband asked for a settlement all I had to do was give him a bill and any balance that might be left, and that would be whether he'd been to America or not, which wasn't any real business of mine.

But that wasn't the point. That hit-or-miss, by-guess-and-by-God sort of service isn't the kind on which we pride ourselves. Reputation—even if Iago said it long ago—is far more than money. Also we handle nothing that isn't absolutely open and above-board. That's why we insist on personal interviews with possible clients and try to sum up both their problems and themselves. Anything suspicious or any withholding of essential information and the client is politely turned down. And Tynworth, or so it seemed to me, had made more than one conflicting statement. He'd been miserly with information and had imposed crippling limitations.

The buzzer went.

"That enquiry, sir," Bertha said. "Lord Tynworth *was* on that plane without any doubt whatever. His destination is New York."

I let out a breath. I felt, in fact, like a suddenly deflated balloon. The bright boy of St. Martin's, as George Wharton had once sneeringly called me, had tripped over his own heels.

"Thanks, Bertha," I said. "Come in in a minute, will you?"

I gave her the notes to deposit at the bank as soon as her relief reported, and I said I thought I'd have some lunch myself.

I had a more or less regular seat at a nearby pub where they provide an old-fashioned square meal and some really good beer. As I chewed I would now and again give myself a kind of wincing, reproachful sneer and I could damn that flibberti-gibbet brain of mine. Tynworth was on his way to New York. Everything was open and above-board, even if I'd been left to see through a glass darkly. He had his own reasons for the vari-ous secrecies he'd imposed, and it was worse than foolish of me to go nosing round for something queer or shady. I'd accepted him as a client, and from then on it was up to me to try to earn his money.

Which shows how hypocritical one can be. It was rather like cheating at patience. On the surface I could force myself to be reassured and all the time there was something deep down over which I kept skating, and whenever it emerged through the thin ice I surreptitiously footed it under again. That something was the inner knowledge that I never ought to have taken that case. What Norris would say when he heard about it I couldn't guess. Maybe, since I was the boss, he'd keep most of his thoughts to himself. All the same, I couldn't see him doing a couple of exuberant cart-wheels at the news.

The office that afternoon was somewhat stagnant, and between jobs I happened to remember something that had occurred to me when I had first heard Tynworth's name. Some-thing had vaguely stirred. I thought I had heard it before, though in what context I didn't know. Heaven knows there are scores and scores of peers of whose names one has never heard. Was it through racing, I now asked myself, that I had heard the name? Some big winner? Some sensational event or other? I didn't think so. It is true that that crossword brain of mine encompasses and registers most things, so that when I am doing a puzzle I am often amazed at myself for finding clean up in the blue some answer which I had long forgotten I ever knew. And there was something else—that name Finder. It also rang the faintest of bells and yet for the life of me I couldn't think of a Finder I had ever known. *Finders are keepers*, went through my mind, but my mind hadn't retained any trace of a Finder.

Bertha sent in a cup of tea and some biscuits, and as I munched I had a good look at that photograph of the missing lady. She was a Finder, and still something wholly unfamiliar. I didn't know the date of that photograph, but she looked about thirty; a blonde with a photographic smile, beautifully regular teeth and a face that was pretty in a banal sort of way.

"I'd known her for years," Tynworth had told me. "She'd been singing with a well-known band and doing very well for herself. I still can't think why she agreed to marry me."

Which looked as if he'd been pestering her for years. As for her agreeing as a kind of favour, it looked to me more the other way. Doubtless the title had at last attracted her. But the whole set-up began to give me ideas, and I was still working on them when Norris came in.

Chapter II
PREPARING THE GROUND

TEA arrived for Norris and we began talking business. I made him acquainted with what had been happening during the couple of days he had been away, and I ended, of course, with the Tynworth commission. I told the story as a straight one and waited for his comments.

"A useful job," he said, "now things are a bit slack. It isn't often we work for the peerage."

He was evidently feeling a certain gratification and I hadn't expected that as his line of reaction. He had visions, perhaps, of ancestral halls and wide acres and coronation splendours, so I told him what I had gathered about Tynworth's actual position.

"Ah, well," he said, "I suppose times have changed. But if he's a racing man in a small way where do the valuables come in?"

"Apparently they're not to come in," I said. "We've got to regard them as something he let slip. Or perhaps he let that information trickle out as justification for the urgency of finding his wife."

"I see. And what's the best line to take?"

I said that ostensibly she'd either left her husband for another man or else had gone back to crooning—or a hope of it. If the former, then we had practically nothing to go on. Every source of enquiry had been closed. If the latter, then we might get some news through the bigger dance bands: *bigger*, because Tynworth had said she'd been doing very well before her marriage.

"But suppose she didn't use her own name?"

I hadn't thought of that.

"There's always the photograph," I said. "I think we should rush some copies, then we might put a couple of men on the job."

He said he'd see to it.

"Meanwhile, if you agree," I said, "I'd like to do some preliminary scouting around. Tom Holberg, for instance, might know something about her. Also I'd like to find out a bit more about Tynworth, especially that little racing stable of his. I'll go into Bertha's room and try to get Tom Holberg now." I got Holberg practically at once. He said he could spare me a minute or two at five o'clock, and that didn't leave me a lot of time.

"Something I forgot to tell you," Bertha said. "It was to do with that enquiry at the airport this morning. It was a girl who took the query and I distinctly heard her say to someone, 'Funny, that's the second this morning.' I thought I'd better let you know."

"Interesting," I said. "What'd you make of it?"

"Well, that we were the second who'd been enquiring if Lord Tynworth was on that plane."

"Couldn't it have been that ours was the second enquiry that morning about the actual plane?"

"Don't think so," she said. "They must get heaps of enquiries about planes. This followed on so pat and just as if it was something unusual."

"Maybe you're right," I told her. "Thanks for telling me, Bertha. By the way, a package of some sort should come for me any time now. See it's sent straight to the flat. It's from Mr. Harstead."

The early evening fog was there when I went out: not yellow and dense but just enough to taste. The visibility was about fifty yards, which meant hardly enough to see and halt a taxi. But I was lucky to get a bus on the corner and I made it to Holberg's place just on time.

Tom's a very old friend of mine and one of the biggest agents in the business. He's the sort of man with whom you feel you could never conceivably have an angry word: quiet, more than knowledgeable, patient, tolerant and genuine as they make them. That late afternoon he looked so glad to see me that I might have been there to pay a long-due bill.

"I'm not going to keep you many minutes," I told him. "All the same, I don't know why you don't give orders to keep me out."

He looked almost shocked.

"Every time I drop in here it's to ask for a favour."

He beamed.

"Why not?"

"Because you won't let me pay for information."

He spread his palms.

"Maybe I will have them keep you out. Whenever you come you pester me about paying. So I should charge you. Very well. One day I will charge you. Charge you plenty. Cigarette?"

I lighted his and my own. I told him what I wanted to know.

"Sarah Finder," he said. "How do you spell that name?"

"Like Finders are keepers."

He frowned in thought for quite a minute. He shrugged his shoulders.

"No. Never heard of her. With a big band, you think?"

"Yes," I said. "My information is that up to three years ago she was making big money."

"At what?"

If it had been any other man I'd have suggested that he had a dirty mind.

"Ostensibly at singing with a band. She made enough to own a mink coat."

He shook his head.

"If she was in the big money, then I'd have known her. And there'd have been broadcasts."

I opened out. Tom could be trusted implicitly. If he ever wrote an autobiography, as he told me, he'd have to hire himself a bodyguard.

"Tynworth," he said. "No. Never heard the name."

I got to my feet.

"That's that then, Tom. Maybe I'll have to work out some other angle."

"Wait a minute," he said. "How many times have you asked me something I couldn't answer? It's all right by you if I think it over? Maybe I give you a ring some time soon?"

"That'll be fine," I said. "I shall be at the flat all the evening. More than grateful, Tom. Or mustn't I say that?"

He patted my shoulder as I went through the door.

Bernice was in. I told her I'd had tea, and when I'd cleaned myself up a bit I joined her at the fire. We chatted for a minute or two about this and that, and then she went on with her book. I started on the *Times* crossword. Somehow it had been a trying day, if only because the normal routine had been upset since dawn, and when I'm mentally tired there's nothing that eases my mind like a crossword or a good detective novel. But that evening it didn't work out like that. For one thing the crossword was the not too frequent, easy kind when you can fill things in almost as quickly as you can write. It even began to bore me, and as I sat there doing nothing I was almost at once back in Tom Holberg's office.

"Darling, you're scowling most horribly."

I came back with a jerk.

"Am I?" I smiled feebly. "Just something I was thinking about."

I didn't really mean to go on, but I did.

"Just a job we have in hand. Something to do with a girl named Finder."

"How do you spell it?"

"Just the ordinary way. The same as you'd spell *binder* or *reminder*."

"Are you sure you'd pronounce it like that? Oughtn't it to be Finder? Like *tinder*?"

"Good lord, yes!"

I wondered what on earth could have made me pronounce it in any other way. All that upsetting of routine, perhaps, and a day's tough mental work. And a careless taking of things for granted.

"I'm pretty sure you're right," I said. "All the same, I still don't know a girl called Finder, and something keeps telling me I ought to."

"But you did!"

"Did?" I said, and stared.

"But of course. Don't you remember that holiday we had at Kettlebourne?"

Kettlebourne. Sussex. Holiday. The year of the War. The White Horse. The Finders.

"Well," I said, and I was smiling feebly again, "fancy forgetting that!"

"It seems almost ages ago," she said. "That dreadful time just before the war. But I do remember Molly. The people were awfully nice, too."

We began talking back those fourteen years ago. We had been strongly recommended the place by a friend and we put in a fortnight there. The White Horse was hotel and guesthouse: a long, rambling sort of place with a wonderful view along the downs. The food had been magnificent. Everything had been cosy and comfortable, and the service the kind you never find today.

"Wait a minute," I suddenly said. "You don't happen to remember the Christian name of either the proprietor or his wife?"

"No," she said, "I don't think I do. The daughter's name was Molly. She was about eighteen. Used to spend most of her time with the riding stable. Remember how she tried to induce me to do some riding?"

"Yes," I said, and my fingers were moving up towards my horn-rims. "Wasn't there another sister?"

"Of course! Sally. You remember. She was just older than Molly. She'd got herself a job in the chorus of some musical show. We never saw her. But didn't we promise to go and see the show, and never did?"

"That's right," I said, and I was getting to my feet. It couldn't be wrong. It just had to be. Moira must be Molly, and Sarah must be Sally. And a musical show. And Molly the horsewoman. Or was there something wrong about that? If Sally married Tynworth, ought she to have been the one who was mad about horses?

"Now I come to think of it, I believe I can find something," Bernice was saying. "I saw it only the other day. I think it's in a drawer in my room."

I went quickly to the telephone and dialled Holberg's number. His secretary said he was still in. I was put through almost at once.

"Ludovic Travers again, Tom. I've discovered that that girl might have called herself Sally. And the name rhymes with *tinder*. Sally Finder. And she had a job in the chorus of some musical show that was on in town in the early summer of 1939. If I find out the name I'll let you know. Will that be a help?"

He said it'd be all the help in the world. I went back to my chair and waited for Bernice, and I was wondering what it was that she'd produce. Women are magpies—that's my experience. There's little that Bernice will ever part with, and on the plea that it's bound to "come in" some time. There isn't a drawer or cupboard in the flat that isn't chock-a-block with Bernice's miscellanea.

What she did triumphantly produce was the brochure of the White Horse, Kettlebourne. There was a photograph of it on the front page and underneath I read the final confirmation— *Proprietor, M. Finder*. And M. stood for Maurice.

"And there's this," Bernice was saying. "I saw it in the paper at the time and I cut it out and I meant to tell you about it. It must have slipped my mind."

It was a notice of marriage, and probably from *The Daily Telegraph*:

> TYNWORTH—FINDER. On June 7th at Chelmsford, Lord Tynworth of Tynworth to Sarah, daughter of the late Maurice and Kathleen Finder of Kettlebourne, Sussex.

"Just what I wanted," I said. "It ought to be very useful."

That's one of the excellent things about Bernice—she can be told so much without asking for more. When she knows it's an agency matter, that is. So for the next few minutes we were only trying with the help of that brochure to get back to those incredibly distant days of 1939. I had just one question to ask before Bernice put that brochure away, but she still couldn't remember the name of that musical show. And then that package from Harstead arrived from the office.

I glanced through the various clippings and extracts, but it was not till after a service dinner that I got down to what Harstead had sent. The accompanying note apologised for the scrappiness of everything and said some stuff must have been discarded after the obituary had appeared. It took me a solid hour to extract what looked like being of any use to me. The following was the fresh information I now had about James Bolfray the elder.

He was the son of a foreman builder in Tynworth. He had a council-school education and then went to an uncle who had a job in a racing stable at Pontefract. One gathered that his original ambition had been to become a jockey (collated with extract from Hansard) but had grown far too fast. He came home and did office work in the firm that employed his father. Attended night school and graduated to charge of costs, etc. Became a partner and then married the only daughter of the owner of the firm. Went in for local politics.

He took over the business on his father-in-law's death, and thanks to various war contracts, expanded it enormously. He finally sold out to Cutbury and Co. soon after being made a peer. *Note by Harstead*: "I tried to get information in the City office about this. Think His Nibs got well into six figures. He left only £30,000 nett. £10,000 to his eldest son's widow."

There was a further note about the kind of man James Bolfray had been. An obituary by a fellow Labour peer was chiefly clichés: an early stalwart of the Party, unswerving loyalty, natural dignity, the cause of the workers at heart, one whose counsels would be greatly missed, and so on. He was definitely right-wing and became more so towards the very end. *An ironic note by Harstead*: 'Funny how property can shape a man's politics.' I imagined he meant that, as a moneyed man, Bolfray was opposed to schemes or policies of penal taxation designed to level-off incomes. Certainly he had been a man of very personal views which he hadn't been afraid to express, and, occasionally, to the consternation of the Party itself. He dropped out of things in 1944. The shock of his son's death, followed by that of his wife, brought on an illness from which he never really recovered.

With these notes on James Bolfray were the beginnings of compilations for his sons. Both had been educated at Tynworth Grammar School. James had gone into business with Cutbury and Co. Thomas had gone into partnership with a man who ran a small stable at Malton. It looked as if the war had killed it, for in 1940 he joined up. He ended the war as a captain in the Tank Corps. There was a clipping about the sale of the family house at Tynworth. Since it made only £4,500 Bolfray must have lived in a very unpretentious way. Another clipping mentioned the purchase of Old Farm, Herndown, by the new Lord Tynworth for the sum of £15,000. It was a hundred and fifty acres including gallops, and there were various buildings besides the house.

That was all that I could glean, and it held no explanation of those valuables with which Tynworth's wife was supposed to have decamped. As I saw things, Tynworth must have started his small stable with very little capital. Various outgoings, such as the buying of horses, must have left little margin till money began to come in. All that I knew about racing told me that small stables depended on at least one or two good coups a year. Inferior stock won inferior money, and the answer lay in betting, and what one made from betting wasn't taxed. Had the valuables been bought from some such coup?

I had a sudden brainwave. Five minutes later I was talking to Harstead at his private address. I thanked him for what he'd sent me and said that in the very near future I hoped to stand him a first-class lunch.

"Any hope, by the way, of having a word with your racing correspondent?"

"I doubt it," he said. "He's a bit too high up in the scale. Also he won't be in in the morning. Racing's supposed to be certain at Newbury."

"No one else I could see?"

"Why not try Jack Mallow? He knows it all. You'll have to be pretty smart, though. He'll probably be in at about nine."

"May I mention your name?"

"I'll try and get him for you straight away. Unless you hear to the contrary, you get hold of him at about nine. He'll be going down to Newbury later."

I put the Bolfray dossiers away in my desk. It was practically bedtime and I knew I'd be glad to get to sleep and have a few hours free of Tynworth. The very last thought I had was about what Bertha had told me. Sleep must have been delayed for quite a few minutes while I wondered who it was that had also been interested in Tynworth's actual departure for America.

I was in Fleet Street well before nine. I had a quarter of an hour to wait before being shown into Jack Mallow's cubbyhole of an office. He was a thinnish-looking chap of about forty: a face tanned with weather and racing written all over him. It turned out that he was "Diomedes", above which pseudonym appeared a paragraph or two each day as a kind of appendix to "Mandeville", the chief racing correspondent.

He didn't seem in any great hurry: at least he took some time to ask me just what I wanted. Then I had to make it clear that whatever he told me would be treated with the utmost confidence.

"That's all right," he said. "Harstead told me about you. Depends, of course, on what you want to know."

"What I want is everything you know about a little stable run by Lord Tynworth at Herndown."

He gave a quick look, licked his bps and flicked the ash from his cigarette.

"You financially interested?"

"Not in the least. I'm working on a case which mustn't have a breath of scandal attached to it. It's all hush-hush. Tynworth's indirectly connected."

"I see."

What he saw I couldn't guess. It was a good minute before he said anything else, and then he asked another question. "What d'you know yourself?"

"About Tynworth's stable? Nothing. I know it's small and it's at Herndown, and that's all. I also happen to know that at the moment he's in New York."

His eyebrows lifted.

"Permanently?"

"Supposed to be back in a week's time."

"Only supposed?"

"Only supposed."

He grunted. He lighted another cigarette from the stub of the old and pushed the packet towards me.

"Well," he said, "I can't give you many facts. Let's say I'm giving you some rumours. That stable's had a heap of bad luck lately. Well, over the last two years. You knew Tynworth had a partner?"

"I didn't."

"A chap named Yale. Youngish chap. Ex-Army Captain. Axed Indian Army, in fact. Said to've been a pal of Tynworth's lady. Came in about three years ago. It's also said they haven't been getting on together."

I think he wanted me to do a bit of questioning, so I did. "You don't happen to know where Tynworth's wife was before he married her?"

"No idea. Believe she was a crooner or something. I saw her once or twice with Tynworth at a meeting. And with Yale."

"And how's the stable doing financially?"

"I told you they'd had a lot of bad luck," he said. "They thought they'd move up the scale a bit. Bought a two-year-old named Quick Cash. A nice colt. Quite a good mover. By Precipitation out of Pot of Gold. Cost them a couple of thousand guineas. It was being sprung at Hurst Park in a certain big handicap. After the money was down, it just died on 'em, which meant no insurance. Then there was another misfire last autumn. Beaten out of a place in a photo finish. A blanket would have covered the four. That's when Howard Rill moved in."

It was I who raised eyebrows.

"Rill," he said. "Stalmans. The commission agents. You've seen their advertisements?"

I suddenly remembered. Advertisements, whole-page ones, in the glossy, sporting weeklies. Scene a race-course. One top-hatted gent telling another that he'd make a packet over that last race. And he'd get his money. Reggie Stalman and Co. had never been known to let a client down.

"I think I begin to get you," I said. "Reggie Stalman is really Howard Rill."

"That's it. And he's moved in. Tynworth's supposed to have owed him a lot of money. Heavy betting to get himself out of a hole. Rill's got a couple of horses down there now. The last thing I heard was that he was about to take over the whole caboodle— lock, stock and barrel. Yale might be clearing out and Tynworth might just be his head-man. That's what I heard." He waved the cigarette stub in a deprecatory gesture. "Not that you can always believe what you hear."

"Naturally." I gave a dry smile that matched his own. "All the same, there's no doubt that Tynworth's in a bad financial way."

"That's it."

"And that's why you were interested to hear he was in New York."

He gaped slightly. He took his time stubbing out that cigarette end.

"You're pretty smart," he told me.

"Not a bit of it. It just seemed like that to me. After all, you can't transact racing business—run a stable, should I say?—from New York. Might I suggest he's gone there to raise money?"

"How could he?"

I shrugged my shoulders.

"You got a better suggestion?"

"Maybe. It's putting him a long, long way from his creditors."

"He's got a small son," I said. "What's going to happen to him?"

He had a quick look at his watch and got to his feet. I took the hint.

"Well, there we are," he told me, and the thin lips spread to a bit of a smile. "Rumours—just rumours. And those who live longest see most."

We shook hands. I thanked him and repeated that nothing that had been discussed would ever get back to him. I went down the lift and out to the street to wait for a bus. The air was misty and no more. Maybe the fine afternoon of the weather forecast was on the way, and Mallow would be catching a race train for Newbury.

A bus drew up and I went on top. That brain of mine began darting about from this piece of information to that and seized for the moment on nothing. All I felt was a slow depression. Something was telling me that everything was far from open and above-board in the Tynworth case. Those valuables, for instance: why had a man who was desperate for money not parted with them long ago? Where did Yale come in—the Yale who'd been a pal of Tynworth's wife? What about Rill? Did he know Tynworth was in America? Was it he who had rung the airport?

Then I did have an idea, though it was pretty fantastic, even for me. Was the wife's departure some sort of collusion? Had a divorce been agreed on? Was there some moneyed lady in the

States whom Tynworth was hoping to marry? Had he gone there to talk things over? Was the present Lady Tynworth to be well paid for her part in the collusion?

That's what I was thinking till a last question stopped me in my tracks. If so, why did Tynworth want his wife found? Why was a man, and a man pressed for money, prepared to produce almost casually a couple of hundred pounds to have her found? Why had he made the matter one of urgency? Hadn't he expected her to leave? Had the valuables been a kind of private cache unsuspected by either Yale or Rill?

I was tying myself in knots, and the bus in any case was nearing Charing Cross. A couple of minutes and I was walking the few yards to the flat. I'd rung the office earlier and hinted that I might be along in the mid-morning. Now I changed my mind. I told Norris I was running out to Herndown and expected to be back in the early afternoon. He said those photographs should be ready by then.

I wasn't too interested in photographs. I was thinking of Herndown. Nothing in what Tynworth had said had barred me from at least going to Herndown, and quite a lot ought to be picked up there. I looked up the place in the Guide. Population, 1,700. A one-star hotel—the Dog and Partridge. I looked up the best route. I thought that if the patchy fog had quite gone I might be there in just over an hour.

Chapter III

A MR. CONN

It was eleven o'clock when I saw the first houses of Herndown. I'd just overtaken a postman riding a bicycle, and I drew up and waited for him.

"Will you tell me where Old Farm is? Lord Tynworth's place?"

"You've passed it," he said. "It'll be the first turning on the left about a quarter of a mile back. It's a narrowish road." It wasn't all that narrow. Two cars could pass if they went dead slow. The countryside was absolutely flat, and, but for scrub oaks in the hedges, one could have seen quite a way across. I came to a fork and drew the car in at the left. I reversed, and was ready to move straight back the way I'd come. I moved over to the verge and mounted a slight bank and began focusing my binoculars. I picked up the house at once, over to my right: quite a big place with what seemed like modern additions. But it still looked like a farmhouse: red-tiled, and its plaster walls coloured a faint pink. A white gate was open on a semi-circular drive. There was no sign of life.

Hedges and shrubberies obscured the view to the left, but I could see a line of horse-boxes, and a smallish man was sweeping a kind of yard in front of them. I moved the glasses still farther round. I could see the white pickets of a paddock. Beyond them something was moving along the line of a hedge. There were three horses and all I could catch of them were heads. A man was on the first and youngish lads on the others. I guessed they were coming in from the gallops.

I swivelled back to the house. But I didn't get that far. By the horse-boxes I picked up a man and a woman. I couldn't follow them clearly; and as soon as I had them held for a second, movement would hide one or other. But the man was big: six feet at least and immensely broad. The woman with him looked by comparison almost a child. She was in riding breeches, with a tweed coat and no hat. Something told me I was looking at Molly Finder.

The man who had been sweeping had gone. I lost the couple for a moment or two, then picked them up again more in the clear. They stopped clean in the open. The man had his back to me and it looked as if he had gripped her arm. His other hand was waving furiously as if he were threatening her. The woman made an angry gesture—she was free now of his hand. And then another movement caught my eye. Those three horses were in the space by the boxes. The big man turned towards them. The woman left him and was almost running towards the house. The big man turned back towards the horses. He didn't hurry, and his shoulders were hunched and his hands deep in the pockets of his heavy overcoat. The horses had gone. Then he went, too. I moved a few yards along the lane, but I couldn't get a sign of him in my glasses. I wondered who he could be. A man of that weight wouldn't be Tynworth's partner Yale. Could he be Howard Rill?

That left fork into which I'd backed seemed to curve round like a boundary to Old Farm. It struck me that from farther round I might get a better view, so I slowly backed the car round the bend of the lane till I was out of sight of the fork. I got out and had another sweep with the glasses. The only thing that was much more plain was the front of the house. The sun was full on it as it faced south, and now I could see a car just outside the drive gate: a large, low-hung car it looked, and it was being wiped down by a man—probably the one who'd been sweeping in front of the horse-boxes.

There was a movement at the front door. A woman came out—a nursemaid probably—for she was carrying a child in one arm and manipulating a small tricycle. She set the child on it. I could just faintly hear her voice as she talked, and once I heard the happy laugh of the child. A woman appeared at the door, still in riding breeches, but now wearing a turtle-necked brown jumper. She must have called the child, for the nurse turned the tricycle back. Two women, just outside the door, laughing and playing with Tynworth's small son.

Then, like suddenly frightened birds, the three were no longer there. The nursemaid picked up the boy and wheeled the tricycle on and round the corner of the house. Molly Finder, as I thought of her, had disappeared inside the door. The big man appeared, shoulders still hunched and hands in overcoat pockets. He went through the open door and into the house.

Five minutes later, at ten minutes to twelve by my watch, he came out. He made for the car. The man who'd been cleaning it stepped back and raised a finger to his forelock. The big man gave a curt wave of the hand. He started the car. I nipped back to my own car and eased it on till I could just see the fork. There was the toot of the horn and the big car swept round into the straight. I followed, and at the end of the short straight stretch saw him turn right towards the village. I trod on the accelerator and was about fifty yards behind him when we came to the first houses. A couple of hundred yards on he slowed. He waved me on, but I slowed too. He turned into the yard of the Dog and Partridge. I drew up outside the small hotel itself. I locked the car and went in by the saloon-bar door.

It was a cosy room, with easy-chairs and a cheerful fire. Two men were standing at the bar talking with the barman: elderly men who looked like local tradesmen. A superior sort of man in brown tweeds was sitting by the fire reading a newspaper. He glanced up at my entrance and at once resumed his reading. I placed him as a retired army man.

I asked the barman about the local bitter and ordered a half-pint. There were friendly good-mornings with the two elderly men, and I took my beer to the fire.

"A lovely morning now," I said to the man in tweeds.

"A grand morning." It was a bluff, hearty voice, well lubricated in the course of years. Little purple veins ran by the rather bulbous nose, and against the red of his cheeks the outer skin was an unhealthy white. The hand that picked up his tankard was shaking slightly.

"Haven't seen you in here?"

"Just passing through," I told him.

He'd given a wave of the hand to the chair alongside his own. I took it. His tankard was empty.

"Have another drink," I said. "What shall it be?"

"Just the same," he said. "Fred'll know."

Fred, the barman, heard. He brought another pint, took my money and the empty. Mr. Tweeds and I drank each other's health.

"Know this place at all?"

"First time I've seen it," I said. "Looks a nice little place."

"Not bad," he said. "Handy for Dunmow or Thaxted if you want to get out of it. I've been here five years now. Born quite near. Name's Porter. Colonel Porter."

"I'm Travers," I said. "Born in Suffolk but living in London. But tell me something."

I lowered my voice slightly as I asked him if there was a racing stable just as one came into the village. I thought I'd seen a small string of horses.

"That'd be Old Farm," he said. "Belongs to a feller called Tynworth. Lord Tynworth, I suppose he is. Father was one of those Socialist peers. A bricklayer once, so they tell me."

"Useful place to have in a village if you're a racing man. Ought to be a good tip or two from time to time."

He snorted.

"Not from him there aren't. The place has gone clean down the hill. Good as done for, so they tell me."

A door at the far end opened and a man came in. He was that man I'd seen at Old Farm: the owner of the Jaguar which I'd tailed. He made straight for the bar, and I had a good view of him before he turned away from me. I put him at nearer fifty than forty. His height was just over six feet and his shoulders immense. Deep grooves ran along the slightly beaked nose and down past the chin. Maybe it was the bulk and the set of his jaw, but there seemed a superb dominance about him. The two elderly men at the bar actually drew back as he came striding up.

"Double whisky."

"Yes, sir. Soda, sir?"

"No," he said. He turned to the two men.

"Nice morning, gentlemen. You'll have a drink with me?" The colonel leaned across to me. He spoke in a whisper. "You don't happen to know who that chap is? Seen him in once before. Tuesday, about eleven."

I shook my head.

The big man put just a little water in his whisky. He waited for the other drinks. Healths were drunk. The three began talking. Fred began polishing glasses. The colonel was talking to me and pricking his ears for the talk at the bar.

"What were we talking about? Oh yes—"

I headed him quickly off. Whoever the big man was I didn't want him to know I was interested in Old Farm. I cut in with a question about Dunmow and the best way from there to Ipswich. Then something happened.

There was a lull in that bar conversation and one of the elderly men was saying he'd have to be going. The big man turned and looked round the room. He seemed to be smiling at something that had been said. Then he caught sight of me and the smile froze. If ever a man was surprised at the sight of anyone, he was at me. He looked away.

"Ever been to the Dunmow flitch ceremony?" I asked the colonel.

"When I was a young feller-me-lad. All damn foolery now, if you ask me."

The big man had taken another look at me, just letting his eyes run over me and beyond. That far door opened again. The man who looked in was probably the manager or owner.

"Your lunch is ready, sir."

The big man just waved a hand, finished off his second whisky and went through the door. He didn't seem to hear Fred's "Good morning, sir".

The colonel waited only a second or two.

"Who's that feller, Fred? Seen him in here before."

"A Mr. Conn, sir. I think he's connected with Old Farm. That's what they say."

"Probably buying the place."

Fred didn't answer.

"Can you get lunch here?" I asked him.

"At one o'clock, sir. That gentleman who's just gone out had his lunch ordered special."

"Would you be so good as to order it for me? I've just got to slip along to the post office."

The colonel said he was lunching, too. And there wasn't any hurry except that the post office closed at one.

I bought some stamps at that post-office-shop and then rang the office. Norris was in. I told him about the car—a 1952 black Jaguar: registered number LCP 8517. The driver was a man named Conn. I wanted to know if he was the owner, and I also wanted his address.

*

I deliberately made it after one o'clock when I got back. Conn must have been a quick eater, for his car had gone. The colonel was still in the saloon bar. He ordered two tankards for the lunch-room and we went through. It was a mediocre lunch and the room was none too warm. The colonel didn't grumble, so I said nothing. What I wanted was to get him back to Old Farm.

I learned very little that was new. The place had been run before the war by an ex-jockey who'd done very well out of it. He'd sold the place purely as a farm in the first year of the war when no one quite knew what was going to happen to racing. That new owner had died in 1946, when Tynworth had bought it. Tynworth's partner, Yale, was described as a taciturn sort of chap. He and Tynworth's wife were often in the saloon bar of an evening, and, so I gathered, chiefly when Tynworth himself was away.

Tynworth raced both on the flat and over the sticks. One had to, the colonel said, to make that kind of stable pay. Not that it had paid. A lot of bad luck, so he said, or else bad management. Tynworth's wife hadn't helped. She was a spender if ever there was one. The other woman there, Tynworth's sister-in-law, he called a nice little body, but one never saw much of her. A fine horse-woman. The best on the place. Tynworth himself did no riding now. He'd had a nasty spill or two in his time.

"Something a bit fishy, if you ask me, about those two women being sisters. Soon as Tynworth married, the place started to go down. May be a coincidence, but there you are. Wonder what this chap Conn'll do if he buys it. Mortgaged up to the hilt, so they say."

That was about all, except that in the house itself there was a sort of cook-general and a nursemaid. Lady Tynworth, still according to the colonel, never did a hand's turn. He added that he'd like to smack her backside. I didn't ask why.

We sat on till after two o'clock. Just as we were going the owner came in.

"Tell me, Percy," the colonel said, "is that chap Conn buying Old Farm?"

I'd gone through the door and I left them talking. The colonel was a gossip, a kind of *Herndown Morning and Evening News*: the sort of man who had to be in the know. Of such, I thought, is village gossip made. Much of what he'd told me I knew for truth, some had been definitely untrue, and the rest could be evaluated later.

I went out by the side door to the yard and round to the front. I didn't know if the colonel was about, but I'd said I was going on to Thaxted, so I went straight on. I went into Thaxted and then turned, thinking I'd take the second-class road home by way of Epping. Then I changed my mind. I'd let the colonel gather I was going on to Ipswich, but something was telling me I ought to have another quick look at Old Farm. I could still get home before any likelihood of fog.

It was just past half-past three when I drove through Herndown. As I neared that side turning that led to Old Farm I saw two women ahead of me, and I knew them for Molly Finder and the nursemaid. It was Molly who was pushing the perambulator. I drew up just ahead of them, ten yards short of the lane. I got out.

I lifted my hat, and it was to Molly I spoke. I wondered if it were she after all. I'd last seen a girl of eighteen. This was a woman of thirty-two. Her face was thin and rather drawn, but it was what I'd call a good face, full of character.

"Pardon me, but am I on the right road for Bishops Stortford?"

"Yes," she said. "Keep straight on. You can't go wrong."

I frowned slightly.

"Please don't think me rude, but I'm sure I've seen you before."

She smiled. Her face was suddenly different. I actually did remember her.

"I don't remember seeing you—"

She paused. She frowned, too.

"My name's Travers," I said. "Ludovic Travers. I live in London."

"But of course!" she said. "I remember you. You stayed at Kettlebourne. When was it now? Just before the war. You and your wife."

"Good lord, yes," I said. "I know who you are. You're Molly Finder!"

We shook hands, I don't quite know why unless it was that all at once we were both part of an ineluctable past. Or it might have been that we suddenly knew each other for someone who was immensely likeable, or at worst a someone whom it was wholly good to see again.

"It's Molly Bolfray now," she said.

"And is this your boy?"

"My sister's," she said.

"And you live in Herndown?"

"Just down the end of the lane there." Her face lighted again. "Do come along and have some tea."

"Well—"

"But you must. I'll ride with you and show you the way. Daisy can come on."

I smiled down at the boy, a bonny-looking chap with fair, curly hair. A teddy-bear much bigger than himself faced him at the other end of the perambulator.

"How old is he?"

"Getting on for two, sir," Daisy said. She was rather a lumpy girl of about eighteen, in a dark-blue sort of uniform. A Herndown girl probably.

I gave them both a smile. We were at the car and I opened the door for Molly. Tynworth had warned me not to go to Old Farm, but to hell with Tynworth. A man has a right to chat with a very old friend.

In that short drive she began telling me about herself: her marriage, her husband's death and how she had come to Herndown in 1947 to help her brother-in-law out. We turned into the drive. I saw an ill-kept lawn and flower-beds untended since the autumn. There was nowhere a smell of money.

We went into a hall with a cloakroom. I found myself giving her my coat and hat and she laid them on the oak settle.

"In here," she said, and went through a door to the right into a roomy lounge.

"Do make yourself comfortable. And see to the fire for me. I'll see Mrs. Drew about tea."

It was an open fireplace with a stack of logs in the recesses. I stirred the fire and made it up. I stood with my back to it and looked round the room. It was comfortable but no more. There wasn't a piece of furniture I'd have liked to take away—but, as I said, it was cosy. There were a few books in an oak case and some photographs on a side table and on the top of an upright piano. One of them was Tynworth. There was no mistaking, even at a distance of ten feet, the outswept moustache.

Molly came back.

"That's a nice fire," she said. "Tea'll be here in a moment or two."

She was quite near and I smiled down at her from my six-foot three.

"Do you know it feels extraordinarily good to see you?"

"It's nice to see you, too."

She shook her head as if she were thinking back. In that moment or two there seemed something pathetic about her, and there was an urge to do something about it. Then she was smiling again.

"Let's sit here, shall we? Then we shall feel the fire."

I helped her draw the settee nearer. Then tea came in. It was plain, as she said, and there hadn't been time for scones. Bread-and-butter, I told her, was good enough for me, let alone what looked like homemade cake.

"Mrs. Drew made it."

The middle-aged woman who'd brought tea in smiled at that. When she'd gone Molly said she was rather superior and had to be humoured. Heaven knew what would happen if she ever left.

We talked and talked. Her father had had his place taken over by the Government in the September of 1939. He and his wife had gone to Southampton, where they had been killed in the big air-raid. She herself had joined the Women's Land Army and had ultimately gone to near Tynworth where she had met her husband. Sally had worked for ENSA. She had met Tynworth at Herndown, where she had come to see her sister in 1947.

"I never actually saw Sally."

"She's away at the moment staying with friends," she said. "Tom's in America, as I said. But tell me more about yourself. Weren't you writing a book? Or am I wrong?"

That was how she was with Sally—always sheering away when I managed to get the conversation round to her. And the last thing I wanted was to show an undue interest. So I did talk about myself and Bernice, letting her assume I was still writing books on obscure subjects; then we got back to Kettlebourne and then to herself again and what she did at Old Farm.

"Seems to me you practically run the place," I said.

"Not a bit of it," she said. "We just can't afford to have more help. Besides, I like it. I always did, as you know. I was riding a pony when I was three."

"But keeping an eye on the house! What's Sally doing? Oughtn't that to be her job?"

"You know how it is," she said, and I thought there was a touch of bitterness. "Some women never do like housework, and I just hate to see things get in a muddle. What about Mrs. Travers? Does she like housework?"

"There's not so much in a flat. But what you ought to have done was to take a holiday with your brother-in-law in America."

She didn't answer that unless it was to smile faintly.

"If it isn't a rude question, has he relatives there?"

"He has," she said. "I oughtn't to be telling you this because it's supposed to be secret, but it's a cousin he's seeing—his mother's brother's son. His father did very well for himself out there. Tom wants his cousin to come over for the coronation."

I began to see daylight. The cousin might be asked for a loan.

"The coronation," I said. "That reminds me. Tom—if I may call him that—ought to qualify for a seat in the Abbey. Was his name in the draw?"

"It was," she said. "And he was lucky—or unlucky."

"How do you mean?"

"Well, he hated the idea. He'd rather be plain Tom Bolfray. It was Sally who talked him out of all that. What about you? Have you got a seat anywhere?"

I said I wasn't worrying. Perhaps I was like Tom, not one for pageantry unless it was on television. Then Mrs. Drew came in and collected the tea-things. Molly stirred the fire to a blaze. Outside, the first dusk was in the February sky. I ought to have been going, but there was something else I wanted to know. It was hopeless, I realised, to try to worm out any more about Sally.

The firelight fell on Molly's face. It heightened the cheek-bones and accentuated the hollows, and yet somehow the very softness of the shadows made the face strangely beautiful. It brought to mind a picture and by whom I didn't know: some Italian Primitive, perhaps, and the face of a madonna.

"You know, Molly, you used to be an uncommonly pretty girl."

"Did I?"

She smiled, and the moment seemed very intimate.

"You certainly did. Now you look tired. Worried. Are you worried?"

"Aren't we all?"

"We needn't be," I said. "And I'm almost old enough to be your father. Sure there's nothing I can do to help?"

"Nothing," she said. "It's just one of those things. A week or two and I'll probably be laughing about it."

And then something happened. There was a sound at the door behind us. It opened and a man came in, and I could see him in the mirror above the fireplace. He was wearing a rather old British warm, and his pork-pie hat was still on. Molly had looked round. She sprang to her feet.

"Arthur! . . . Where on earth have you—"

She stopped. She moistened her lips. I'd got to my feet.

"Mr. Travers, this is Arthur Yale. Arthur, this is a very old friend of mine whom I haven't seen for years and years."

"Since just before the war," I said. "How d'you do, Mr. Yale."

"How d'you do."

The tone was non-committal—almost curt. He reminded me rather of Mallow, that racing reporter I'd seen at the newspaper office: tallish, thin and hardbitten. There was blue stubble on his jowl and what looked like a bruise on one cheek.

"I ought to have been off long ago," I told Molly.

"No need to hurry," Yale told me evenly. "Cigarette?"

"Thanks, no," I said. "But I really have to go. It's quite a way back to town."

He lighted himself a cigarette with what seemed the last tear-off from a folder. He flicked the folder towards the table.

"I'll see you off," Molly told me. "I shan't be long, Arthur."

"Goodbye then," I said to Yale. "We may meet each other again some time."

"Perhaps we will."

He flicked his hat towards the settee and moved along to the fire. Molly went through the door. I saw something white just short of it and stooped to pick it up. It was that folder that had missed the table. Something on it made me slip it into my pocket.

CHAPTER IV
GETTING NEARER?

THERE seemed a change in the weather as I drove back to town. The sky was very overcast, but there was merely a faint mist that didn't really hamper driving. I was glad the fog had gone. I had a lot of thinking to do, but I couldn't do much of it till I was on the main road through Bishops Stortford. I rang Bernice from there and said I ought to be back by seven. She told me Tom Holberg had rung that morning after I'd gone and later he'd sent round a letter.

It was Arthur Yale who was most on my mind as I drove on towards town. Molly had been startled at the sight of him— and relieved. He'd been away, and where she didn't know. I wondered where he'd been, and why. Wherever it was he'd either been in a scrap or had fallen, for as he had passed near me in the lounge I'd seen that bruise quite plainly on his cheek. He wasn't tight, but he'd been drinking, and yet the face hadn't been what I'd call dissipated.

Shaved and cleaned up generally he'd have been quite a good-looking chap. He was probably about thirty-five, and there was something about him that I couldn't quite register to my own satisfaction. He looked like someone off the top shelf, and as I thought that I knew where I'd seen him before—not in the flesh but in those advertisements for high-class tailorings: lean sahibs at race-meetings, for instance, displaying the latest in overcoats. That was Arthur Yale, that and a touch of Mallow. Yale, Tynworth's partner and perhaps the stable jockey in the jumping season.

I thought about Conn and that scene I'd witnessed with Molly Bolfray. Why had Conn been so angry? At the absence of Yale? And was Conn, as that chatterer Colonel Porter had assumed, the virtual owner of Old Farm? I didn't know. In fact it struck me pretty ruefully that, though that day I'd been practically in the heart of Tynworth's affairs, I'd also learned practically nothing about his commission—to discover the whereabouts of his wife.

Or was Yale the clue? He'd all along, according to my information, been a friend of that lady. Mallow and Porter had both hinted that they were still a little more than friendly. And Yale had been away. Since when?

Could it be that Sally had left unknown to him, too? Had he been double-crossed somehow, and had he gone off on the Tuesday morning to find her? Had he found her with some other man? Had there been a fight? And had he come back knowing that she was now out of his life for good? And, if so, could I get Yale to lead me somehow to her?

It seemed like a ray of light, and then there came something that obliterated it like a thick curtain. Somewhere something was badly wrong. It was Sally who had made Tynworth stick to his title. It was Sally who had insisted that he should accept that luck of the ballot so that she could be one of that choice company at the crowning in Westminster Abbey. And yet she had thrown all that up and gone away. Something surely was wrong. Had Tynworth misled me for his own reasons? Was the departure merely temporary? And there was the son, the small Peter. Wouldn't there have to be some tremendous compensation for the loss of him if she had really gone for good?

The whole thing was more than confusing, and driving a car through the first suburbs wasn't helpful in sorting it out. The thoughts kept running through my mind, and I kept pushing them back. It scared me once when I realised I'd driven for quite a way by instinct, and after that I really kept my mind on the road. It was just after seven when I went up to the flat. As I took off my overcoat I remembered something—that folder I'd picked up from the floor of the lounge at Old Farm.

It was rather better than the ordinary folder, though simple enough: white, with a gilt surround, and embossed in its centre the gilt lettering:

THE
MONTEREY CLUB
Marshall St., W.1

The Monterey Club. I'd been there once, about two years ago, with John Hill, the secretary of United Insurance for whom we worked. The food had been magnificent, but I'd been glad it was he who was paying the bill. There'd been a well-known dance band, the name of which I'd long forgotten, but which Hill had said must be costing a small fortune. And there'd been a he-crooner and a she. The she, I did remember that, hadn't been Sally Finder. It couldn't have been, for she was then married to Tynworth and doubtless carrying her boy.

Bernice was seeing to service dinners, and I opened the letter which Tom Holberg had sent round.

> Tried to get you but your wife said you'd be away all day. The lady in whom you were interested called herself Sally de Freece when she left ENSA.
>
> She was with ENSA till 1946. With Hal Prew and his Pirates till 1948, then with Carlo Romano and his Latin

Rhythm. Several broadcasts. Married a Lord Tynworth in 1950. Hope that's enough to carry on with.

It was and it wasn't. I wondered if it would be too tricky to try to get a line through the Romano with whom she'd last worked, but dinner was coming in and I had to have a quick wash and clean-up. Over the meal I told Bernice about Molly Bolfray—the general news and no more. I did add that Molly had suggested we both go to Herndown some time when things, as she had enigmatically put it, had sorted themselves out.

I rang the office, but Norris was at home. I got him there.

"Yes," he said, "I got what you wanted. The car's registered in Conn's name. Wallis Conn. He lives at Willoughby Road, Hampstead. A detached house, name of Winburg. I didn't know what you wanted exactly, so I sent a man along for a look round. A nice little place. Conn got there at about five. Left his car in the garage and went out again at about six to the Underground station. Only five minutes away."

"That's fine," I said. "Wonder if you could have the same man there soon after eight tomorrow morning. He doesn't look the type who goes very early wherever he goes. I'd like him tailed to wherever he lands up."

Norris said he'd see to it, but there'd better be a couple of men, and a car—just in case. That was that. It was getting on for nine o'clock and I hoped I could call it a day.

I didn't go to the office in the morning. Norris was going to ring me when a report came in about Conn. But I did go out early as far as the bookstall at Charing Cross Station, where I bought a copy of *London Amusements*. The Monterey Club had a short paragraph. The band was Francisco Bernardo and his Brazilianos, and it was a name which I thought I had seen in the *Radio Times*. The week was described as their final one. Next week the band would be George Kraft—just that and no more. His name I'd also seen in the *Radio Times*. The singers with Bernardo were Luize del Ray and Tony Marre—names that conveyed nothing.

It was still well short of nine o'clock and I went along to my tobacconist and bought a box of cigars. Tom Holberg liked a good cigar after dinner at home, and these were certainly good. The fifty cost me almost twenty pounds, but I reckoned I still owed him money. Years before, I'd done him what he thought was an inestimable favour, and ever since then he'd resolutely refused to be paid for the frequent calls I'd made on him, even when I insisted they were for the firm.

Tom wasn't in but was expected at any minute. His secretary told me he had a list of appointments with never a moment till five o'clock. He was even lunching in the office. But she knew how Tom and I stood and I was actually let through to the office itself. Two minutes after nine Tom came in. He seemed just as pleased as ever to see me.

"Shan't keep you more than a minute or two," I told him. "These are for you, by the way, not for the customers. And thanks for what you did about Sally de Freece."

"These names," he said. "I don't know how they think them up. What's wrong with Sarah Finder—if she can sing?"

"Which reminds me. A Francisco Bernardo has a band at the Monterey Club. Know anything about him?"

His fat face wreathed in smiles.

"I knew that boy when he was Frankie Bowen. A Hoxton boy. His old mother had a paper stand in Old Street." He shook his head approvingly. "Not a bad boy. Came up fast. Played tenor sax with Harry Sanders before he was twenty. Went to the States just before the war. Maybe he guessed what was coming. Played with—"

Tom would probably have gone on for minutes.

"That's fine, Tom. What's he like?"

"In the profession? Pretty good."

"That's praise, coming from you. And in himself?"

He spread his palms.

"Been divorced twice. The last about six months ago."

"One for the women apparently. That's about all I want to know, Tom. But you couldn't get me his private address?"

"Any hurry?"

"Before lunch, if possible."

He pursed his lips.

"I'll put Miriam on to it." Miriam was the secretary. "Ring you where?"

"At the office. Thanks a lot, Tom. Much obliged."

"It's nothing," he said, and began unwrapping the parcel I'd laid on his table. Maybe he'd thought it a box of cigarettes, but as I went through the door he was calling me back. I went down the stairs at the double. I didn't want his thanks.

I hopped a bus for the office. It was a quarter to ten when I got there. A message had come from Davis, one of the operatives who'd been at Conn's house. Conn had left on foot, presumably for the Underground. Rosen, the other operative, had followed him and there might be a report at any time. Norris had told Davis to try a few enquiries, and just then Davis reported in. He said he hadn't picked up a lot. There was a kind of daily house-keeper at Winburg and occasionally a man for the garden. Until about a year ago Conn's father had lived there, too, but he'd died.

Davis stood by. A few minutes later a call came through from Rosen. He was at a call-box near Guiver House, just off Moorgate Street. Conn had gone into the office of Stalman and Co. The firm occupied the whole of the second floor.

"Stay there," I told him. "Davis will join you. If Conn comes out, keep him in sight."

As I told Norris, I wasn't surprised. Rill was said to have a controlling interest in Old Farm. Conn had been there, and acting as if he were the boss, so he and Rill just had to be connected. What I was wondering was if it got us any farther.

"If I may say so," Norris told me, "I still think working the big dance bands is the best thing. Here're the photographs, by the way."

They were good. I pocketed a couple. But, as I told Norris, I wished she'd been in evening dress: the sort of rig-out she wore when she was crooning.

Norris was busy and I went out to pass a half-hour over coffee. Norris, I thought, was probably right, and yet I couldn't afford to turn down a hunch, and that hunch was that if I knew just why Sally de Freece had married Tynworth, then I'd know where she was. She must have known all about Old Farm and what she was in for. It was true that up till that time the stable hadn't had its spell of bad luck, and maybe there'd been a certain glamour about racing. Maybe, too, Tynworth had painted too glowing a picture. Hard money and late hours at crooning set against an easy time and easier money from the bookies. And there'd been the title. Lady Tynworth would be a someone: a someone to flash in the eyes of old friends. A status, too, among the local gentry.

I very much doubted if they'd ever called, unless they were the sporting type, definitely interested or hoping for tips straight from the owner's mouth. Colonel Porter had put the situation plainly enough when he'd *supposed* he ought to call Tom Bolfray Lord Tynworth, and added that the first peer had been a bricklayer. What a nation of snobs we are!

And yet—well, think it out for yourself. Look at the almost incredible contradictions. Sally insists on her husband keeping his title. She insists on his taking his chance in the official ballot for seats in the Abbey, and yet she throws all that up—and after he's been successful in that ballot—and disappears, and I'm told that there's more than a likelihood of her having gone off to some other man.

Why the absolute change of ideas? I tried to find an answer. She'd married Tynworth, and almost at once she must have been pregnant. That meant almost a year of the three that had constituted her life at Old Farm. After that she had sometimes gone to race meetings. There had been the devastating series of misfortunes. Tynworth had tried to recoup himself by heavy betting, but Sally still had her mink coat, and she still had the company of Yale. Had she seen there was no future in life at Old Farm? Had sheer boredom and the quarrels between her husband and Yale been the real cause of that sudden decision to throw it all up? Plus another man, of course, and that man definitely not Yale?

And what about that boy of hers? Lines of that hymn which I'd known almost from my own nursery days went suddenly through my mind.

> *Can a woman's tender care*
> *Cease towards the child she bare?*

And as suddenly these lines brought an idea. The marriage had been in June 1950. From then till now was two years and eight months. But Peter Bolfray, according to Daisy, was getting on for two. Surely that phrase meant that he was very near two? I wondered. I gulped down the last of my coffee, paid my bill and went out to the street. I picked up a taxi and told the driver to take me to Somerset House. A quarter of an hour later I had a copy of the birth certificate of Peter James Bolfray. *He was an eight-months child.*

As I sat in the bus that was taking me back to Broad Street I knew that was pretty staggering news. Or was it? In the reasonably normal course of events there are eight-months babies, or even seven. And yet the circumstances seemed to suggest that the set-up at Old Farm wasn't normal. Had Sally de Freece suddenly yielded to the importunities of Tynworth because she knew she was pregnant? If so, who was the child's father? *Was it Yale?*

But it wasn't with Yale that she'd gone away. Everything as I'd seen it said that she'd double-crossed Yale.

Her going had been as much a surprise to him as to her husband. It wasn't too much to assume that he'd had a vague idea as to where she'd gone and had tried to find her. Molly had been worried about him. She'd had no idea where he'd been. But he certainly hadn't been successful.

Norris had plenty of news. Tom Holberg had sent a message. Bernardo's address was Flat 7, Surrey Court, Westminster.

"What makes you think he's involved?" Norris asked me.

I told him about that match folder. The Monterey Club looked like one of the places where Arthur Yale had been making enquiries about Sally, and it seemed to me he must have had something definite to go on. Norris nodded as if he agreed.

"Rosen just rang," he told me. "Conn came out at about ten and took a taxi for Holborn. He went by the Piccadilly Line to Cockfosters, to a house called Embridge, quite near the station and the golf course. Davis is taking the car out there."

I hardly needed to consult the telephone directory, but there it was. Embridge was the house of Howard Rill.

"Seems according to schedule," Norris said. "Conn must be an employee of Stalman's. He's gone out there to report."

It was getting on for midday when another report came through. A doctor's car had driven up to Embridge. The doctor had stayed only a few minutes and Conn had come out with him. The doctor had given him a lift to the station. Conn presumably was going back to town. Davis wanted instructions.

"Come straight back here," I said. "Mr. Norris will give you instructions—both of you."

Davis I knew as a particularly good man. Norris said Rosen was good, too. He was newer and I didn't know him so well.

"Bernardo, as he calls himself, doesn't come on at the Monterey till nine o'clock," I said. "I want his flat kept under observation. It'll be a tricky job, but he's got to be followed when he comes out. I'm gambling that that won't be till this afternoon. Whether he comes out or not, he's also to be followed if anyhow possible after he leaves the Monterey Club tonight. It's quite possible he knows where the woman is. He may drop in on her."

Norris wrote it down. If Bernardo had left the flat, then he could be picked up later when the Monterey closed down.

"That's it," I said. "Davis and Rosen can work together. A report won't matter till the morning. You arrange any details."

"Where can I get hold of you if necessary?"

"It shouldn't be necessary," I told him. "There's no actual hurry. If Bernardo has the woman parked anywhere, she won't run away. If anything's really and desperately urgent, then I'll be lunching at the Monterey Club till about half-past one. After that I don't know. In all probability I'll drop in here again in the late afternoon."

I took a taxi, for I wanted to get to the Monterey early. The dance floor would be closed but the restaurant open, and even that wouldn't be busy till nearer one o'clock. The mere fact that you're lunching there at all shows you've got leisure. The clientele there doesn't wolf down food in an hour's break for lunch, and most of them would have quite a goodish preliminary spell at the bar.

It was a long room with at least fifty tables, but at a quarter-past twelve there weren't a score of people having lunch. I'd by-passed the bar, and the head waiter had handed me to a somewhat elderly underling who took me to a table in the corner. I chose that one of the two seats that had its back to the room. I wasn't interested in my fellow-lunchers, and I didn't particularly want them to be interested in me.

The waiter, spry enough in spite of his years, had all the time in the world. He made suggestions about my meal. I took them critically. I also had a half-bottle of Rosé Tavel. It was my own suggestion and it was treated with respect. I was being marked down as a man of discrimination and means, good, no doubt, for a superlative tip. The soup arrived, brought to the table by yet another, and very young, underling.

"Pity I couldn't have made it dinner," I said. "Bernardo's pretty good, isn't he?"

"Very good, sir. You'd have seen him himself, sir. I mean he had a slight accident and has been away for a night."

"Maybe next week," I said.

The waiter smiled regretfully.

"Ah! Next week, sir, he won't be here. I think he has a longish engagement in the provinces: Birmingham and Manchester and so on."

The Potage au Cresson was good. The Ragoût de Veau that followed it was superb. So was the Soufflé aux Pommes. The Tavel was perfection.

"Coffee, sir?"

"Yes. Black."

"A liqueur, sir?"

I thought for a moment.

"Yes—a kümmel. And bring the bill with it."

They came. The bill was three pounds eighteen shillings. I put a fiver on the plate. I also slipped something into the waiter's hand. Inside a pound note was a note of a different kind.

Can I speak to you anywhere privately this afternoon.

The thanks stopped in his throat as he read that note. I was looking at my coffee as I stirred in the sugar. He had suddenly gone.

It was a good five minutes before he came back.

"Your change, sir."

He had deftly inserted something under the plate before he drew respectfully back.

"That's all, thank you," I said, and pushed the plate towards him.

My fingers closed over the note. It said he'd be at the Piccadilly side door of Swan and Edgar's at half-past three.

When the time came I brought my car round from St. James's so as to be on his side of the street. I wouldn't have known him in his dark overcoat and smart grey hat, and it was he who spotted me as I leaned over. He looked a bit nervous as he got in.

"It's all right," I told him. "You're not being kidnapped. We'll park in Leicester Square, then we can talk."

I drew up by the Odeon. I passed him my cigarette case, and up to then he hadn't said a word.

"You're not a tec, are you, sir?"

"Do I look like one?"

He had to smile at that, and no wonder.

"Well, sir, you never know these days, with police colleges and so on."

"There'll be nothing for you to worry about," I told him. "This is a purely private matter between you and me. As soon as you've answered a question or two you can forget about it."

I'd taken a fiver from my wallet, uncreased it and put it tantalisingly in the locker in front of me.

"The fact is," I said, "I'm worried about a niece of mine. She's gone away and we don't know where. This is a photograph of her. Have you ever seen her at your place?"

From an inner pocket he produced a pair of spectacles. "Yes, sir," he said. "I've seen her several times. Not just lately, though."

"Know her name?"

"Can't say I do, sir. We get so many."

"Remember who she was with?"

He frowned. He shook his head.

"Ever see her with a thinnish, clean-shaven man of about thirty-five? Had something of a racing look about him. Be about five feet nine or ten. Good-looking chap."

"Yes, sir. I think I remember the man."

Then his mouth gaped slightly. There was an involuntary jerk of his hands as he removed his glasses.

"Only two more questions," I said. "All this is strictly between you and me, as I said. But did there by any chance happen to be a row of any sort at your place this week?"

"A row, sir?"

His voice had a shocked incredibility.

"I don't mean the actual public rooms. In the band's dressing-room, shall we say."

He cleared his throat.

"Oh, that, sir. I believe there was. Can't say I know much about it, only what I was told."

"Well, tell me what you were told."

He said it wasn't really anything. Someone had asked round the back to speak to Mr. Bernardo and Bernardo went out to the passage. The man attacked Bernardo, and members of the band threw him out.

"It's worth a pound extra if you can remember the man's name."

"Well, sir, the rumour was that his name was Yale—Captain Yale."

"What night was it?"

"Wednesday, sir, just after we were closing down."

I handed him the notes. He waited for me to say something more.

"That's all," was what I did say. "I'm very grateful to you. Now forget all about it."

"I will, sir. Thank you, sir."

I drove slowly on to the garage. Everything fitted. Yale had probably spent some time at the Monterey on the Wednesday and had challenged Bernardo after the show. Bernardo was supposed to have had a slight accident which had prevented his appearance on the Thursday night. A black eye, probably, that had now been doctored or painted. I'd seen Yale on his return to Old Farm on the Thursday—yesterday—afternoon.

Twelve pounds of the client's money gone in an afternoon. I hoped it would be worth it.

CHAPTER V
THE LADY FOUND

I TOLD myself I was right in keeping strictly to the point with that waiter and not pressing him for more than the minimum of information. That way he'd probably expect me to see him again and ask more questions, and that should mean he'd keep his mouth shut and not mention me in the course of some chatty conversation with a colleague. At this stage it was urgent that Bernardo should not know that anyone had shown an interest in that little scrap on the Wednesday night, for if it was he who had Sally parked somewhere, then he'd be more than careful about giving her whereabouts away.

My idea was that she might possibly be going with him on that provincial tour and that he'd then work her into his band. She'd probably tell Tynworth to get a divorce, after which she could marry Bernardo. I admit those ideas were hazy and taking a deal for granted, and yet somehow I seemed committed to action based on their lines. If they turned out to be utterly and fantastically wrong, then at least I could claim that I'd been spending Tynworth's money in perfectly good faith. If, that is, the accounts were ever questioned.

Bernice was out so I made myself a pot of tea. I rang Norris, and he said Bernardo had left his flat when our men got there, but he'd be picked up later from the Monterey Club. That left me at a loose end, so I got out some paper and began jotting down some questions as they occurred to me: questions you have heard me ask before; questions whose answers were always contradictory. That brought me to something of which I'd rather lost sight.

Why had Conn seemed so startled at the sight of me in the bar of the hotel at Herndown? Why had he kept surreptitiously running an eye over me? I was certain that we'd never met. I admit that my appearance is one that you'd probably remember, but I was certain, as I said, that I'd never run across him or he across me. Yet he appeared to know me. What was the answer to that?

I couldn't find one. I'd only come into the case early on the Wednesday morning. Tynworth hadn't seen me till then and he hadn't had time to tell Conn about me. Why should he in any case tell Conn about me? Wasn't that American trip somewhat secret? Hadn't Molly Bolfray, in connection with it, said something like, "I oughtn't to tell you about this, but. . ." Or suppose Conn, as having virtual control through Rill over Old Farm, had had to be told why Tynworth would be away, I'd still gathered from Tynworth himself that no one—not even Molly Bolfray—knew that the Broad Street Detective Agency was being employed to find a missing wife. I'd gathered, too, that everyone—and that would include Conn—was being told, just as Molly had told me, that the wife was staying with friends.

I just couldn't understand it. But it brought me to Howard Rill. An idea came. I looked up his number and rang. A man's voice answered.

"I'm just ringing up to ask about Mr. Rill," I said. "I only just learned he'd been ill. Who's speaking, by the way?"

"Plumer, sir. Mr. Rill's man."

"How is he, Plumer?"

"It was nothing, sir. Just the influenza that's being going about. He's hoping to be out in a day or so."

"Glad to hear it," I said. "Tell him I rang."

I hung up before he could ask me for a name. But there'd been nothing suspicious about that. A reporter on one of the popular dailies, thinking it necessary to describe me in connection with evidence I had given at the Old Bailey in a murder case, had called my face patrician and my voice a pleasant baritone. That, as the Bright Young People of the nineteen-twenties would have said, was definitely sick-making; all the same, if the voice part were true, then among Rill's friends, acquaintances and clients must have been many who fitted the bill for the solicitous gentleman who had enquired about his health.

And what had I learned? Only that Rill would soon be on his pins again. And that Conn's call on him had been in the way of business. And it had also been business that had taken Conn to Old Farm where two of Rill's jumpers were now trained. What it didn't explain was why Conn had grasped Molly Bolfray by the arm, and why she and the nursemaid Daisy had disappeared at the sight of him coming later on towards the house.

I left it and went back to Bernardo. A minute or two and I was ringing Tom Holberg's office.

"That you, Miriam? Ludovic Travers here. . . . Listen, Miriam. I don't want you to disturb Tom on any account, but could you tell me who handles Francisco Bernardo whose band is at the Monterey Club?"

She told me to hang on. I didn't have to wait long. The name was Willis and Trant at an address in Charing Cross Road. I made a note that I'd have to send Miriam some flowers.

In five minutes I was looking at a board which said that Willis and Trant were on the second floor. I went up the stairs to the second-floor landing. A door said ENQUIRIES. I knocked and went in.

It was a smallish room. One girl was typing and another, a nice-looking brunette, was reading a book at the desk. She shot the book into a drawer.

"Yes, sir?"

"Look," I said, "I'm afraid you're going to think me an awful fool, but—well, isn't Francisco Bernardo one of your firm's clients?"

"Yes," she said, and looked a bit puzzled.

"Good," I said. "It's about a niece of mine who's crazy about dance bands. She saw Mr. Bernardo at the Monterey Club and wanted to get his autograph. She lives in Birmingham and has heard he's coming there shortly and she wrote me today and asked me to find out. Seems a bit silly, perhaps, but there it is."

She smiled.

"He'll be there next week. That's right, isn't it, Doreen?"

Doreen said it was.

"I'm very grateful to you." I tried a special, sophisticated smile of my own. "There must be something special about him. You don't happen to have a photograph I could see?"

"I think so, if you just wait a minute."

I waited. Doreen typed stolidly on, though now and again she shot a look at me. Her colleague came back.

"Here're two," she said. "Plenty more, of course, but I thought these might do."

One was of the great man himself and the other of him with his band. If you gave Rudolph Valentino a black streak of a moustache, then you'd have Bernardo—that's what I thought. He looked about thirty-five. I'm no snob, but his was the kind of face that I loathed: that shaven-down moustache, hair well below the ears, the showy glamour and the synthetic smile with just the right glimpse of pearly teeth.

"A good-looking chap."

"Oh, he is. That doesn't really do him justice."

"And these costumes are genuine Brazilian, are they?"

The question seemed almost an insult. I didn't know. I've never been in Brazil. I did know that the trees and mountains behind the group of Bernardo and his band was none too realistic a back-cloth.

I gave the photographs back. Again I was most grateful. Even Doreen smiled as I backed out of the door.

*

When I arrived home Bernice was in and she reminded me that I'd promised to take her to see an Italian movie about which the critics were raving. So that accounted for my evening. In the morning I rang Norris early. Bernardo had gone straight home after his session at the Monterey Club.

"The men are on duty again?"

"Not till ten," he told me. "Apparently the gentleman concerned never makes an appearance till about eleven o'clock."

I took it easy, and it was after eleven when I turned up at the office. Norris and I talked about one or two matters, and it was just after half-past when a report came.

"Davis here, sir, speaking from the Langton Hotel in Morland Street. I lost him on the second floor."

"Rosen with you?"

"Yes, sir. At the side entrance."

"You've got to find what room he went to," I told him. "Look, flash your card to the manager. Say we've had a tip that a hotel swindler may be there under an alias. Make up a convincing story, but be sure to have a look at the registrations. Keep an eye out for single women, then the initials S.F."

I knew the Langton well. It isn't one of the big caravanserais and it isn't an old-type family hotel: it's a cross between the two but big enough. Big enough, that is, for anyone who wants to be virtually unnoticed and whose callers would be unnoticed, too. Norris and I were having hopes, but, whereas he had work to do, I had nothing to do but wait. It was over half an hour before Davis rang again.

"I think I've got her, sir. A Mrs. Stanley French: Room 128."

"Right," I said. "Keep the place under observation and do nothing till the caller's gone. Then let Rosen go to the room and apologise for knocking at the wrong door. Anything so long as he has a look at her. If you're sure you've got a better scheme, then use it."

An hour passed and nothing happened. Norris went out to lunch and I had something brought in. At two o'clock Rosen reported that unless there was some other way out the caller was still in the hotel. The afternoon began to wear away. At four o'clock Rosen reported again to the same effect, adding that even if the caller had gone the woman hadn't come down.

Nothing happened till just on six o'clock.

"Davis here, sir. The couple have just gone out. The man went first. After five minutes the woman left by the side door. They went off together in a taxi he'd had drawn up. This is the number."

"Never mind the number," I told him. "What about the woman?"

"Her all right, sir. Made up to the nines, but there wasn't any mistaking her."

So the gamble had come off—so far. If it hadn't, then we'd have tried tracing her through her car, which she must have garaged somewhere, but that would have meant either far more men or a lot of time, unless we had stupendous luck. But everything wasn't over yet.

According to Davis she'd booked in at the Langton on the Thursday morning although she'd arrived in town in the early hours on the Monday. But that wasn't hard to figure out. It was all a question of a ration book. If she stayed at the first hotel for three days, then that book would have had to be produced, with its revelation of a false name. So she moved from the first hotel to the Langton, and it followed that, her three days there being now over, she would have to find yet another hotel.

Unless, of course, she were going to Birmingham with Bernardo. If he was opening in Birmingham on the Monday, then he'd definitely be travelling on the Sunday. That meant keeping the Langton under observation, and reliefs for Davis and Rosen. But it was now Saturday evening and operatives would be available, so that didn't worry us. What was exasperating was that we hadn't discovered her whereabouts just one day earlier. Now that advertisement couldn't be inserted in the *Telegraph* till the Monday morning for Tuesday's issue. The fact that it was the client's money we would have to spend was only a part of it. Wherever she was, we had to produce her at the time that message appeared. Now, this very evening, we could so produce her. Tuesday might be quite a different thing.

What did happen is largely irrelevant. The main events are these. Sally, Lady Tynworth, returned to the hotel alone at about half-past ten that Saturday night. At eleven o'clock on the Sunday morning she left, still alone, and in a taxi with quite a lot of luggage. She took the eleven-forty from King's Cross to Birmingham. Davis and Rosen went with her.

Late on the Saturday we'd contacted a Birmingham agency and asked them to stand by. Now she was on the train we arranged with them to have a car ready and another man. At about half-past three that Sunday afternoon we were rung by Davis. The party had booked in at the Archdale Hotel on the corner of New Street and Sawley Street and was occupying Room 35. It had been engaged in advance.

"Don't think we haven't every confidence in you," I told Davis, "but from now till about Tuesday afternoon is the crucial time. Whatever happens you mustn't lose her."

"She'll be safe, sir," he assured me. "She's there under her ration-book name—Sarah Bolfray."

I said full instructions for making contact with Henry Balfour or his representative would be in the last post. That again was that and there was nothing to do but wait. On the Monday morning the message was handed in at the newspaper office. It appeared on the Tuesday morning.

I was at the office at seven o'clock. It was just after eight when Balfour contacted me. It was a rather smothered voice as if he were trying to disguise it.

"Henry Balfour here. You have some news for me?"

I told him where the wanted woman was. I said a man with a light-coloured waterproof and a light-grey snap-brim hat would be just outside the hotel main entrance.

"Just ask him if it's the Archdale Hotel. It's a silly question but that's how he'll know you. He'll tell you if she's still there. If not, where she actually is."

"I want your man to clear out after that," he said. "I'll handle things from then on."

"Right," I said. "Provided you accept full responsibility. There'll be a small return, by the way, on the advance you made to us."

"If everything's all right—keep it," he said. "Regard it as a bonus."

"And you'll let us know if everything *was* all right?"

"No need to," he said. "If you don't hear from me by this afternoon you can take it it's all right."

"Just one other thing. I'd like to know what train you're taking. There's one from King's Cross that gets you in about midday."

"That'll be the one," he said. "Thank you, Mr. Travers. I'm very much obliged."

Our men reported back at about six o'clock. Davis said it was a taxi-driver who accosted him.

"Everything O.K. That's what I told him. She's still in her room. He went off by Sawley Street and I didn't spot anyone special coming back. I waited for about half an hour, then reported to the Birmingham agency."

That was the end, or so I thought, of the Case of the Missing Lady: thought, that is, after two more days had passed and nothing had been heard from Henry Balfour.

I should have said that it was the end as far as the Broad Street Detective Agency was concerned. As far as I myself was concerned, I hated the whole business. I knew, though I didn't unburden myself to Norris, that about it there had been something remarkably fishy. It had left behind it questions that demanded answers: questions that kept nagging at me and making me absent-minded at home and an irritation to my own self. It was as if someone had asked an intriguing riddle and had given you what you knew must be the wrong answer, and then the poser of the riddle had gone for good, leaving the riddle itself still there.

Towards the end of the week I suddenly realised that Tynworth was back, or ought to be back. I wondered if he actually were. How to find out I didn't know. I could, of course, make some excuse to ring Molly Bolfray, suggesting a meal with my wife and myself, for instance, in town. And yet I couldn't. I had been definitely instructed by Tynworth not to go to Old Farm, and when I thought of that a sort of cold shiver ran down my spine. Molly would tell Tynworth she'd seen an old friend, a Mr. Travers. It wasn't beyond all possibility that Tynworth would ring or write, claiming some breach of contract. There'd been nothing in writing, of course, but even a complaint from Tynworth would be regrettable.

Hallows, our senior man, happened to be in that afternoon, so I had a private word with him in the operatives' room. It was just short of two o'clock, and I thought that Molly Bolfray might be in the house.

"If Lord Tynworth answers you, pretend there's an interruption your end of the line," I told Hallows, "and make it an excuse to ring off. If anyone offers to fetch him, say it doesn't matter as you'll be coming along in the morning. If a woman answers, just ask if Lord Tynworth's back yet from America. If you have to give a name, make one up and say it's in connection with buying a horse of his."

There was more to it, of course, than that, though I didn't have time to make him wise to what lay behind it all. He went out to do the telephoning, but in a quarter of an hour he was back.

"He wasn't there," he said. "It was that Mrs. Bolfray who answered. She hasn't had any word from him since he left except a cable to say he'd arrived. I gathered she'd expected him home last Monday at the latest."

That was extraordinary. It gave one, as they say, furiously to think. It more than confirmed the suspicions I'd had all along that the whole affair, to put it bluntly, stank. Not that it was any concern of mine. And I didn't have time to elaborate things, for Bertha was saying that Norris wanted me.

"It's Mr. Hill," Norris said, passing me the telephone.

"Travers here, Hill. You wanted me?"

"Yes," he said. "I wonder if you could drop in today or early tomorrow."

"Today if you like," I said. "What time?"

"Four o'clock?"

"I'll be there," I said. "Anything special? I mean, ought I to bring Hallows?"

"Perhaps you'd better," he said.

So some special job was on for United Insurance. I was glad of it. It'd at least take my mind off the Case of the Missing Lady.

PART II
INTERLUDE OF THE LAMMERFORD JEWELS

Chapter VI
THE SURPRISE

HALLOWS and I arrived on the dot, and inside five minutes we were in John Hill's room. He was his usual imperturbable self, and there was no guessing from his looks how important the imminent business might happen to be. There were handshakes and the lighting of cigarettes.

"Something I'd like you to investigate," he began. "No need to tell you people it's highly confidential. It's to do with the Lammerford Jewels."

I didn't say I'd never heard of them.

"The original Lord Lammerford was our ambassador to Russia," he said. "I don't know how exact I am about all this because I only heard it at third hand, so to speak—not that it's important—but I believe there was some matter of a personal service for the Tsar, and the jewels were a strictly private present. Various items. I'll give you the full list later, but there was a tiara, a rivière, a bracelet and a ring or two. Emeralds and diamonds in platinum and gold. Very fine-quality stones.

"The second Lord Lammerford inherited, then they came to his son—an only son. He died in 1935 and there was no heir. His widow sold them in 1939, a couple of years before she died. The family had fallen on rather bad times, by the way. The sale was very private. They were bought by a Lord Tynworth as an investment."

I almost leapt up in my chair. As it was, I had to clear my throat.

"He was a Labour peer, but a man with money," Hill was going on. "A shrewd man of business, too. Knew the war was coming and bought with the practical certainty of security if not considerable appreciation."

"If it isn't a foolish question," I said, "how did he make contact with Lady Lammerford?"

"You mean, why weren't they put on the market? Sold at Christie's, for instance?"

"Something like that."

"Well, the Lammerford place was Knighton Hall, which is quite near Tynworth. Bolfray used to be one of Tynworth's two members of parliament and he knew the family well. Also, old Lady Lammerford wanted the affair kept confidential. Bolfray—Lord Tynworth—bought them, as I said, and he had a good bargain. I don't mean he drove a hard bargain. There was a confidential valuation beforehand which was the actual basis, but the value of those jewels was then just under thirty thousand pounds, which was approximately what was paid. Their value today is over fifty thousand, which is the sum for which they're insured with us. But only in special circumstances. Let me explain."

He smiled.

"I'm afraid I'm getting muddled over this. Let's go back to Lord Tynworth. He bought not only the jewels but also a complete replica which the second lord had had made by a very good firm. The jewels weren't famous in any way. They weren't part of any legend. I'd say nine out of ten men in the highest-class trade have never heard of them. But about Lord Tynworth. I knew him and I knew of him. You know there were rumours about Ramsay Macdonald and his love of court dress? Well, Tynworth had rumours of the same sort attached to his name, though in a very much smaller circle. He was a peer, and he had money, and he liked his wife to be seen in public wearing those replicas. No one except under a glass could tell they weren't the real thing. At any rate he kept the replicas in his own safe. The originals were in the vaults of the Metropolitan Bank in Fenchurch Street. You follow all that?"

"Nothing could be clearer."

"Good. Then that brings us to Lady Tynworth's death in 1944, following on the death of their eldest son. Lord Tynworth's own health broke up and he died in 1946. He left the jewels in trust for any children of his other son Thomas. It may sound complicated, but it isn't really. When the eldest of such children came of age the jewels were to be sold and he or she was to receive a proportionate amount. Put it this way. If there were three children and there wouldn't be the likelihood of more, the eldest got a third. The other two got their thirds on coming of age. The replicas were left to Thomas, the son, absolutely.

"The bank themselves are now the only trustees. The originals are still with them. Or they were. There was provision for that in the will. If in the opinion of the trustees the occasion warranted it, the originals might be used."

He gave that same rueful smile.

"I still feel I'm getting this a bit muddled. The will wasn't too clear though it survived probate. Curious how shrewd men, businessmen, can make what I might call bad wills, but there we are. I think Bolfray—his mind fell away badly before his death— had certain delusions of grandeur. Maybe he was visualising his heir's wife as from the old nobility and likely to attend gala or state functions. I don't know, but that's how I see it. But the hard facts are that Thomas didn't marry that kind of woman. He and his wife saw the jewels one afternoon at the bank, but no occasion ever arose for an application to use them. Until this very year. You see the point? The coronation."

"Exactly," I said. "Tynworth must have had luck in the ballot—or am I guessing wrong?"

"You're dead right," he said. "He wanted the jewels examined and cleaned beforehand, and in the preliminary correspondence Harman and Peake of Old Bond Street were suggested and accepted by him. But once the jewels left the vaults that would be where we came in. Until they were back at the bank they'd be covered by us. Which brings us to the real point."

He drew a scribbling pad in front of him and consulted some notes. Hallows and I took out our notebooks.

"Tynworth received permission to withdraw the jewels and he actually did so on Saturday, February the 14th. We were notified by him just beforehand by telephone, and the provisional premium having already been paid, everything was in order. The actual person who handled things went down with influenza and his papers were left till his return, and that wasn't till yesterday. It struck him at once that he ought to have rung Harman and Peake to make sure the jewels were being attended to and to get the probable date of return to the bank. You see, it wasn't till some time near the coronation that the jewels would be in Tynworth's actual custody. But Harman and Peake said they'd never received the jewels!"

"Good lord!"

"You may well be surprised," Hill said. "We've got to admit a most amazing muddle. Negligence on our part, of course, which is being thoroughly investigated, but gross breach of trust on the part of Lord Tynworth. But things are even worse than I've outlined. I rang Old Farm, Herndown, this morning to speak with Lord Tynworth and get his explanations. I was told he was in America visiting a relative and might be back at any moment. Lady Tynworth was visiting friends in England. Mrs. Bolfray— Tynworth's sister-in-law—said she knew nothing about the jewels, though she'd naturally heard of them."

"Very queer."

"It's more than that," he said. "I had a certain source of enquiry and I was told that Tynworth is rather in Queer Street. It looks as if Old Farm will soon cease to be his at all."

He didn't raise his voice as he fired that bombshell. He just gave us both a look.

"Looks bad," I said. "But Tynworth couldn't have taken those jewels to America to dispose of them. He'd never have got through the customs."

"I imagine it's been done. It strikes me that human nature is such that the very name of a peer of the realm might conduce to a lack of suspicion. The jewels could easily have been concealed about his person."

"If he has disposed of them, then he's in America for good," Hallows said. "He daren't appear back here."

"I know. But we're liable—unless they can be recovered. It'd be no consolation to us if he were sentenced for robbing his own son, which is what it amounts to."

"You say he was heavily in debt," I said. "Any chance of his having handed them over to a creditor?"

"That'll be included in your investigation," he told me. "It'll be a reasonably tactful one. I say *reasonably* because Tynworth has committed a gross breach of trust. We're entitled to take drastic action."

He got to his feet.

"Any questions?"

Hallows, who knew practically nothing about the Case of the Missing Lady, wanted to know more about Tynworth and his circumstances. Hill sat down again and I had to listen to rather less than what I knew already. Howard Rill's name was mentioned as a probable creditor.

A few minutes later we were going, and we had authority to act and a copy of Hill's own dossier of the affair. Hallows and I went back to the office. When he left he knew as much about everything as I did. It had all been a staggering coincidence, but it had been just as well not to intimate to Hill that there'd been any coincidence at all. Tynworth had been our client, for one thing. Also it was just as well to be in a position, even if we didn't recover the jewels, to show Hill that we'd cast our net pretty wide. That it had been cast at almost the same shoal before was no business of his.

From what we knew it looked as if the case was as good as over. Tynworth had stated to me that his wife had taken certain valuables which were not hers to take, and what they were we now knew. We might have sat back smugly and let Hill think we had achieved a miracle by simply confronting Sally Bolfray, threatening her with the police and recovering the property. But that wasn't the way to go to work. If she had taken the jewels, then she'd taken them from Old Farm. Also she might have taken only some of them and Tynworth himself might have taken the rest to America. In any case it was at Old Farm that we ought to begin. It was what Hill had expected.

The previous night we'd rung the Birmingham agency and instructed them to keep Sally Bolfray under observation. Even though there seemed no great danger of her leaving the city— Bernardo was playing there for a fortnight—we wanted the job done very unobtrusively.

Now Norris was ringing Old Farm. It was Mrs. Drew who answered. Mrs. Bolfray, she said, hadn't come in yet from exercise, and could she take a message. It ended by our ringing again half an hour later, and then she was in. Norris explained the situation, that we were acting for United Insurance in a matter about which she had been rung the previous day.

"The representatives for the insurance company would like to see you this morning," Norris said. "What time would suit you?"

"Half-past eleven?"

"Thank you, Mrs. Bolfray—they shall be there. By the way, one of them will be a Mr. Travers. He tells me he's an old friend of yours."

She'd given a gasp of surprise, Norris said, and then she'd said that that would be very nice.

"Said you were very charming," Norris told me with a grin. "Probably you'll be able to charm something out of her."

We left at ten o'clock. Hallows had his little private box of gadgets and I an attaché-case with a formidable series of documents, chiefly for show. It was a grand morning. That later February and the first half of March were to be dry and almost consistently sunny. I mention that, because the weather was to have a considerable bearing on the case itself and the developments that arose.

We drew into the drive dead on time. Molly must have been listening or watching for the car, for she was at the front door as we got out.

"How nice to see you," she said, and she meant me. I introduced Hallows. We went into the lounge and seated ourselves.

"You mustn't mind me talking to Mr. Travers," she told Hallows, "but we're quite old friends. And why didn't you tell me you were connected with an insurance company?" she asked me accusingly. "Letting me think you were still an author."

There was an unnatural pertness about her. The slim person in the jodhpurs and high-necked sweater had something of the *gamine* about her that morning. Could she be putting on an act?

"That's only for my leisure," I said. "I still have to live. And don't ask me why."

She laughed as if it was the birth of that senile joke. Mrs. Drew came in with coffee. She gave me and Hallows quite a close look.

"I was sure you'd like coffee," Molly told us, and proceeded to pour it. Making everything friendly from the start, I told myself, and wondered just what it was she was anxious to conceal. That was why, as soon as I'd sipped my coffee and said it was good, I got right down to business.

"Mr. Hill told us you had no idea that certain articles of jewellery were here in the house?"

She was taken aback. I didn't think she'd expected to be questioned so quickly.

"No," she said. "No, I didn't. I knew Sally wanted them cleaned and got ready, but I didn't know they were actually here."

"Did Sally?"

"I don't know," she said. "I mean, if I knew that Sally knew, then I'd have known myself. Wouldn't I?"

That apt retort seemed to give her confidence.

"All I know is what I told Mr. Hill and what I've just told you."

"Look, Molly," I said, "I want to assure you that everything that's said here and now is absolutely confidential. You believe that?"

"Of course—if you say so."

"I do say so. I also have to add that the apparent absence of the jewellery will have to be explained by somebody, otherwise it will be a matter for the police. It's as serious as that."

She frowned. She said she didn't understand. I enlightened her. I made her see just where Tynworth stood.

"I'm sure it'll be all right as soon as he comes back," she said, and it was puzzling me why I hadn't succeeded in scaring her.

"Oughtn't he to have been back a day or two ago? Has he cabled you about it?"

"Well, no," she said slowly. Then she brightened. "But he's an erratic sort of person. He might walk in at any minute."

"Let's hope for his sake he does. But now a very personal question. Supposing you'd known that jewellery was here—or, rather, let's put it another way: now you know the jewellery *was* here, do you see any connection between it and your sister's surreptitious departure?"

She stared at me. She was frightened.

"How d'you know that?"

"A big insurance company has ways and means of finding out things. Remember it has fifty thousand pounds at stake."

She was in a corner. From then on she wouldn't know just how much we knew. But she knew she'd have to talk and she told me about Sally's departure.

"That tallies with what we know," I said. "But if the jewellery *was* here, where might it have been?"

"Possibly in the safe," she said, and she'd nervously moistened her lips. "Actually there're two safes: one in the office, and one upstairs in another room that Tom used as an office. Anything valuable was kept there because we once had a burglary in the outside office."

"You got a key to the safe upstairs?"

"Of course not. Tom had the key."

"Your sister had one?"

"Not that I know of. In fact I'm sure she didn't."

"Mind if we have a look at that safe?"

"Not at all. I'll just tell Mrs. Drew to take these things away."

We waited at the foot of the stairs while she went to the kitchen. I guessed it was all an excuse to steel her nerves against a new crisis.

"A pretty woman," Hallows whispered.

"And a scared one."

"Wonder what the safe'll be like."

She was coming back along the short passage. We followed her up to the first landing, where she opened a door on the right. It was a comparatively bare room of some twelve feet by eight: its only furnishings a table, chair, a metal filing cabinet and, in the far corner, a medium-sized safe that looked as if Hallows should have brought a tin-opener.

"You see to the safe, Hallows: we'll wait outside."

"Just old family secrets," I whispered to Molly. "The tricks of the trade. It isn't everyone who can open a safe."

I could feel her trembling as I took her arm.

"This the nursery?"

The door was open and we went through.

"No nephew?"

"He's out with Daisy," she told me, and she actually smiled. "I like him to have plenty of fresh air."

It was a fine, airy room with a cot, a play-pen and quite a few toys. That big teddy-bear I'd seen in the perambulator lay in the play-pen, legs grotesquely in the air. A rag book was with it and some bricks.

"You're very fond of him, aren't you, Molly?"

"Yes," she said, and very quietly. "He's always been more mine than Sally's. You don't mind me telling you that?"

"Why should I? It makes me know more than ever that you're a very nice person."

There was a call from the door. We went back to the office.

Hallows had the safe open. Even from where we stood we could see it was absolutely empty.

"Well, there's nothing there," I said fatuously. "But it brings us to something else. There were replicas of the jewellery. You knew that?"

She hesitated for a moment before she said yes.

"Who kept those?"

"Sally did. After all, they were hers."

"She took them with her?"

"She must have done. She left nothing behind except some clothes she didn't want. I mean, she wouldn't have left them if she'd have wanted them?"

"Mind if we have a look at the room?"

"Is that necessary?"

"Well, no," I said. "Not at this stage. You've been through the room yourself, I take it, and you'll guarantee they're not there?"

"I'm positive they're not there. Not even the empty cases."

"And do you know where your sister actually is?"

Again she hesitated. She bit her lip. I thought that tears were pretty close, but she fought them back.

"Yes," she said. "A letter came this morning for Tom. I opened it. I didn't know if it might be something for me to do—as he's away. It's in my room. I'll fetch it."

Hallows raised his eyebrows questioningly. I shrugged my shoulders. Molly came back.

"At Birmingham," I said, looking at the envelope. Then I drew out the letter. It was written on hotel stationery.

Dear Tom,

I have gone for good and don't expect me to come back because I shan't. If you want evidence for a divorce you can get it here. The less fuss you make about it, the better for everyone. Provided you act quickly I shan't want anything in return and there won't be any trouble about Peter.

SALLY.

Short and sweet, I was thinking; and then I heard a sound. Molly was crying.

"That's all right, Molly." I put my hand on her shoulder. "Take it easy. Looks to me as if everything's for the best. After all, you will still have the boy."

She suddenly turned away. She was almost running through the nursery door. Probably to her bedroom. Hallows and I stood there and we didn't look at each other. Then I nodded and we went slowly down the stairs and into the lounge. It was a good five minutes before Molly came in. Her eyes were still red.

"I'm sorry," she said. "I oughtn't to have given way like that."

"Nonsense. A good cry does you good. We're not keeping you much longer, in any case, but do you think we might have a word with Mr. Yale, Tom's partner? Pardon my calling him Tom."

"He might be back at the stables by now. Shall I see?"

"Do, please. And you might ask him to look in that other safe. He has a key to it?"

"Of course," she told me from the door. "But I'm sure there's nothing there."

From the window I saw her hurrying towards the stables.

"Won't she have time to cook something up?" Hallows said.

"You don't trust her?"

"I do and I don't. I don't think she's likely to be mixed up in anything crooked, but I think she knows quite a lot she hasn't told."

"Don't want to press her at this juncture," I said. "Just let things move along easily."

I began telling him from the window what I knew about Yale. I hadn't quite finished when the two were at the door. Yale was a surprise to me, and not because he looked vastly different from the surly, unkempt Yale of my previous call. He actually looked most friendly. He was smiling as he held out his hand.

"Seeing each other again sooner than we thought."

"Yes," I said. "Sorry it has to be about business. Also I'd like to assure you that when I turned up the other day it was absolutely genuine. Nothing to do with business, as I called it."

"Sure of it," he said. "Cigarette?"

Hallows had one. I had a pipe.

"What about a spot of sherry? Or gin and something?"

"Only just had coffee," I said. "Good of you, all the same. Also we have to get back to town."

He leaned back cross-legged in the easy-chair.

"Molly's been telling me about this jewellery business. Looks like a pretty bad show on the face of it, but Tom—my partner—will doubtless explain."

"I hope for his sake he will," I told him, and I also told him just why.

"A damn silly thing for him to do," he said. "If he ever had the stuff here, that is."

"You knew nothing about it?"

"Never a thing. I did know that Sally was nagging a bit about getting the stuff ready for the coronation. And that was all damn nonsense, too, if you ask me. The belted-earl stuff and all that."

"Not perhaps from her point of view. Women—I speak as a married man—rather like shows and occasions."

"Why not—if you can live up to it? And if so, why the hell did she suddenly bolt? Molly's just told me she's in Birmingham with some other man."

There'd been a slight sneer in the tone. Or was it pity for himself?

"Yes," I said. "I hope you were told also that our firm has fifty thousand pounds at stake."

He whistled.

"Honestly? I never dreamed they'd be worth so much. Did you, Molly?"

"I'd no idea. I did know they were valuable."

"You can take it from me that that's the value of the missing jewellery," I said. "And that Lord Tynworth will have to answer some mightily unpleasant questions when he comes back."

He shrugged his shoulders. He asked what they could do about it, with the hope, apparently, that I'd admit there was nothing they could do at all.

"Two or three questions you might answer," I told him. "For instance, do either of you know a Henry Balfour?"

They interchanged blank looks. Neither knew anyone of that name.

"Then who are Lord Tynworth's solicitors?"

"Waller, Highes and Waller, Bank Chambers, Chelmsford," Yale told me. "They acted in the sale of the property here and Tom took them on. Handy to have a reasonably local firm."

I got to my feet.

"You're busy people, and I won't keep you longer. Just one other thing. Would you both care to give me your word that you won't communicate with Lady Tynworth in Birmingham and warn her that she's going to be questioned?"

"You can certainly rely on us both for that," Yale said.

"And one other thing. Lord Tynworth's in America. Does he know his wife's left him?"

"I rang him first thing in the morning after she'd gone," Molly said.

"Where was he?"

"At the New Regality Hotel."

I thanked her and said we'd be going. And I hoped they'd both regard the visit as purely friendly.

"Hasn't it been?" Yale asked me.

"Of course it has," Molly told him. "Mr. Travers has been most considerate."

"Nice of you to say so. The only other thing is that we'd be very grateful if you'd ring the head office if anything you consider important should occur to any of you. You have our card, Molly."

We said goodbye to her. Yale went out with us to the car. He asked only one question.

"What was it that Molly was telling me about the police being likely to get mixed up in all this?"

I asked him to work it out for himself and I told him how and why. I did add that if Lord Tynworth did turn up in the course of the next day or so he ought at once to get in touch with us. I could see there were other questions he had on his mind, but I gave a farewell wave of the hand and moved the car on. I still had an eye his way and that was why I caught a glimpse of someone round the corner at the back of the house as we went slowly by. It was Mrs. Drew. At the sight of the car she shot back out of sight.

"That cook housekeeper—the woman who brought in the coffee. Wonder what she was watching us for?"

"Probably waiting to put lunch on the table," Hallows said. "Wanted to make sure we'd gone."

CHAPTER VII
THE LIARS

"WHERE now?" Hallows asked as we turned left into the main road.

"Chelmsford. I'd like a word with Tynworth's solicitors."

I hadn't much time to spare if I wanted to ring them before one o'clock, but we were in Dunmow with ten minutes in hand. The earliest appointment I could have, I was told, was at two.

It was only thirteen miles to Chelmsford. We parked the car in the hotel yard and had lunch. Hallows asked me how I was feeling now about things. I waited till I heard what he thought about Yale.

"Seemed on his best behaviour," he said. "I'd expected something different after what you told me. A good-looking chap. Real racing type of gentleman I suppose you could call him."

"Why not?" I said. "But he's a brazen liar. He was hand-in-glove with Sally Bolfray. I think it's a certainty she had him on a string until the very last moment and he was as staggered as anybody when she disappeared. Yet he swore he knew nothing about the jewellery. And another thing. He was a member of the family, so to speak. They all ate together. The jewels must have been talked about."

"What about Mrs. Bolfray?"

"Maybe I'm a bit prejudiced, but she seemed open enough. I had an idea earlier she was trying to conceal something, or scared. I think she was worrying about that letter from her sister. She'd had it only this morning. But there's one other thing, and about Tynworth. Why did he stay at a place like the New Regality?"

"Yes," Hallow said. "Hardly in his class, you'd think, even if he was hard-up. Central, of course, for the West End."

"It's a modern rabbit-warren," I said, "and not all that cheap. The food's conveyor-belt stuff. It's the sort of place you'd apologise for if you had to mention it to your friends."

"In fact you don't feel happy about things."

I told him I felt very unhappy, and partly because I just couldn't say exactly why. But I was glad to leave the whole thing and talk over what should be said to the solicitors. Everything had to be governed by Tynworth's return. Would he strongly resent an approach to those solicitors? Would he try to make something of it? We didn't think he'd dare. His conduct had been highly reprehensible, though he might claim it had been only forgetfulness.

"Mind if I get this clear?" Hallows asked me. "Tynworth went to town on the Monday afternoon and everyone knew he was going to the New Regality. He left his main baggage at the Airport Building and then went to the hotel. The jewels were then in that safe I opened this morning."

"According to the way I interpreted his statements—yes."

"Then early the next morning Mrs. Bolfray got hold of him at the New Regality and told him about his wife. He went back to Herndown and found the safe empty, though his was the only key. But he suspected his wife of having a key—that'd be simple enough—and he got hold of that Henry Balfour to take over. Balfour advised using the Broad Street Detective Agency. And didn't Tynworth also see the solicitors?"

"That was inherent in what he told me. It was possible even to assume that Balfour was either connected with the solicitors or had been in touch with them."

"Then why shouldn't we pick the solicitors' brains? Tynworth probably told them more than he told you. He may have given them proofs that his wife took the jewels."

But things didn't work out like that. Waller was a man of about sixty: a typical senior member of an old-fashioned firm of country solicitors. I introduced myself and Hallows, showed my credentials and came to the point. Waller was struck with horror at Tynworth's breach of trust. I could see he was suspecting even worse.

That was where I became deliberately vague. I'd been at Old Farm, I'd said, and the company I represented had made other enquiries and so—purely in confidence and without prejudice—I'd be grateful for an answer to a couple of questions.

"For example, Mr. Waller, we've learned that Lord Tynworth was using a friend of his, in his own enforced absence, to try to recover the jewels—a Henry Balfour. Do you know him?"

"Balfour? Balfour?" He shook his head. "I don't know any Balfour."

"I see. And did Lord Tynworth acquaint you with the facts on the Tuesday before his leaving for America?"

He clicked his tongue.

"My dear sir, I can assure you that we haven't seen or heard from Lord Tynworth for at least some weeks. Everything you've said comes as a complete surprise, not to say shock."

I got to my feet.

"Then we needn't trouble you any longer. We're most grateful for taking up your time."

"But wait a minute. Wait a minute." He was all of a fluster. "From time to time we handle certain business for Lord Tynworth and if anything emerges from this it's likely he'll be consulting us. He isn't back yet?"

"He isn't. He should have been back at least two days ago."

He clicked his tongue again.

"Shall we leave it?" I said. "And would you care to be informed, strictly in confidence, of any developments?"

"I certainly would. But Lord Tynworth must be back soon. Won't that clear the whole matter up?"

I said we certainly hoped so, and with that we shook hands and left. Waller was looking most unhappy.

"I don't like the look of it," Hallows said to me as we walked back to the car.

I said I hated the very sight of it. Everywhere was nothing but lies. Even Tynworth had thought it necessary to use a quota.

"One thing we can't get away from, though. There *was* a Henry Balfour. He saw the *Telegraph* message, he rang as arranged and he went to Birmingham."

"And yet nothing's happened as far as we know. Lady Tynworth's still at the Birmingham hotel."

"Yes," I said. "Strikes me that the sooner we get to Birmingham and hear her side of the story, the better."

It was well after four o'clock when we got back to the office. I'd rung Norris to try to check up on something—Lord Tynworth's registration at the New Regality. When we arrived he had still more disturbing news for us. Neither a Lord Tynworth or a T. Bolfray had been registered there for the night in question. Which made Molly Bolfray also a liar.

It made me angry. Bertha got Old Farm on the telephone and I spoke to Molly.

"Travers here, Molly. Something peculiar's turned up. You're dead sure your brother-in-law did spend the Monday night at the New Regality?"

"But of course! I rang him there on the Tuesday morning. At eight o'clock."

"What name did you ask for?"

There was a silence. There was no sudden click, but the line went dead. I joggled and joggled, but nothing happened.

I buzzed through to Bertha and asked her to get the Herndown number again.

It was Mrs. Drew who spoke. She said she'd find Mrs. Bolfray. I waited a couple of minutes.

"So sorry," Molly said. "Someone must have cut us off. What was it you were saying?"

I tried to keep the annoyance out of my voice.

"I was asking what name Lord Tynworth used at the New Regality."

"Oh, that," she said, and laughed. "He used his mother's name. Waterford. He didn't want publicity, and he hadn't much money—poor dear."

"Much obliged," I said. "But tell me something else while we're talking. What was the name and address of that cousin he was seeing in America?"

"Waterford," she said. "John F. Waterford, Junior; The Drive, Oakville, Long Island."

"Did your brother-in-law have a return ticket?"

"I don't think so. He didn't know how long he might actually be staying."

"But he expected to be back inside a week."

"That's what he told me."

I thanked her and rang off. As I told Norris and Hallows, I liked it less and less. Molly Bolfray was playing some queer game or other. And so was Tynworth. There was no point in using his mother's maiden name at a huge caravanserai of a place like the New Regality. If he didn't want to use his title, who on earth would care a red cent about a T. Bolfray, for instance.

"We'll check on the Waterford name," Norris said. "What train are you proposing to take to Birmingham?"

We looked it up and the six-thirty seemed the one.

"Get hold of that John F. Waterford," I said, "and find out when Tynworth arrived at his place. It's even possible that Tynworth might still be there. Never mind the expense. We can hear all about it when we get back tomorrow afternoon. Try to book either a twin-bed or two single rooms at the Archdale. Give me a ring about it at the flat."

An hour later Norris rang to say a room with twin-beds had been reserved in Hallows's name. He added that Tynworth had registered at the New Regality under the name of T. Waterford.

It was after nine o'clock when we got to the hotel. We'd had dinner on the train and, as I wasn't anxious to be seen, Hallows did some scouting around. I'd turned in by the time he'd got back.

He'd discovered that Sally Bolfray wasn't in her room, and that Bernardo's room was two doors away on the opposite side of the corridor. Bernardo and his Brazilianos were the star attraction that week at the Empire, which meant two shows a night. The following week they were at the Palace Hotel. Of the two singers he'd had in town at the Monterey, Tony Marre remained. Luize del Ray had been replaced by a Carlotta Marini.

"Probably a stand-by," he said, "while Sally Bolfray or whatever she'll call herself is getting the hang of things. Fake South American accent and all that. And some of the real stuff, learning it like a parrot."

In the morning we took our time. The lady wouldn't probably appear till pretty late, so it was not till after nine o'clock that we began settling down in the reception hall behind our newspapers. We had a long wait. We'd had mid-morning coffee, and it was after eleven o'clock when the lady appeared. Bernardo followed just behind her. He made for the newspaper kiosk. The lady sank into a chair. I made for her, with Hallows just behind me. I gave what was intended for my best smile.

"Lady Tynworth?"

"Well—yes," she said.

There seemed something very wary about her look, as if she were trying to remember me or estimate just what that sudden appearance might imply. I was seeing her for the first time. That photograph I had seen had been good, though now I could see a slight resemblance to Molly. But she was a genuine blonde: her hair a couple of shades lighter than Molly's, and her face harder and the eyes a cold bluey-grey. There was an indefinable cheapness about her.

"I wonder if you could spare us a minute or two, Lady Tynworth?"

She seemed still groping for some recollection of me. Then her lip drooped.

"This isn't anything to do with my husband, by any chance?"

Bernardo was there. I hadn't heard his steps on the thick carpet, but I'd caught a whiff of hair-cream, and there he was.

"Good morning."

He wanted an introduction and to be in things. At close quarters and in a tweed suit he wasn't the radiant cavalier of the photograph. His face was sallow and the eyes a bit puffy. Just one more step down the ladder and he'd have been a rather prosperous spiv.

Let's call the woman Sally and save the pseudonyms. It was she who spoke.

"I don't know who they are, Frankie, but I think they're here about you-know-who."

"That's fine," he said. "Just what do you want to know, gentlemen?"

A couple were going by and I waited till they were well past.

"I'm afraid you're wrong, Lady Tynworth. I represent United Insurance—"

"Good God!" He laughed. Then he waved a hand. "Look, we're busy. We don't want insurance. Go and peddle it some place else."

I'd have liked to smack him across the mouth.

"You're still wrong," I said. "We're here to see if you can give us any information, Lady Tynworth, about your husband. He's apparently disappeared."

"Disappeared?" It had startled her—but only for a moment. She looked up at Frankie and laughed. "They don't know he's in America."

"We know it perfectly well," I told her quietly. "But he should have been back days ago. Nothing's been heard or seen of him. We wondered if you could help us."

That set her back on her heels. She looked at Frankie. He shrugged his shoulders, but it was he who made the suggestion.

"What about talking this over upstairs?"

He moved, then turned back. His eyes narrowed.

"This isn't some dirty trick, by any chance?"

"No trick at all. What I've told you is absolute fact. Lady Tynworth has only to ring her sister and verify it. We can wait."

"Right then. Let's go up."

"Mr. Bernardo is a very old friend," Sally confided to me as we went up the stairs to the first floor. "If what you've told me is true, I think I ought to have someone to help me, don't you?"

I agreed. I'd have agreed to anything provided it ended in talk. And it looked like it. Frankie apparently had a suite—sitting-room, bedroom and bath. He unlocked the door and we went straight into the sitting-room. A saxophone was on the table and a couple of instrument cases and various little stacks of music-sheets. There was more music on the floor.

"A bit crowded," he told us. "My name's Bernardo, if you didn't know it."

"The well-known band-leader?"

"Well, maybe I *am* well known."

I said he certainly was. I introduced Hallows and myself. The name conveyed nothing.

"Sit down," he said. "Might as well be comfortable. You'll have a drink?"

I said we'd only just had coffee. I gave him and Sally an official card.

"Still don't see what an insurance company's got to do with it?"

"I'll explain."

There were seats for just the four of us. He lighted two cigarettes and gave one to Sally. I waited till they'd settled down again, and then, with no preliminaries, I flung the whole thing at them—Tynworth, the jewels, fifty thousand pounds. No need to ask who was the cat and who the pigeons. They didn't even dare look at each other. Frankie was affecting an utter indifference.

"You see the seriousness of everything, Lady Tynworth? Would you mind—"

"For God's sake cut out that Lady Tynworth!" She was all on edge and she'd practically spat at me. "Call me anything—if you have to talk at all."

"Steady, Sally. Nothing to get upset about."

She shrugged her shoulders.

"I'm sorry." She turned to me. "What is it you want to know?"

"When you saw those jewels last."

"When? On the Saturday evening when they were brought home. We all saw them."

"Who do you mean by all?"

"Just all. I and Molly. And Arthur Yale, if you know him. Wasn't it natural we should want to look at them?" She shrugged her shoulders. "What happened to them then I don't know. My husband probably put them in the safe."

"But your sister Molly says she didn't see them."

"What!" She almost shrieked the word. "The dirty little liar!"

"And the replicas which were your own property? You have them here?"

"I have not," she told me with dignity. "My husband asked me to let him have them for a time. I thought he was going to have them seen to with the others. That's the last I saw of them."

"Then both the originals and the replicas have gone," I said. "Can't you give us any ideas about it?"

"Isn't it obvious?" That was Frankie cutting in. "He took both sets. Either working some swindle or disposing of them in America. It's plain as the nose on your face. That's why he's missing!" He turned triumphantly to Sally. "He never intended to come back."

"He was up to his ears in debt," Sally said. "Or didn't you know that?"

There'd been just a bit of a sneer. I said I *had* known it. But could she give me any evidence in support of her husband's intentions?

"He'd be far too clever. More brains than money—or so he thought."

Frankie got to his feet.

"Look, there's no point in going on with this. You've been told and told again the lady knows nothing about it."

"Just a minute. I've merely been asking in a friendly way if she could help us. But now I'll tell you something else."

I had her in the corner of my eye. She was absolutely motionless: just waiting and wondering what I'd say.

"Someone else thought Lady Tynworth knew where the jewels were."

He took a step towards me.

"Just what are you insinuating?"

"Nothing. I was about to tell you facts—that our information is that a certain party employed a detective agency to trace Lady Tynworth. She was traced to here from the Langton Hotel and the party was informed. He at once came here and saw her in her room. What transpired I haven't yet learned, but I'm hoping to."

"I can tell you," she told me shrilly. "Nothing did. No one saw me here about any jewels. It's an absolute lie."

I shrugged my shoulders.

"Well, if that's your attitude, I can only thank you and go. The next step will be for the police."

That shook her again. Frankie tried more bluster.

"What right have you to pester her with questions? You're just a bloody insurance agent. Get out of here."

"I wouldn't take that attitude, Mr. Bernardo," Hallows told him quietly. "The police mightn't be so friendly as we are."

"Oh, for God's sake!" That was Sally again. "Can't you get out of here? Bring the police. Bring the whole damn force. I still don't know anything."

"If the lady has a nervous breakdown I'll hold you responsible."

He grasped my arm and began moving me towards the door. I shook him off.

"Keep your hands to yourself." I waited a moment. "Good-morning to you, Lady Tynworth. I'm afraid you're going to be sorry about all this."

We went out—there was nothing else for it. What could we do? We had no powers. They'd have been within their rights if they'd refused to talk at all. There was no law behind us. Frankie's cheap sneer hadn't been too far out. We weren't much more than insurance agents.

Lunch was on, so we had it, and we were going back by the two o'clock. I was still furious. Hallows was taking it quite philosophically.

"We know they're both liars. If they haven't got the jewels they know who has. Our time'll come when we're in the witness-box."

I felt I'd handled things badly.

"Nothing derogatory about you, Hallows, but I wish to heaven you were George Wharton. He'd have turned that couple inside out."

"Well, he'd be the law."

"I know. But I ought to have led up more cunningly to our friend Henry Balfour and why he saw her here. I might have trapped her into telling me his real name."

"I doubt it," he told me.

I went on with the meal and I hardly knew what I was eating. I thought of something else.

"'Do you know, I think she was right about something? Those women, and probably Yale, *must* have seen the jewels. Tynworth couldn't have brought anything so staggering, so attractive to women, into the house without their having a good look."

"But that makes Mrs. Bolfray a liar."

"She is," I said. "The difference is that she's covering up for someone—probably Tynworth. Yale's a liar, too. They're all liars."

"I don't know," he said. "I liked Mrs. Bolfray. The other one hates her. You could hear that when she called her a dirty little liar."

"All liars are dirty."

He smiled dryly.

"Except us."

I had to smile. It gave me a sense of proportion. It made me forget that face of Frankie's and the feel of his hand on my arm.

Our two friends didn't make an appearance in the dining-room. We caught our train and all the way to town we were busy compiling a detailed report to date. When we got to King's Cross I had yet another idea. Just a few steps and we'd be at the Piccadilly Line. It was still early, so why not have a word with Howard Rill.

By luck there were two telephone booths free. Hallows was to ring the office for news. I'd try to get hold of Rill.

Plumer came on the line, so I slipped my handkerchief between my teeth.

"This is the United Insurance Company. May I speak to Mr. Rill?"

"Sorry, sir, but Mr. Rill's playing golf."

In practically the same breath he was asking me to hold on. He thought Mr. Rill had just come in. A couple of minutes and Rill was on the line.

"Rill speaking. Just what is it you want?"

"This is United Insurance, Mr. Rill. District manager speaking. We'd be grateful if you'd see a couple of our representatives."

"But I'm not insured with you? I'm insured elsewhere."

"I know, sir. This is something quite different. We understand you may be able to help us."

"Help you? What about?"

"A very confidential matter, sir. I'll merely mention the name of Lord Tynworth."

There was a tiny grunt as if he'd given a start. He didn't speak for quite a few seconds.

"I still don't understand. However"—the tone had been pompous—"there'll be no harm in hearing what you have to say. When do your representatives want to come?"

"Almost at once, sir. It's rather urgent."

"All right," he said. "It's now—let me see—it's a quarter to five. Shall we say an hour's time?"

"That will suit us admirably. We're much obliged, Mr. Rill."

Hallows was waiting outside. Bertha had said Norris was out but he might be in at any minute. She believed there was news but she'd rather he told it himself.

"Get her again," I said. "Say we're going out to Cockfosters and we'll be at the office before eight o'clock. Ask her to let my wife know."

Norris still wasn't in. We had plenty of time for a cup of tea and a bun. We even had to take it slowly from Cockfosters Station to Rill's house.

CHAPTER VIII
THE THUNDERBOLTS

WE WERE shown into a room that was a cross between lounge and private office. It was a large house in large grounds—we couldn't help seeing that even in the scant light of an early February evening—and this room was quite large enough for its purpose. It was slick, modern and yet comfortable, but the only thing I'd have liked in it was the Regency bracket clock on the mantelpiece of the showy marble fireplace. The sporting prints on the walls looked like reproductions.

We'd hardly time to look round us when the far door opened and I was looking at Howard Rill for the first time. He was in a dark suit with a grey tie, and at first sight I saw something of a Colonel Blimp. But he wasn't quite that in spite of the reddish purple of the face and the handsome white moustache. He was taller, and he had only the slightest of middle-aged spreads. A handsome man in a florid way, urbane in manner and his tone inclined to the unctuous.

His hand went out as he came nearer. I introduced myself and Hallows. A queer, quick look went across his face at the mention of my name, or so I thought.

"A drink before business, gentlemen? What shall it be?" I said sherry. Hallows said sherry. We all had sherry. We drank each other's health from the depths of the big leather chairs.

"Have a good game of golf, sir?" I asked him.

"A capital game. You play yourself?"

I said I'd played a lot in my time but nowadays I was usually too busy. We must have gone on talking golf for the best part of five minutes and I wondered why he wasn't anxious to get down to business. Then there was a small diversion. A tap at the door and Plumer looked in.

"What is it, Plumer?"

"It's all right, sir. I'll see you later."

Rill looked annoyed at that barging in.

"The damn fellow. He knew you were here. But to get down to business, gentlemen. What brings you here? Something, did I understand, to do with Lord Tynworth?"

I said that was so.

"But why the connection?"

"That's not our business," I told him. "We merely receive our orders. We understood you might be able to help us."

"He's insured with you?"

"In a way, yes."

"I still don't understand. Do you mean he's given my name as a reference?"

"Nothing of the sort, sir. This is our card, by the way. I take it that whatever is said here is in the very strictest confidence?"

"Most decidedly." He smiled. He gently tapped his pink forehead. "I can assure you that somewhere here I have confidences that would surprise you."

So I began to talk. His look of surprise became one of bewilderment and utter incredulity. He was bursting to interrupt, but he let me finish.

"Astounding!" he said. "It's like a fairy-tale."

"It's hard fact," I told him. "Everything I've told you is well authenticated. Our firm stands to lose fifty thousand pounds. And Lord Tynworth's still in America. He can stay there as far as we're concerned, provided we recover the jewels."

Then I looked him clean in the eye.

"I hope, sir, you'll take this in the right spirit, but since Lord Tynworth was in debt to you—or that's our information—we wondered if by any chance he might have deposited the jewels recently as some sort of security."

"Utterly fantastic," he said. "Another sherry?"

We both refused.

"Whisky?"

We still refused.

"Well, I'll have one myself. I need it after what you've been telling me. Looks as if I might be a considerable sum of money out of pocket, too."

But it wasn't too stiff a drink he poured himself, even if there was only the shortest squirt of the soda. He took a gulp and brought the glass to the low table by his chair. Then he told us what we already knew. Tynworth had done some heavy betting. He owed best part of ten thousand pounds.

"Ours is a big firm," Rill said, "and I've had quite a bad turn of 'flu lately. I didn't really realise Tynworth was in so deep. One gives some latitude to a peer of the realm, in any case. He's expected to be a strictly honourable man. . . ."

He went on and on. I knew it all for something thought up a bit too hastily in that hour since I'd rung him from King's Cross. It wasn't chronological but all over the place, like that mentioning a recent influenza which hadn't really a thing to do with Tynworth's debts of at least weeks before.

"We're not the blood-suckers people take us to be," he was saying. "I could have made trouble for Lord Tynworth. He'd have lost his licence." He spread his palms. "But what good would that have done me? That's why I sent him a couple of horses. At least some of my money's coming back. He's had bad luck, but he's a good trainer. I wouldn't be surprised if we don't ultimately square our account. But this America business!" He spread his palms again. "It makes you lose faith in human nature. And risking taking those jewels through the customs—"

"Just a moment, sir. We've no evidence as to that."

"What else could have happened? For all I know—I haven't made enquiries—he may owe money elsewhere." He smiled sadly. "No, my dear sir. I'd be prepared to lay a considerable sum that you'll never clap eyes on him again."

"You'd no idea he was going to America?"

I don't know why the question took him by surprise, but it did.

"Wait a moment. I rang him about those horses of mine. One's going at Lingfield next week. There was something he said." He frowned. He allowed himself to smile. "Yes, I remember. He said he hoped to have a happy surprise for me in a few days. That was it. A happy surprise. I naturally asked if he was talking about the horse, but he wasn't. He was hoping to pay me a considerable sum of money. That's what he said. According to you it was just before he left. I'm pretty sure it was the Monday week before he left."

"You think his little secret was this trip of his to America?"

"Either that or he was just fobbing me off."

"But you never had the faintest idea he was going to America?"

"Not the faintest."

"And you never heard of the Lammerford Jewels?"

"Never."

I let out a breath. I said it was a bad business. He agreed. "That partner of his—Yale. I suppose he's up to the ears in debt, too?"

"No," he said. "It's more complicated than that. Yale sweetened up the business with five thousand when he came in. He's a grandson of old Lord Ampling, by the way. He won't come in for the title, but he's bound to be left a goodish packet. Yale's refused to put any more money in. He never owed us more than five hundred at any time and at the moment he owes nothing."

"Know anything about Lady Tynworth, sir?"

"Practically nothing. Never concerned with her. I know the sister-in-law rather better—the Honourable Moira. A nice little woman. Helps a lot in the stable. A thorough good horsewoman."

We got up to go. He tried to press a drink on us for the road. He insisted on having us driven back to the station. The bell was pushed for Plumer. He was to bring the car round at once.

I had a closer look at one row of prints. They were a well-known set of eight, and quite good.

"You're an authority?" he asked me.

I said I wasn't, but I liked what I liked. Then I heard a car, and somewhere in the drive. Its brakes squeaked slightly, but it was going away. Rill began talking about the prints again. A couple of minutes and our car was really at the door.

"Might I ask a favour?" Rill said as we went through to the hall. "Could I be kept informed? In strict confidence, of course?"

"I think that could be arranged," I told him. "Shall we leave it that if you don't hear from us, then there's nothing worth reporting."

"That'll be excellent," he told me.

I thanked him and we shook hands. He came with us to the door. The light was on above the circular porch. Plumer opened the rear door for us and we got in. Rill waved a hand as we moved off. He was still standing there as we went out of sight round the bend of the drive.

*

We stepped straight into a train only a few seconds before it moved off. It was rather noisy for talking, and by the time we were at Finsbury Park our carriage was packed. We got out at Leicester Square and walked round to the flat, and I left my case with the hall porter. Then we took a bus at Charing Cross. There was plenty of room on top.

"What'd you make of Rill?" I asked Hallows.

"A smooth piece of work. Butter wouldn't melt in his mouth."

"Anything peculiar strike you?"

"Only that he talked about golf for the very devil of a time."

"And until when?"

He thought for a moment.

"I get you. Till that chap Plumer came in." He smiled. "It couldn't have been a signal of some sort?"

"Let me tell you how I work things out. I was sitting nearer the window than you, but a little time before Plumer came in I heard a car drawing into the drive. Then, just after Plumer received his orders to get the car for us I heard a car going away."

"I heard that. Sounded like a powerful car."

"Then why shouldn't things work out like this? I mentioned Tynworth's name on the phone and then Rill didn't hem and haw any longer. He told me to come out in an hour's time. That gave him time to contact Conn and get him there, too. The golf-palaver was marking time till Conn got there. Plumer's little entry was a signal that Conn had arrived. When Plumer went out to get the car he told Conn we were just going. Conn went first."

"Sounds all right to me," Hallows said. "But why shouldn't Conn wait till after we'd gone and then talk things over with Rill?"

"I'd say because some action had to be taken. Or Conn may have parked his car where I'd see it and recognise it. Must have been a shock when he heard my name. Maybe the car was only taken out somewhere till we'd gone, and then Conn went back."

"He was listening to everything that was said?"

"Undoubtedly. And don't ask me why."

"Yes, but why should Rill send for him?"

"My idea of Conn," I said, "is that he's the real executive. A kind of strong-arm man. As for why Rill sent for him, the answer must be that they're both in this business up to the neck. The mere mention of Tynworth's name got me an entry."

"Yes," he said. "I can see Conn in it from what you've told me about him, but Rill—"

"What *about* Rill?"

"Well, he must have plenty of money. Look at that place of his. Would it pay him to be mixed up in anything shady?"

"Depends on the risk," I said. "I've no tears to shed for Rill. Commission agent, turf accountant, call it what you will—it still spells bookie. Did you ever hear of a home for indigent bookmakers? Rill was putting up a front with us tonight. I didn't like him. I still don't like him. I'd trust him as far as I could throw a battleship."

We got off at the corner and walked the few yards to the office. Norris was waiting for us.

"You're well on time," he told us. "Get anything out there tonight?"

"Don't know till we've sifted it," I said. "Most of it, and at Birmingham, was hot air and lies. What about this end? Anything happened?"

"Happened?" he said. "You'd never guess. You'd better brace yourself for a shock. It's about Tynworth. I couldn't get in touch with that Mr. Waterford till late last night, nearly midnight our time. What d'you think he told me? *That he hadn't seen hair or hide of Tynworth!*"

I couldn't say a word.

"He said Tynworth cabled him that he was coming over practically at once. Gave the Thursday morning as the probable date of arrival. Probable, mind you. That's why Waterford didn't meet him at the airport. Since then he's been expecting him or to hear from him every day."

"But he was on the plane!"

"I know he was. The whole thing's the very devil."

"Looks to me," Hallows said, "as if he did manage to get those jewels over there and that he's not coming back. The business about seeing his cousin was only a blind."

I was trying to think things out. Then suddenly I made up my mind.

"The first thing in the morning, Hallows, you'll come to the flat where we can get down to a detailed report for the insurance company. Let Hill make the decisions from now on. And if he wants my advice I'll tell him to go to the police."

But the night wasn't over. Something else was to come as a shock, and different from the one that Norris had sprung on us. It happened so quickly that any words I take to describe it would use more time than the happening itself. I'd got off the bus while it was held up just short of Charing Cross Station. I crossed the road and went past Duncannon Street. Further on there was a short cut that came out near the garage where I always kept my car, and from there it was only a minute or so to the flat.

The short cut was a kind of alleyway with walls each side, and about seventy-five yards long. The light was reasonably good from the main end where the traffic was going by, but at the other end, to which I was going, it was a bit dim, with only an old-fashioned light high up on the wall. As soon as one got through to Sylvester Street it was light enough again, though there was rarely any night traffic.

Well, I was nearing the Sylvester Street end and I was thinking about what had happened that night, when all at once I heard a zipp and a whine. I couldn't think what the devil it was, but I halted and half turned. That may have saved my life. I don't know. I do know there was a second zipp and a second whine and that was when the unbelievable truth dawned on me and I suddenly flopped down. It was a kind of instinct from military training. I know that I saw a dark something disappear at the far end I'd come from. I knew, too, that someone had taken two shots at me, and that the whines had been the ricochets as the bullets struck a wall.

It had been a matter of maybe five or six seconds. I'd heard no one behind me, so whoever had fired those shots must have worn rubber-soled shoes. Mind you, I didn't think of that at once. I was too shaken. My legs felt a bit wobbly as I got up and made quickly for the lights of Sylvester Street. I waited there a minute and dusted my knees before I went on to the flat.

There was a note for me from Bernice saying she'd not be in till just after ten o'clock. I was glad she wasn't there, for she might have noticed my shoulder. I wouldn't have noticed the overcoat myself if I hadn't felt a slight pain as I took it off. A hole had been drilled clean through it and the layers beneath it, and had grazed my shoulder, just drawing blood.

I dabbed the graze with iodine and stuck on some plaster, then I poured myself a stiff drink. I'd been hungry, but now I didn't feel like a meal. All I knew was that someone had wanted to kill me. And because of what had happened since I'd been working for United Insurance. Because I knew too much or was suspected of knowing too much. Because my elimination might finally and definitely bog down the whole case. And the only one who could have fired those shots was, or so it seemed, the man who had hurried away in his car from Rill's place: the man who, as I had told Hallows, had an urgent job to do. And that was Wallis Conn.

I must have been picked up at the office. He may have been on the same bus with me and on my heels and closing the gap as I entered the alley. At that time of night it wouldn't be often used. As for the noise of the shots, that wouldn't be too noticeable against the traffic. And, of course, the whole thing had been a matter of seconds and the planned getaway even more quick. But it was a nasty experience. A foot to the right with that first shot and I'd have had it, and there's very little fun in a morgue.

I felt a bit better after the drink, but I poured myself another and rang down for sandwiches. I think I was reasonably normal when Bernice came in—at least she noticed nothing odd about me. Thanks to a long day, I slept like a log. It was when I made my first conscious turn at the sound of the alarm clock that I felt that graze again.

I made the early tea, ordered breakfast and dressed and went out to the end of Sylvester Street. A van was just a few yards on, unloading stuff for a greengrocer.

"Lost something, guvnor?" one of the men asked me.

I said it was nothing in particular and gave the search up. Looking for two pieces of grey metal in Sylvester Street might be a morning's job. I did wonder if I should ring Norris and ask him to put a man on the search, but I turned the idea down. That street is pretty busy in daylight; besides, those bullets had been real enough. I had a graze on my shoulder and an overcoat, jacket, pullover and shirt to prove it. And what use would flattened bullets be when I'd never be likely to lay my hands on the gun.

Breakfast was early. Hallows and I were at work at eight and it was over another hour before we'd made the full draft of the report for Hill. When I'd come to that final bit about the attempt on me the previous night Hallows looked as if he could hardly believe me.

"This business must go pretty deep," he said. "There must be more in it than just those jewels."

I'd come to think that way, too, and yet I didn't know. Fifty thousand pounds might be a motive for murder.

"But won't whoever it was try it again?"

I didn't think so. I wasn't going to give him a chance. I don't say I was scared, but the grave's a mighty lonely place and death has a chilling finality. And if the attempt had been made by Conn, or for Conn, then I could stop everything at the source, for as soon as Hill decided on putting everything into the hands of the police I'd ring Rill and tell him so. There'd be no fear of any attack on me when the police knew as much as I.

"I wonder if you'd mind doing something, sir? You'll probably think the idea silly, but would you find out if Tynworth did come home?"

I rang Norris, even if I did think it most unlikely. Everything pointed to the fact that Tynworth had disposed of those jewels in America. To return to England after that would be sheer lunacy. But I asked Norris to question the air line; and then I began dictating the report while Hallows typed it in triplicate. It was about the most comprehensive we'd ever submitted. Nothing was left out. We said what we knew and what we thought we knew. Where we had only suspicions, we gave full reasons.

We'd been at it an hour when Norris rang.

"This case fairly beats me," he said, "but our friend did come back. He had a return ticket and he used it. Just under a week over there, as he said. Got back early on the Thursday morning."

It was perfectly staggering. Tynworth had been back in England for some days and yet he hadn't communicated with anybody. Or *was* it staggering? If he'd sold the jewels in America and had now come home, wouldn't he lie doggo? Wouldn't it be in the strictest secrecy that he'd communicate with anyone—Molly Bolfray, for instance—whom he was sure he could trust?

That's what had flashed through my mind.

"Get hold of Old Farm," I told Norris. "Insist on speaking to Mrs. Bolfray."

We got on with the report again but only for a minute or two. I suddenly stopped.

"What gave you the idea that Tynworth might have come back?" I asked Hallows.

"I was just wondering who might have fired those shots," he said. "I ran over likely people and he happened to occur to me."

"Well, he *is* home," I said. "That complicates things, and it doesn't look so pleasant for me. He might have had that crack at me. He might be fool enough to think I was the only one who guessed he'd sold the jewels."

That was the first thought. The second and third made it far less feasible. He couldn't have been such a fool. What kind of people did he think the bank and the insurance company were? Why had he come back at all when, as far as he knew, he might be on the wanted list of every police force in the country?

"Let's leave it," I said, "till we hear from Norris."

That was not till an hour later. He'd had Mrs. Drew on the line and she'd said Lord Tynworth wasn't back and that as far as she knew nothing had been heard from him. As for Mrs. Bolfray, she was out on the far gallop, half a mile away.

"I told her she had to be fetched and that she was to ring me," Norris said. "She did ring me, just a few minutes ago. Said she hadn't heard a word and was scared to death. She sounded genuine enough to me."

We finished that report, bringing it bang up to date, at half-past twelve. Then I rang Hill. I hinted that I'd pretty grave news for him and he asked me to come along at once.

When we got to Hill's room a Mr. Tabard, representing the bank-trustees, was there. Hill had had sandwiches and coffee brought up, but before I began reading the report he wanted to know what the grave news was. I told him the news about Tynworth. I went a little way back and told him about that attack on myself. It was incredible, he said. He even quoted this twentieth century and a civilised country at me, but he didn't let me get so far as showing him that graze on my shoulder.

It was lucky I'd brought all three copies. Hill had one, Tabard one, and I read the third. There weren't many questions, but it was two o'clock when the last page had been read. Hill congratulated us, and that was something. He said we'd not only moved fast but to very real purpose.

"You're reporting that attack on you?"

"If you mean independently, certainly not," I said. "I may be called over the coals for not reporting it, but that's nothing. That attack's an inherent part of the report."

Nothing was decided there and then. Tabard had to consult his people, but it was plain that within a few hours things would be in the hands of Scotland Yard. The bank, as trustees, would make the final decision. Hallows and I were thanked again, I took our file copy of the report, and that was that. There ended, as I might say, the Case of the Lammerford Jewels.

What I didn't anticipate was that on the following Monday a wholly new angle was to open that case again.

PART III
THE VANISHED LORD

CHAPTER IX
THE OLD FIRM

I'VE written a good many times about George Wharton, so I won't risk your boredom by covering that ground again. You may see him in your mind's eye: the six feet of him, the broad shoulders, the huge weeping-willow of a moustache, the dark hair brushed cunningly across the thinning dome of his skull. A less obvious camouflage is the stoop of the shoulders and the look of forlornness that comes with the donning of a pair of antiquated spectacles. They have perfectly plain glass, but they do give him the look of a kindly if somewhat harassed representative of the law: one who ought by rights to have picked a vocation far less onerous.

I've worked with him for the best part of twenty years. Bernice regards him as the perfect uncle. I like him, and there can be times when I loathe him. He can infuriate in one minute and have you wagging your tail in the next. He can be maddeningly secretive, smoothly open, suspiciously ingratiating. He loves the dramatic and producing rabbits from a hat—his own hat. All that seems to add up to the word mountebank. If you thought so you'd be wrong. A man doesn't rise, and the hard way, to be Chief Superintendent at the Yard by anything but sheer merit. Eccentricities are only the basic ingredients of that queer thing we call personality.

It was on the Monday morning when he rang me. I'd known that our report had been sent to the Yard. I'd also taken the precaution of telling Rill, as I'd promised, that the Yard now knew as much as myself.

It was actually during a leisurely breakfast that he rang.

"What's this I'm hearing about you?" he said.

"Heaven knows," I told him. "Don't say my best friends have been talking at last."

He snorted.

"That report with your name at the bottom. I've only just seen it. Is it true about that attack on you?"

You see the kind of infuriating questions I have to listen to?

"Didn't you say my name was at the bottom?" I countered dryly.

He gave another snort, a mild one.

"How are you? You weren't really hurt?"

I lowered my voice. Bernice knew nothing about it. I'd had to smuggle certain articles of clothing to my tailor for slight repairs.

"Well, I'd like to see you," he said. "Can you make it in an hour's time? By then I'll have gone a bit more thoroughly into this report."

An hour gave me time to see Norris. I know George's pertinacity, and the question was whether or not, in view of the extraordinary circumstances, we ought to withhold information about the Tynworth who'd been our original client. Norris, ex-Chief Inspector himself, didn't hesitate. It'd be wiser in the long run to put on the table every card we'd ever had. If Tynworth, in some unforeseen way, could prove himself in the clear, he'd still have only himself to blame for a divulgence of the customary confidences.

So I went up to the familiar room. It was a lovely day outside, warmer than in George's den, though a fire of sorts was going. Sergeant Matthews was there—another old friend, and in his case I don't hesitate about the word friend. Matthews is about thirty and has managed to keep a sense of humour. You have to if you're going to devil for George and retain a measure of sanity.

We shook hands. I hung my mended overcoat on the familiar peg, stoked my pipe to keep George company and drew in a chair. George was at the desk, the report in front of him. They'd had copies made, for Matthews had one.

"An extraordinary business, this," George began.

"It's going to be more extraordinary still when I've added some more to it," I said.

"More?" He glared. "You mean to say it isn't complete?"

I began explaining. I hadn't got out a dozen words when he was buzzing for a stenographer. I could see him racking his brains for some reprimand. To him I'm still the raw amateur of twenty years ago. He had to fall back on why I hadn't reported that attack on myself.

He wasn't any happier when I told him that would explain itself. Then the stenographer came in. I began a slow recital of what had transpired on a certain Wednesday morning, and how we'd run Sally, Lady Tynworth, to earth at the Birmingham hotel. George's face was a kaleidoscope. He has a secret loathing of detective agencies, whether members of the Federation or not. It's a kind of mental arrogance. He can even make me feel mentally shabby. He's like the owner of a big department store who sees a spiv selling nylons under the store's own windows.

The long recital came to an end. He had to admit that it supplemented admirably the report. But he'd been taking his own notes and began firing questions. I had to extemporise thumbnail sketches of Molly Bolfray, Yale, Bernardo, Lady Tynworth, Conn and Rill.

"What was that training establishment like?"

"Don't know," I said. "I didn't go over it. I had no authority to demand it. I didn't even see the need for it. I got what I could and it turned out to be enough."

The look on his face doubted if there could be anywhere one so credulous and even careless as myself. He talked about the value of backgrounds and work which would now have to be done unnecessarily.

"Look, George," I said, "give me a hundred lines and forget it. I've told you all I know. If you don't want me any more I'll be pushing along."

That's the only way to treat him—to stand up to him. To look him clean in the eye and show you're not going to be pushed around. It worked, as it generally does. Why was I getting on my high horse? Wasn't his bark worse than his bite?

"I don't like this," he said, and flicked a finger across the report. "I don't like it at all." He leaned forward. "Do you realise we may have to ask ourselves whether or not this Tynworth is still alive?"

I said I'd thought of it. But what could I do?

"You're free for a day or two?"

"Absolutely."

"Right," he said. "I'll make arrangements. Anything to suggest except covering the whole ground again?"

I said he might get into touch with the American cousin and learn everything about the relationships between him and Tynworth: if that cousin, for example, could say why Tynworth had proposed to visit him. And if the cousin had heard of the Lammerford Jewels.

That was all I could think of at the moment. Matthews seemed to be remembering something.

"Excuse me, sir, but don't I remember something to do with that name Rill? Didn't we see some report or other a month ago?"

George didn't remember, and that was something it was hard for him to admit. He prides himself as being better than a herd of elephants. He said he couldn't be expected to recall something to which he'd probably been asked merely to append a signature.

"Look," he told me. "I'll have copies made of that supplementary report of yours and then I'll be seeing the C.C. What about turning up here again about two?"

I said I'd be there. Matthews gave me a surreptitious wink, which might have been just exuberance of spirits. I felt quite pleased myself as I waited for a bus. But for the way things were turning out I might have had to spend the rest of my days with a whole heap of nagging questions unanswered. And now I was probably going to get some of the answers and be paid for it. That's why I treated myself to a lunch at Romani's.

George wasn't back when I returned to his room. Matthews was there. He was still pleased with himself. He said it must be almost a year since we'd worked together on a case. It'd be quite like old times.

"I found out that bit about Rill," he said. "There was a local complaint or hint dropped or something about parties going on there. They thought the place was being used for gambling. Turned out a mare's-nest: or at least Rill himself owned he had friends in for a game of cards. Bridge parties. Never more than eight including himself, so everything was in order. He even offered to supply names."

"Wonder if Tynworth's was among them."

"We'll never know unless he tells us. He sounded a specious sort of cove, though, according to your report." He gave me a grin. "I'd like to see the Old General have a crack at him."

That was Wharton's nickname at the Yard, and at that moment he came in. He, too, was looking quite pleased.

"Full speed ahead," he told us. "No time for Herndown. Might as well tackle Rill."

Rill happened to be at the Guiver Street offices. Wharton said he'd be there almost at once. And he'd be grateful if he could see Mr. Conn at the same time.

Stalman and Co. must have been doing well, judging by their floor space. Rill's own room was beautifully fitted: it looked like the small lounge of a highly exclusive club except for the battery of telephones and the office communication system. Rill himself looked worthy of it; in fact, with his black jacket and shepherd's plaid trousers, he wouldn't have disgraced the House of Lords.

I doubt if he'd expected three of us. Wharton explained me away as still representing the insurance company.

"Well, make yourselves comfortable, gentlemen," Rill told us. "Mr. Conn will be here in a moment. I'll see if he's—"

The far door opened and Conn came in. It was very nicely timed. He was wearing a well-cut brown tweed suit and a neat and rather darker tie. He looked vastly different from the Conn of my report. As he came forward he was smiling with a kind of courteous affability. When Rill introduced Wharton and the two shook hands I thought how alike they were in build, but there the resemblance stopped. Conn, in spite of the Savile Row suit and the affability, looked rough-hewn and big business. Wharton, in his old blue overcoat with the velvet collar, looked almost shabby. As Matthews told me afterwards, he might have been an applicant for a night-watchman's job.

"Haven't I seen you somewhere before?" Conn said when I was introduced. There was no screwing up of eyes: just the same affability.

"Yes," I said. "We were in the saloon bar of that hotel at Herndown."

"Of course."

The smile passed on to Matthews. Rill was there, too, with a handsome silver cigarette box. It was a minute or two before we were all sitting down.

"Well, sir," Rill said, "what is it precisely that you want?"

Wharton grimaced.

"To tell you the truth, I hardly know. This is just an exploratory visit with the hope that you can help us. I have a very detailed report, by the way, of Mr. Travers's interview at Cockfosters, but, frankly, I'm not too concerned about those missing jewels. I'm concerned about Lord Tynworth himself."

The old ground was covered. Rill and Conn were certain Tynworth was in America and that he'd sold the jewels there. Wharton let them theorise.

"That sounds logical," he said. "But may I tell you something?"

So after an assurance of the strictest confidence they heard that Tynworth was back in England. They couldn't believe it.

"I was at his place yesterday," Conn said, "and they'd heard nothing of him then."

"Well, there we are," Wharton said. "I assure you he's been back now for some days. He's lying doggo. Why? Didn't he raise that money he as good as promised you, Mr. Rill? Is he ashamed of meeting you?"

Rill shrugged his shoulders. Conn said that didn't explain why he hadn't gone to Old Farm.

"Exactly," Wharton said. "So you see why I'm worried. Old Farm is his life. His young son is there. His wife left him as soon as he'd started for America, so he has all that on his hands. He has to try to get himself out of financial troubles. And that reminds me. Would you mind explaining exactly how he got himself so heavily in debt?"

That was George at his most typical: a fact or two, an obscuring with verbiage, and then the firing of a question.

Conn and Rill looked at each other. Rill made a gesture and Conn took over. He said he did so because Rill would hate to tell the facts himself.

"No, no, Wallis," protested Rill. It was a lovely bit of acting, Conn insisting on divulging that Rill had taken a great liking to Tynworth, and Rill, smiling modestly and even looking, as his almost besotted kindness of heart emerged, so embarrassed that he didn't know where to put himself. Finally he had to cut in.

"No, really," he said with a modest wave of the hand. "There *was* a certain amount of business. I admit I liked Lord Tynworth and I tried to help him. And I admit that when I was talking to Mr. Travers I hated him to think I'd—well, I'd been a soft-hearted fool. That's why I might have given the impression that his debts were purely betting ones."

Wharton put on his spectacles and began turning over the leaves of the report, using his attaché-case as a desk. It was all by-play and I wondered what was coming.

He looked up mildly. Rill and Conn were watching him as closely as if he might produce a bomb from that case and with the fuse well alight.

"You could let me have a statement of accounts?"

"Unfortunately, no," Rill said. "Nothing was ever entered in the books. Everything was personal."

"Well, that doesn't so much matter," Wharton said casually. "But you did put a certain amount of pressure on him?"

Rill smiled deprecatingly.

"No, I wouldn't call it that. I'm not a poor man, but on the other hand I'm not excessively rich. Who is, these days? I had to call a halt and Tynworth agreed. He also took two horses of mine, both four-year-olds. They'd each won on the flat and he was to school them as jumpers."

"You don't hold a mortgage on Old Farm?"

"The farm part has always been let," Rill said, "with an agreement to supply the stables and with full rights over the jumps and gallops. There is a mortgage on it, I do know that, but who holds it is a different matter."

"Right," Wharton said. "Perhaps you will let me make a summary. Tell me if I'm wrong, but you had a high personal regard for Lord Tynworth. I might almost call it affection."

"Well, yes," Rill said reluctantly.

"He's too modest," Conn added.

"Well, it did him credit," Wharton said. "It cost you money, but money which you could reasonably afford. When did you last see him, by the way?"

"Oh"—he dragged the word out—"I suppose it was a month ago. I telephoned occasionally."

"And you, Mr. Conn?"

"On the Saturday. The one before he left for America."

"The meeting was—er—amicable?"

"Why not?" He smiled broadly. "It wasn't me he owed money to."

"And you didn't know he'd gone to America?"

"Well, I did. I was down there that day when I saw Mr. Travers in that saloon bar and I heard it then."

The spectacles were still on. Wharton was looking at the report again.

"But you didn't mention it to Mr. Rill?"

That was something they hadn't had time to plan. For a second or two one saw a kind of panic. Conn took over.

"I'm sure I told you."

"You didn't. I was down with influenza if you remember."

"Ah, that," Conn said. "Maybe I meant to and then thought I had."

Wharton closed the attaché-case.

"I think that's all—for the moment. You neither of you have the least idea where Lord Tynworth now is?"

Neither had.

"But if you get even the slightest inkling, you'll let me know?"

Both would be delighted to.

"And neither of you has ever heard about those missing jewels?"

Neither had. Rill said that part of things had come as a tremendous shock. It was a breach of faith. It made one dubious about any trust whatever in human nature.

We all got to our feet. Wharton put the spectacles in their antiquated case.

"They say there's no fool like an old fool," Rill was going on, "but this will certainly be a lesson to me. An expensive lesson."

"We all have to experience it sooner or later," Wharton told him sadly. "But I'm very grateful to you two gentlemen for your candour and help; and that you'll inform me at once if you get wind of anything."

We began moving towards the door.

"By the way," Wharton said, and his tone couldn't have been more jocular, "they tell me you're a bit of a bridge player."

I wasn't looking at Rill. Matthews said the remark set him right back on his heels.

"I don't know," Rill said after a moment or two. "I admit I like a game. At my time of life one should take things a bit easier. It's one of my hobbies. I like having a few friends in occasionally."

"And just for family stakes."

"Exactly. A modest sixpence a hundred. Just a principle of mine. I don't like people losing money in my own house."

There was hand-shaking all round. A little of the gloss had been rubbed off the affability as far as Rill was concerned. Conn, as they say about the racing fillies, was cool, calm and collected. Nothing could have been warmer than his goodbyes to myself. He even hoped he'd be seeing me again, somewhere, some time.

"Where to, sir?"

Matthews was driving the car. Wharton and I were in the back.

"Out to Cockfosters," Wharton said. "I'd like to run my rule over that house of Rill's."

The car moved off. We settled comfortably back. I began telling George that Rill and Conn had been putting on a big act. That was the reason for the discrepancies between that afternoon and the report.

"You think I didn't spot it?" he snorted. Then he chuckled. "Couldn't have bettered it myself. As much concentrated humbug in a half-hour as I've heard the last six months."

"The benevolent bookie."

"That's him. But I took that smile off his face before we left." He frowned slightly. "That chap Conn's a different proposition. He's tough. Notice how he handled things?"

I reminded George about something in that voluminous report—the brow-beating of Moira Bolfray by Conn.

"I had it in mind," he said. "No point in putting the screws on, though. When we've made the rounds we may be seeing our two friends again."

He gave what I always call that Coliseum smile of his—the one where the lion spots a plump Christian. And we left it at that till we were nearing Cockfosters. I told Matthews the way. We stopped just short of Rill's house. We went slowly by it. We stopped again just past it. We moved on again.

"Rich but not gaudy," George said. "A nice place. A bit of class about it but not enough to excite the income-tax commissioners."

We drove on by the golf course and then headed for home.

"What chink do you think of making for in that yarn of theirs?" I asked George.

He said it was going to take time. He might get a look at the firm's tax accounts and see if Tynworth's debts had been included against profits. But the morning's trip to Herndown might be more immediately productive. We arranged that he should pick me up outside the National Portrait Gallery at nine o'clock sharp. That was where I was dropped.

It had been a superb afternoon, with a sun that was genuinely warm, and the weather was to continue like that for some weeks. A little fog here and there, and some frost at night, but what I'd call amply compensatory weather for that damnable and destructive winter. I didn't expect to find Bernice in, and she wasn't, so I made myself a pot of tea. Just after six o'clock I thought I'd put in an hour at the club.

It was just one of those things. I have a dislike of the word coincidence, and maybe because of a cussed streak in me that has always made me regard it from what I might call the other end—the occasions when we might have met an old friend, for instance, if only we'd happened to be at a certain time where we hadn't been. But that evening I was held up through watching what looked like a coronation try-out of street decorations, and when I at last moved on I knew I hadn't time after all to go to the club for a worthwhile visit and get back at the seven o'clock of the note I'd left for Bernice. And at that moment I was passing the bar of Delaney's.

I dropped in. There weren't a dozen people there, though towards seven o'clock it would probably be crowded. I made for one of the high seats at the bar itself, draped my long legs round it and asked for a Dubonnet with a touch of gin. I had a look at myself in my portion of the big mirror that ran each side of the array of bottles. I let my eye run along it, and all at once I was holding my breath.

Two stools away from me on my left were two men. They were half facing each other, and each had an elbow on the bar. There was a voice that I recognised: I couldn't help recognising it. It was the one of the man with his back to me.

"No, no, old boy. You're wrong there. I'm sure you're wrong."

I cleared my throat noisily. I wanted him to swivel round so that I could see his face. He did turn slightly, and then his eyes happened to lift towards the mirror. He said something to his friend and, before I could pull myself together after the shock, he was off that stool and making for the door. I took the rest of my drink at a gulp. When I got out to the street there wasn't a sign of him. I tried an old trick and went across the street for a look each way. But he'd gone, and when I'd got back to the bar the other man had gone too.

I nodded the waiter to me.

"Know who those two men were who were just sitting here?"

He shook his head.

"Are they often in here?"

"Can't say I remember them, sir."

I went out. I quickened my steps back to the flat. I rang the Yard and got George. He didn't seem to believe me.

"There wasn't a doubt," I said. "I actually saw the little mole near his nose. Couldn't mistake his voice either. I know he'd shaved off his moustache, but I'd bet my immortal soul it was Tynworth."

George grunted.

"Shaved off his moustache, eh? Then he *is* lying doggo. But we'll pick him up sooner or later. We'll get a photo in the morning. That might do the trick."

I didn't know. I felt as if I didn't know anything, except that I'd had one of the most incredible encounters of my life.

CHAPTER X
OLD FARM AGAIN

A WORD of reassurance. Wharton was about to probe into matters about which enquiries had already been made. But there wasn't to be any repetition. That report of ours was accepted as a basis, but naturally he wanted to see with his own eyes and form his own impressions. Also he had drawn certain deductions of his own and he wanted to test them. What those deductions and theories were we weren't likely to know till the testing had been done; all the same, one could gather quite a lot from the nature of his leading questions.

As we came near the house that morning I caught sight of Yale standing by those front boxes. I told Wharton who it was, and Matthews drew the car up just short of the drive. Yale began coming towards us. We met him halfway. I introduced Wharton and Matthews.

Yale was in riding-breeches and sweater. He began apologising for them.

"Not at all," said Wharton heartily. "Every man to his trade. A big place you've got here, Mr. Yale."

"Too big," Yale said as we walked towards the stables. "The man here before the war had a pretty big string. We've got only six, and a couple of them aren't our own."

"Look," Wharton said, "when you're a fool the best thing to do is own up to it. I'm a racing fool. Tell me all about it."

Yale gave a wry smile. It was a tall order. I thought he was looking not unpleased with himself that morning. Maybe it was the morning, but he looked to me like someone who's pretty sure of himself and can afford to regard the misfortunes of others with a certain equanimity.

As we strolled round, Yale tried to enlighten Wharton. The staff consisted of a couple of stable-lads and two apprentices, both local. There was also a sort of handy-man—the man I'd seen on my first visit, sweeping the yard by the front boxes. We saw the actual horses, four of them; the other two were at exercise. Yale was very optimistic about a three-year-old named Diamattic. He said he'd been hard to train, but in the late spring he ought to win a good race.

"This is Castle Carton," he said. "He's one of Mr. Rill's. Going at Lingfield pretty soon. You know Mr. Rill?"

"Yes," Wharton said thoughtfully. "A friend of yours, is he?"

"Rill's a friend of everyone—if he has money."

"Yes," Wharton said again. "I've gathered that. But strictly between ourselves, just what do you think of him?"

Yale's lip drooped.

"Strictly off the record?"

"More than that," Wharton told him. "Not even near the record."

Yale didn't speak for a moment. He looked at Matthews and me. Matthews was stroking the head of the handsome animal looking out above the half-door of the box. I also tried to look indifferent.

"Rill," Yale said. "He's one of the absolute and complete bastards. You've heard about the bad luck we had here? No one could believe it. The hell of it was it began as soon as I came here. Nothing ever went right. Rill took advantage of it to wriggle his way in here. Now he's the old man of the sea—he and his friend Conn."

"Nothing underhand?"

"Not that you could actually prove. You know there's occasionally some gambling arranged at that place of his at Cockfosters?"

"Really?" Wharton looked shocked. "And did Lord Tynworth go there?"

"Only once, to my knowledge. If you ever run across his wife, though, she might tell you things."

"Thanks for the tip," Wharton said. "I'll bear it in mind. You've been very helpful, Mr. Yale, so let me tell you something. I shall be seeing Mrs. Bolfray in a minute and telling her the same thing. Your partner's back from America."

Yale gaped.

"He's been back some days."

"I don't believe it."

"Oh?" said Wharton. "And why don't you believe it?"

"Because if he were back, then he'd come here. Everything's crying out for him to come here."

"Nevertheless, he's back. He had a return ticket and he used it. What's more, he's been seen. And don't ask me where he actually is, because I don't know. He was seen in London last night, and disappeared before he could be spoken to."

Yale looked knocked all of a heap. He said it was sheer fantasy.

"Listen, sir. He went to America to get his cousin to come over here for the coronation. He'd be staying here for a bit, and what was wanted was for the cousin to take a share or make a loan so that Rill could be got rid of. Bad luck just can't go on. There's money to be made once you get rid of the hoodoo."

"Well, there're the facts," Wharton said. "But what about these missing jewels that Mr. Travers here is so concerned about. Know anything confidential about them?"

"I'll tell you the absolute truth."

His opinion was that something queer had been going on. He knew about the jewels, and he knew that Tynworth's wife had been pestering him about that coronation business and then having the jewels cleaned. He also knew of the replicas. He had seen Sally wearing them, or some of them—earrings and bracelet principally—when he'd happened to be with her in town. What he definitely didn't know was that the jewels had been brought to Old Farm.

Yet he had an idea that something queer had been in the wind. He lived, of course, in the house and had his meals there, and towards the end of the week before Tynworth left for America there seemed a lot of secretiveness. Just something from which he was being excluded.

He owned that he'd since learned from Molly Bolfray that the jewels were apparently missing, and the replicas, too.

"You knew Tynworth's wife had left him?"

"We did," Wharton said.

"Then she probably has the replicas. They're hers. As for the originals, God knows where they are."

He gave a wry grin.

"It's the very devil. Tynworth couldn't have done any—well, monkey business with 'em. He's not that sort. He and I haven't always seen eye to eye over running this place, but he'd never go in for that kind of thing. Believe me, I know. If anyone's behind it, I'd say keep an eye on Rill."

"Or Conn."

"Yes. And Conn."

"Did you have a key yourself to that indoor safe?"

"Never."

"Anyone else have one but Tynworth?"

"Anyone could have had one," he said. "He was a careless devil. Used to have his keys on a ring in his breeches pocket. When he changed he forgot them half the time. There were a couple of safe rings on that chain, by the way—or were the last time I saw them. Far as I remember that was a pretty long time ago."

"I'm more than grateful. Hope to see you again some time. And don't worry about your partner. He'll probably be turning up today. And with all the answers."

"Hope he does. I don't mind telling you he's had me badly worried."

"And better luck to you both next season," Wharton told him.

"Thank you, sir. We're going to need it."

He shook hands with Wharton, and actually gave me a smile. Then he turned back.

"Just one thing, sir. You know your own business, of course, but could you go easy with Mrs. Bolfray? She's a bundle of nerves. All this business, you know. It's worried her."

Wharton said he'd more than bear it in mind. I looked back as we neared the corner of the stables. A lad had brought Castle Carton out of his box. Yale was running a hand down his fetlocks.

"A nice chap that," Wharton said. "Nice manners. You can always tell one of the Nobs."

George professes to hate snobbery, but he's as big a snob as you'd find. It depends on the angles. He can talk with scorn of what he calls the Big Bugs and quote Cambridge at me when I seem to fall short in the line of brains, and yet he's capable of dragging into a conversation some business he's had with a real live peer of the realm.

"You're telling Mrs. Bolfray about her brother-in-law?" I asked him.

"Have to," he said. "Nerves or no nerves. Might perhaps leave it till the last."

The same lounge, Molly with her hands folded on her lap; the same entry of Mrs. Drew with the coffee, and the same wary look round at us from that cook-housekeeper. She set down the tray.

"Sorry, madam, but I think I ought to run down to the grocer's. There's some things I want."

"Do," Molly said. "Oh, and bring me a book of stamps."

The preliminaries had been finished with before the coffee came in. Wharton sipped the hot drink and said it was good.

He wiped his huge moustache with sweeps of the voluminous handkerchief.

"We're not going to be any nuisance to you, Mrs. Bolfray," he said. "Just want you to explain one or two little things and then we'll be going."

I hoped he was speaking the truth for once. Molly looked pale and desperately worried for all the brave show she was putting up.

"Might I see a photograph of Lord Tynworth, for instance?"

"Of course," she said, and fetched that framed one from the top of the piano. "This was taken just before he was married. There aren't any wedding groups. It was a very quiet wedding. At Chelmsford Register Office."

Wharton had a good look, then passed the photograph to me. Tynworth looked thinner than when I'd seen him, and the photographer had touched out that mole on the side of the nose. Matthews looked and passed the photograph back.

"I just like to see people," Wharton said. "Names are nothing. But I wonder if I might be very personal. I understand your sister has left her husband. Could you tell me how they got on together? Whether it was unexpected to you or not?"

"It was," she said. "Six months ago it wouldn't have been. She was utterly bored here and she was terrible to get on with. Even Tom used to get angry sometimes and he was absolutely besotted. You must forgive me for talking like that about my own sister. I hadn't any patience with her. She was unbearable. She never seemed to care about the boy or anything but herself. Used to go to town quite a lot. Then she suddenly changed. I think it was that business about the coronation."

"But you still didn't trust her?"

"It wasn't exactly trust. I was relieved, really. It made everything much more pleasant."

"She had money of her own?"

"She never told me. She used to hint sometimes when she was in one of her worst moods that she could get on without any of us. She must have had money. That mink coat of hers was worth at least a thousand. And she never helped Tom out with money. Always used to plead poverty."

"She sounds like a mass of contradictions to me, Molly," I said.

"She was." I don't know why she gave me that little grateful smile. "And she fooled us all right up to the last. I just happened to wake up and hear what I thought was a car and then I found she'd gone. The next thing was that letter you saw—days after."

"And you rang your brother-in-law early the next morning."

"Yes," she said.

"And he came here." Wharton had taken up the running.

"Here?" she said.

"Didn't he come here?"

"Why should he?" she said. "What could he do? Besides, he had a most shocking cold. Tonsilitis he said it was. I was worried about him."

"You didn't meet him in town?"

"But why? I mean, look what I had to do. And there wasn't any reason. Everything was fixed up before he left. I know Sally's going was a shock, but how would seeing him help at all?"

"You're right," Wharton said. "I may keep this photograph for a day or two? I'll see it's sent back. And might I look at the upstairs safe?"

We traipsed up, the four of us.

"Not too strong a job," Wharton said as he frowned down at the safe. "I suppose your brother-in-law left the jewels in it, nevertheless?"

"I don't know," she said. "I think he must have done. He couldn't have taken them with him. I helped to pack his bag."

There were all sorts of implications there. Wharton slurred over them. He cocked an ear at the sudden noise.

"My nephew," Molly said, and smiled. "He has a bit of a cold, so we're keeping him in for a day or two."

Wharton allowed himself to beam.

"I'm a grandfather, you know. Might I have a look at him?"

"Do," she said, and opened the nursery door. George and I went in. Matthews stayed out.

"Looks a bonny boy," George said, still beaming. "Who's he like? His father or his mother?"

Daisy peeped in, blushed and disappeared again.

"More like his mother," Molly said. "The hair will darken, of course."

"Looks a lucky young fellow to me," George said, still the grandfather. "If I'd had one of these toys when I was his age I'd have been happy. What's his favourite?"

"Teddy, perhaps. He sleeps with Teddy. He also likes his clockwork train. He can be an absolute pest making you wind his clockwork toys. We'd better get out before he begins."

"I'll tell you something," Wharton said as the door of the nursery was closed. "Don't forget that I'm more than old enough to be your father—that's why I think you'd give a good deal if he were your own."

"I don't have to," she said, and smiled gently. "He is my own—now. He always was more mine than Sally's."

We didn't go into the lounge again but said our goodbyes in the hall. I was hating the moment when Wharton would have to tell her about Tynworth, but he didn't.

"Still speaking almost like your father," he said, "I don't want you to worry. Everything's going to be all right." Then as we moved off from the porch:

"Forgot to tell you, but Mr. Yale may have some news for you."

"Turn towards the village," I told Matthews as we came to the T-head at the end of the lane.

I explained to Wharton. We might do worse than go to the hotel for a drink while Matthews flashed his card at the post office and made certain enquiries about telephone calls that morning. If Mrs. Drew had been curious about things, then it hadn't been on behalf of herself. And that excuse to go to the village on the arrival of yet two more strangers was possibly the least bit thin.

Wharton said we'd go past the hotel and Matthews could walk back. At the moment he preferred not to be too noticeable in Herndown. So Matthews went back, and George and I sat on in the car just past the last house northwards from the village. It was cosy in the car, with the sun shining outside. We stoked our pipes, and I was asking George what he'd thought of things. He said he'd liked Molly Bolfray. She'd struck him as a reliable witness. As George claims to be able to spot a liar from a mile distance, that was praise.

"She's definitely worried about her brother-in-law," he told me. "My view is that she knows he took those jewels. And how're you going to reconcile that with what Yale said about him being incapable of any hanky-panky?"

"There's something more difficult to reconcile than even that," I said. "Tynworth explicitly informed me that he'd spent most of his Tuesday at Old Farm. She swears he never went near the place and that there wasn't any need to. Why did Tynworth tell me that? If he didn't want me to make enquiries there, why didn't he say so? He was the client. Why did he tell lies?"

Wharton didn't know. All he could say was that he had a hunch that everything was wrong. Everybody had done the unexpected. Tynworth, claimed by Yale to be above duplicity, had thought fit to tell me unnecessary lies. Tynworth's wife had been playing her own game at Old Farm in order to get the jewels there, and she'd disappeared as soon as her husband had left for America. Yale had gone chasing her. And why? Because she'd been leading him on? Because he suspected she'd taken the jewels?

"I can understand why Tynworth wanted you to find his wife," George said. "Mrs. Bolfray said he was mad about her. Couldn't do anything wrong in his eyes, so being told she'd left him in the lurch was a shock. But why let fall that she'd gone off with the jewels?"

"It beats me," I said. "How could he know it? Molly Bolfray said she herself could only guess that the jewels might have been in the safe—"

"And a hell of a place to put fifty thousand pounds' worth of stuff. I wouldn't mind betting I could open it with a hairpin."

"I know," I said. "Always the inexplicable. And Tynworth lets fall to me that his wife has gone off with the stuff. Why'd he do that? How'd he know? Molly didn't tell him because she wasn't aware the stuff was in the safe at all. And something else more inexplicable still. Why *didn't* he go at once to Old Farm? If he suspected his wife of bolting with that amount of valuables, why didn't he go there and make sure? He had all day to do it in. His shopping and business couldn't have been so important as that."

"Everything's cock-eyed," George burst out exasperatedly. "And everybody's lying like hell. What we will do is see the wife. About time I put the screws on."

"And there again is something fishy," I said. "Why did Tynworth want those replicas from her? Don't you get ideas, George, as soon as you say those two words to yourself—replicas and originals?"

"I know," he said. "The likelihood of a switch. If so, who's got what?"

Matthews was coming and I wasn't sorry to leave things. He'd had no luck at the post office because the telephone-box was outside and not under observation. A caller didn't get his number, other than a local one, through the telephone at the post office. He dialled O and got the main exchange. But Matthews had the number of the telephone-box and at Bishops Stortford he rang the Yard for a tracing of outgoing calls at about eleven o'clock.

When we got back the calls were waiting for us. There were only three for the morning and two of them to Chelmsford. The third was a Hampstead call. We checked the number. *Mrs. Drew had rung Conn's house.*

"If that doesn't beat cock-fighting," Wharton said. "What d'you make of it? Conn's evidently paying her to keep him informed about what's going on down there. And it can't be about horses."

He didn't take a minute to make up his mind. Matthews was to do some snooping round Conn's place. Matthews wasn't too happy about so vague an assignment.

"Use your wits, man," Wharton snapped at him. "Do you think Conn sits at the end of a telephone there all day? Someone takes the messages. Get an idea who it is. Take a man with you if you want him."

I didn't see how it was going to help. George, it struck me, was all hot and bothered, and he just wanted to be doing something for the sake of something to do. I went out with Matthews, in any case. It was nearer three o'clock than two and we'd had to skip lunch. George had told me to get back in an hour's time.

I made out with an early tea. When I got back George said that photograph of Tynworth was being seen to. If the trip to Birmingham in the morning produced nothing useful, then the *Police Gazette* would have the photograph and a detailed description.

"Last thing tonight I'll have Old Farm rung to see if he should happen to be back. What're you looking so glum about?"

"Am I?" I said. "If I am it's because I'm all at sea. Something tells me there's some little thing missing. Something we've got to find; maybe the right answer to some question or other, and then we'll see daylight. And that's more than I can at the moment."

He went out on some business or other and left me to it. I got a clean sheet of paper and told myself I'd put down the complete series of *whys*: why had So-and-so done this or So-and-so not done that. A couple of minutes and I gave it up. I could have filled the whole sheet with questions, so I tried another angle—writing down a list of those contradictory answers we'd been given. I gave that one up, too. There was no point in it if I couldn't weigh one against another and find an answer of my own. And then Matthews came in, and Wharton with him.

Wharton was pleased. You'd have thought in sending Matthews to Hampstead he hadn't been firing in the dark.

"There you are," he told me, his tone a go-thou-and-do-likewise. "What d'you think? Matthews had one look at that housekeeper of Conn's. He says she's the living spit of that Mrs. Drew!"

Matthews was a bit more modest. He said, after what I'd put in my report, he'd been watching Mrs. Drew when she was in with the coffee. When he went to the door of Conn's house to ask the way to somewhere it'd been like seeing a ghost.

"That little button nose, sir, and the pointed chin, and the eyes and everything. If they're not twins, they're sisters."

"Conn must have planted the Drew woman at Old Farm," Wharton said.

"Olga, the beautiful spy," Matthews told us, and Wharton didn't reprove the levity.

"What're you going to do about it?" I wanted to know.

"Nothing," he said. "In the morning we're going to Birmingham. If we get nothing there, and if Tynworth isn't at Old Farm when we get back, then I'm putting the pressure on. A whole lot of people are going through the hoop."

Matthews was going to Birmingham by the seven-o'clock train and he'd have Sally Bolfray located when we turned up soon after eleven in the morning. I went home resolved to put everything out of my mind. I might as well have resolved to stop breathing.

CHAPTER XI
FRESH THUNDERBOLT

MATTHEWS was waiting for us at the Archdale. He said the lady wasn't up yet.

"What about Bernardo?"

"He isn't up, either."

"Right," Wharton said. "Tap at the lady's door and tell her we're here. Do it nicely, but emphasise the Scotland Yard. Say we'll see her as soon as she's ready. We'll follow you up and have a preliminary word with Bernardo."

We waited a minute or two and went up. Matthews was round the corridor corner at the head of the stairs.

"I told her," he said, "and she looked scared stiff. When she thought I'd gone she slipped on a dressing-gown and went to Bernardo's room. She's there now."

"Right," Wharton said. "Might as well join them."

He knocked at Bernardo's door. Bernardo's voice asked who was there. Wharton merely rapped again. Bernardo opened the door. Wharton put a hand to it and went in. We followed.

"Can't you see there's a lady here?"

Sally was by the window, clutching the dressing-gown about her. Bernardo was practically dressed. He had only to slip on his coat.

"I beg your pardon," Wharton said. "Is it Lady Tynworth, by any chance?"

"It is," Bernardo told him, and he was still glowering. "Don't you think it's a bit steep barging in here like this?"

"Under the circumstances—no," Wharton told him bluntly. "We were expecting to see Lady Tynworth in her room."

He introduced himself and Matthews.

"Mr. Travers, I think, you know. You can probably guess why he's here. I'm here in much the same connection—and about your husband, Lady Tynworth, who's still missing. Perhaps you'll see us in your room."

Her hands were still holding that dressing-gown round her neck. She was trying to be angry. She said she didn't see why it was necessary. She'd told me all she knew.

"You must leave that for me to judge," Wharton told her. "This is a serious business. All we want is your help."

She went flaunting by him. He nodded back to Matthews, Matthews went out with her.

"After I've seen Lady Tynworth I'd like a word with you too, Mr. Bernardo."

"With me?" he said, and squinted round from the mirror where he was brushing his hair. "What good am I to you?"

"Again, that'll have to be for us to judge," Wharton told him quietly. "Are you willing to help, or not?"

"Not now," he said. "I'm due for a rehearsal in ten minutes' time."

Wharton turned to me. The smile was bland.

"Mr. Bernardo has a rehearsal. Fifty thousand pounds' worth of jewels are missing. Lord Tynworth's missing. And Mr. Bernardo has a rehearsal."

Bernardo was looking ugly.

"And so what?"

Wharton shrugged his shoulders.

"Nothing. But it's quite a way to town. You'd rather be questioned at the Yard?"

"You can't do that to *me*."

"Why not? You refuse to co-operate. All we want is plain answers to simple questions. A matter, perhaps, of ten minutes." He shrugged his shoulders again. "It's up to you."

Bernardo licked his thick lips.

"When?"

"When we've finished with Lady Tynworth. There's a telephone by the bed there. Call your rehearsal off. We shall be very grateful."

"I still don't see it."

The tone was less bellicose.

"I know that perfectly well. But give us credit for having reasons. In your own field you're a reasonably busy and important man. We don't bother people like yourself without cause."

Matthews tapped at the door and looked in. Lady Tynworth was ready to see us.

"Any reason why I shouldn't come, too?" Bernardo wanted to know.

"There might be," Wharton told him. "I hope we shan't keep you long."

Out in the corridor he nodded for Matthews to stay by the door. We moved on the few yards to the other door. The Coliseum smile flickered across Wharton's face.

Sally was presentable, even if the make-up looked a bit hurried. She asked if Bernardo might be present.

"Later perhaps—yes," Wharton told her. "But please don't be alarmed—"

"I'm not alarmed. Why should I be?"

"Exactly. All we want are answers to a few simple questions. In the friendly atmosphere—I hope—of this room. We want help and you want to give it us."

There were two chairs in that quite large and well-furnished bedroom. She took the easy one. We remained standing. Wharton offered her his cigarette case. She looked up and gave the ghost of a smile.

"Thanks."

I held my lighter. She took a puff or two.

"Just what is it you want to know?"

"Something personal. Just why did you leave your husband?"

Her head went sideways with a raising of eyebrows. There'd also been a look of relief.

"Don't women leave their husbands?"

"I suppose you might call it their privilege," Wharton told her amiably. "They do do it. Like to tell us why you did it?"

"Why not? I suppose you've been snooping round at Old Farm?"

"Not snooping." He was still most friendly. "Just asking a few questions."

She told us. It came pouring out as if she was glad to have the real truth told: Old Farm, boring to tears; Tynworth a muddler and heading for the rocks; no future in anything.

"I didn't want a scene," she said, "and that's why I left when I did. I could always look after myself in the past and I'm going to do so now. Next week I'll be singing with Mr. Bernardo's band."

"Resuming your professional name?"

"Yes. It's Sally de Freece again."

"What about your boy?"

She flushed slightly. She stubbed out the cigarette.

"I never wanted children. It isn't my fault if I just don't like children. I'm sorry, but that's the way it is."

Wharton adjusted the spectacles. He laid the attaché-case on the bed and consulted his papers. He peered at her over the spectacle-tops.

"I'm giving you some information," he said. "On the Wednesday morning just before he flew to America your husband saw a firm of private enquiry agents and asked them to find you. He said it was an urgent job because you'd taken some valuables with you. He didn't actually say so, but the valuables were the Lammerford Jewels."

"Then he was liar," she told us venomously. "If anyone took them, it was him. And the replicas, which were my property."

"Yes, but what about the other man who had the same idea? The man who came to see you here?"

"It's a lie. I told *him*"—that was myself—"it was a lie."

"Then it couldn't have been a Mr. Conn?"

She gave a little gasp.

"What do you mean?"

"What I say. Mr. Conn didn't come to see you here?"

"Why on earth should he?"

"That's what I'm wondering myself. Still, let's leave it. I want you to tell us everything you know about those jewels. What happened about them, say, in the last couple of months."

I heard nothing new except that now it was said that Tynworth would be getting them from the bank after he got back from America.

"And you didn't even wait to see them?"

"I changed my mind," she said. "I knew I'd been a fool trying to make a go of things. So I cleared out. No fuss, no tears." Her lip drooped. "A pity about the Abbey."

"I don't know," Wharton said. "It'll probably be a bit of a crush. But some news for you. Don't say it can't be true. It is true. Your husband was seen in London two nights ago." Her eyes opened wide.

"In London?" She frowned. "You mean he hasn't been to Old Farm?"

"Exactly. He's been back from America for quite a few days. Up to last night they'd heard nothing from him at Old Farm."

There was a subtle difference about her, no more underlying hostility but a genuine curiosity.

"But how extraordinary! What's his idea?"

Then she knew. You could see it in her face. She had had all at once an idea of her own.

"Yes?" Wharton said.

"Oh, nothing." She gave a little laugh. "Only what I told—I forget your name."

"Travers."

"Of course. Don't you remember I told you that Tom must have taken those jewels to America? Of course, he's afraid to go home if the police are after him."

That hadn't been what she was thinking. That was something that had come opportunely to mind. Wharton let it pass.

"About those replicas of yours. Why did he want them?"

"Isn't it obvious? I think he was trying a trick on somebody. Anything to get money."

"You haven't a very high opinion of him."

"Should I have?"

Wharton switched again and to Yale. He wanted to know how she'd met him.

"Arthur Yale?" She hadn't turned a hair. "I was at school with his sister."

I remembered. The Finders had been nice people. The two girls had been to an expensive school. You could see that in Molly. This one had been around: kicked around too, perhaps. Schooling had worn like a shoddy veneer.

"I met him just after the war," she was saying, "when I was with Hal Prew." The lip drooped again. "I had to make a new start somewhere and Hal was as good as any. Arthur was just a friend."

"How'd he come to join your husband?"

"He didn't like what he was doing—riding, principally. He wanted a place of his own and he could get the money. I knew Tom had talked about a partner, so—well, there you are."

"And you continued just good friends."

"Just good friends." Her look was as level as his own and she emphasised each word. "And did I need one! I suppose you've been to Herndown? Arthur was someone to go out with. We liked the same sort of things."

"He was in love with you?"

She shrugged her shoulders.

"He may have been. I wouldn't know."

"Yet as soon as you'd left Old Farm he went to town to find you. Why should he do that? And get himself into a fight over you with Bernardo?"

"Some lies of that sister of mine," she said. "She and her morals! She's the root of everything, if you want to know. Always nagging. You couldn't have the wireless on. You oughtn't to go to town. Tom this and Tom that. If she wants Tom she can have him. Looks as if she'll be getting a bad bargain."

She reached for her bag and lighted a cigarette. Wharton waited.

"Well, that's really everything, Lady Tynworth. I don't think we shall be bothering you again." He held out his hand. "Thank you for what you've told us. And good luck to you in your come-back—if that's the right word."

She was all of a dither, like a lady-in-waiting chucked under the chin by Henry the Eighth.

"But how nice of you! Honestly, I think that's very nice of you."

I contorted my own face to a smile. Sally was looking ten years younger as we smiled the last goodbyes from the door.

"God, what a woman!" George was muttering as we made the few yards to Bernardo's door. Matthews joined us. Bernardo's room had a haze of smoke and half a dozen butts were in the ash-tray. He'd been lying on the bed reading a newspaper and he was just sliding off as we came in. Wharton should have been blasted by the look he received. But he wasn't. He had never been more genially apologetic.

"Most sorry we kept you so long, but we shan't need to ask for your help after all. Lady Tynworth has told us practically all we want to know. By the way, she's singing with you in the near future, she tells me. Just between ourselves, is she good?"

Bernardo didn't answer for a moment: it took him that long to catch up with the flow of Wharton's words. But even then he wasn't sure. Gratified, perhaps, that we were going, but wondering what lay behind the question.

"Sally? Sally de Freece, you know. Well, yes, I might say she's *very* good. She's coming back with all the experience and, if I may say so, with even more personality. She's got that something most of the others haven't got."

"Can't you capitalise on her title?"

He turned to me.

"Hasn't Gertrude Gilmore got a title?"

"Certainly she has. Whether it's any good as publicity I don't know."

"You're quite right," Bernardo was pleased to tell me. "It's the act that counts."

"Well"—Wharton held out his hand—"I'm much obliged to you and I'm sorry to have dislocated your plans. I've wished Lady Tynworth good luck. May I wish you the same?"

"Good of you. I sure do appreciate it. You won't have a drink before you go?"

So that left two people wagging their tails. Wharton didn't say a thing till we got downstairs. He made for a seat in the open lounge, and snapped his fingers to the waiter. Three Worthingtons came. Wharton took half his at a go and wiped his moustache.

"A nice pair, those two," he told us. "She's probably back in his room and they're laughing their heads off at getting away with it."

"Away with what?" I asked him.

"Remains to be seen," he told us darkly. He finished off the beer, gave the moustache another wipe and got to his feet.

"You'd better have lunch here. I've got a call to make. See you at the train."

He went off to the cloakroom. Matthews wondered what was in the wind. I thought he was paying a courtesy visit to police headquarters—not that I minded. It gave Matthews and me a chance to air our own theories at lunch. But I won't claim that it got us anywhere. Every now and again I'd wonder why Wharton hadn't sat down quietly over his beer and discussed the morning instead of rushing off on what he described as a call. With Wharton you never know, but one thing you do know—that he never acts without both rhyme and reason. But you might bear in mind that call of his. I'd completely forgotten it till the day something arose out of it—something that was to have a vital bearing on the case.

What took it out of my mind was the incredible discovery that came almost out of nowhere when we got back to the Yard that early evening. In the train Wharton had kept away from the case, but he was rearing to get into things again once we were in his room. He rang down to see if the Tynworth photographs were ready, and they were. As he went to the door he told Matthews, or me, that we'd better get that personal description from Old Farm.

"You'd better do it, sir."

"No, you do it," I said. "I don't want to talk to Molly Bolfray. She'll be thinking it was a dirty trick not telling her direct about Tynworth's being in London. You get hold of Yale. If you like, I'll talk to him."

He did get Molly. She told him Yale was round at the stables and she'd try the office. Yale was there. Matthews passed me the phone.

"Travers here, Yale."

"Oh yes—how are you?"

His voice was quite cheery.

"Just alive," I said. "And you?"

"Still hoping. Any news for us?"

"What about you? Tynworth not turned up?"

"Far as we're concerned, he's vanished. Molly's worried to death. I'm a hell of a long way from being happy myself."

"Aren't we all?" I said. "But, by the way, we're just in from Birmingham. Been seeing an old friend of yours."

He didn't answer for a moment or two.

"How was she?"

"Pleased with life. Strictly between our two selves, you had a crush on her, didn't you?"

"If I did, I've got over it," he said. "I'm not the first who's made a fool of himself. Also between ourselves, she's a treacherous, scheming bitch and I'm glad I know it."

"I won't disagree with you. But about why we're ringing you up, and this is most confidential. Molly's not to be told, and you'll see why. We've got to get hold of Tynworth by hook or crook, so we're sending out the alarm. No wireless S.O.S. at present, only the *Police Gazette*, if you know what that is. We have a photograph and now we want a description. Will you give us that?"

"Only too glad to. You want it now?"

"That's right. I'm ready to take it down."

"Well, he's five foot eight and scales about ten-twelve. Used to be lighter, but he hadn't done a lot of riding recently. Had a few breaks in his time and he's got an ankle that troubles him. Dark hair and practically no grey in it. A straight-out moustache—one of the flying-officer type, if you get me. Brown eyes. That's about all."

"Any special features or blemishes?"

"Only a few broken collar-bones and things and you wouldn't call those blemishes—or would you?"

"Hasn't he got a mole by the right side of his nose?"

"A mole? Who on earth told you that!"

"He hasn't?"

"Of course he hasn't. Dammit, I ought to know."

A cold trickle had gone down my spine. Wharton had come in and I was afraid he was going to speak and I waved a frantic hand. I didn't want to lose the thread of the thought that had come into my mind.

"Sorry," I said. "I don't know where we got hold of the idea. But tell me something else. Was he perfectly fit when he left for America? He didn't have a cold?"

"He was fit as a flea. Worried, of course, but never better in his life."

"That's good," I said, and it couldn't have been more inanely. "Much obliged for your help. We'll let you know if anything happens. Meanwhile, not a word to a soul."

"You bet," he said; and then I rang off.

I let out a breath. I just sat there.

"What's happened?" Wharton said.

I told him.

*

I couldn't blame him for the recriminations, but I doggedly refused to blame myself.

"Why shouldn't I have accepted the man as Tynworth? Read the report again. Didn't I state that I knew there was something fishy? And what about you? You knew all that and you also took it for granted the man I saw was who he claimed to be."

"I didn't actually see him, did I?" The snort blew out that moustache of his like a drying sheet in a gale. "And you saw a photograph afterwards?"

I tried to be patient. I'd seen the man who claimed to be Tynworth in a very bad fight. Photographs are unreliable, and I admitted I'd gone chiefly by the moustache in taking the photograph to be that of the man I'd seen. Then I let fly at him.

"You heard the discrepancy when Molly Bolfray told us her brother-in-law hadn't been to Old Farm on the Tuesday as I'd been told. You heard her say he'd tonsilitis and could hardly speak, and yet you had no suspicions. Are you always so right and everyone else wrong?"

"Now, now, now!" He held up a pontifical hand. "You're taking it all wrong. No use crying over spilt milk."

"If it was spilt, then we both spilt it."

"Right," he said, and the voice was almost unctuous. "Maybe I did take things a bit for granted. But you see where we stand now? I may be wrong, but if Tynworth's still alive, then my name's Robinson."

I agreed.

"Let's work things out," he said. "Knowing what you do now, and having met the impersonator, tell us how you see things."

I asked for a minute or two to think. George stoked his pipe. Matthews lit a cigarette.

"This is a rough idea," I said. "Someone knew that Tynworth was taking those jewels up to town, on his way, so to speak, to America. I'd say he was killed on the Monday evening after he'd registered at the hotel. But he hadn't the real jewels. All the murderer got were the replicas. So something had to be done. A man was found—or he might have been the actual murderer—who could pass muster as Tynworth. I wouldn't say if the moustache I saw was real, but that man was sent or went to the hotel late that night. He took over Tynworth's small case with the air tickets and the cloakroom ticket. He was rung in the morning by Molly Bolfray and told that his wife had cleared out. He had to think and act fast, so he put on the tonsilitis act and could only croak. She took it for granted and she was all hot and bothered herself.

"Then the man cleared out. He guessed that Tynworth's wife had gone off with the real jewels, so finally he looked through the advertisements and picked himself a detective agency. He took good care to see me, from that agency, when we'd have only the drive from Liverpool Street to the Airport Building to talk in and when I couldn't keep my eyes on him and the road at the same time. He dropped a hint about missing valuables and fixed that advertisement stunt whereby someone else in the game would tackle Lady Tynworth when we'd found her. Then he flew to America and came back on Tynworth's ticket in case any enquiries were made. His passport photograph—Tynworth's—would be bad, as they always are. In any case, his very title would pass him on a rank bad photograph."

"Yes," Wharton said heavily. "That sounds feasible. And someone did see the Tynworth woman at the Archdale, though she swore blind they didn't."

"She's plausible, George. You know that. She's a fluent liar. An expert. Whoever saw her, she obviously got away with it. She convinced him she didn't have the jewels."

"Did she have them?" That was Matthews.

"I'd say yes," Wharton told him. "And that's being taken care of—when the time comes."

"What time?" I wanted to know.

"When we've got a body," he said grimly. "The jewels are incidental except in so far as they lead us to a possible murderer. Our immediate job's to find out if Tynworth's really dead. The fact that we're now convinced he is is really nothing. We've got to have a body."

"Who was behind it all?" Matthews said. "Surely it must have been Rill or Conn, or both?"

Wharton snorted.

"What about Bernardo? Wouldn't he have been getting his singer and the jewels at the same time? What about Yale?"

"No, no, George. Yale must have had an alibi. He must have slept at the house that night. He must have been there in the morning when Molly told him her sister had gone."

"We've had better alibis before, haven't we? And busted them." He glared at the pipe. He relit it.

"No, what we've got to do is work like moles. No one's to know we suspect a thing. Matthews, you'll check up on everybody in every morgue. We'll give that a day. After that we'll keep it in mind and test out a few alibis."

He was slowly making for the door. We sat there.

"I'll have to have a word about this with the Powers-that-be," he told us. "You'd better get going, Matthews, and take what men you want. You"—that was myself—"had better get home and think things over. Maybe by the morning you'll have some more ideas."

CHAPTER XII

THE BODY

THERE weren't more than two unidentified bodies in the Home Counties, and both of those had been brought out of the Thames—one a woman of thirty or so and the other an elderly down-and-out. That was as far as we'd got by the morning of the second day; and if Wharton was to stick to his original idea, then we were to get busy on alibis. But Wharton was hedging. We had no guarantee, so he now said, that Tynworth was dead. If he were, then we couldn't narrow the time down sufficiently.

He'd been going through that report of mine again and trying to collate it with the rough theory I'd outlined about what had happened to Tynworth after he arrived in town, on the late afternoon of that Monday.

"Let's call the impersonator X," he said. "Wasn't it bad handling to have X come back from New York? Wouldn't everyone have assumed, as most people did till he came back, that he was over there for good? Wouldn't that have been the perfect red-herring?"

I thought X had been caught up in a set of circumstances and they had taken control. For all we knew, he had had to come back. X didn't want to be permanently exiled. He'd come home if only for a share of the possible spoils.

"I know that," George told me testily. "But why not come back under another name—that is, leave Tynworth still there."

"What about a passport? He couldn't use Tynworth's. And unless he wanted to pay a packet for a new ticket he'd have to use Tynworth's."

"You may be right," he told me reluctantly. "I must admit everything's got the look of being hurriedly worked out. Take that mole. X, your report says, looked pale and worried. That was easy enough. A bit of powder on the face and dark under the eyes. But while he was powdering the face, why didn't he powder out that mole?"

I didn't know, unless, as he'd said, things had had to be improvised. And then I thought of something. It was one of those value ideas that pass haphazardly through the mind and then make you suddenly sit up with the realisation that you've got something that's really big. And then, before I could get the idea into focus, the buzzer went.

"Yes?" Wharton said.

I couldn't hear anything but a faint voice that was talking rapidly. But Wharton's eyes were bulging a bit and he laid his pipe down. Now and again he gave an impatient yes. Then he was saying he'd take something down.

"North of Barnet. . . . Lane a mile short of South Mimms. . . . First on right. . . . Lowman Farm. . . . Right. Have a car ready. No driver."

"Might be something," he told me, "and might not. Sounds promising, though. A body in a burnt-out straw-stack."

Inside five minutes we were on the move and I was driving. For once he didn't grumble about an occasional lapse to above the speed limit, but every time I tried to talk he told me to keep my eyes on the road. All I gathered from him was this:

An old stack-bottom had been set on fire and the farmer attributed it to a carelessly dropped match or mischief by boys. He hadn't troubled to remove the burnt pile till that morning, and then because he was going to plough the field. That was how the badly charred body had been discovered, and he'd had the sense to get back home at once and dial Whitehall 1212.

We made better time once we were through the inner suburbs. It was about eleven o'clock when we came to the last lane and one of those stretches of oasis farmland. We could see the farm itself, about half a mile on and set back from the lane. A police patrol car was just short of the house and one of the men was waiting for us. He said we'd have to go by a track across the fields and it'd be better to walk.

The track was dry but rutty. In a couple of minutes we could see a tractor drawn up inside a field-gate and three or four men just standing around. Jewle—Chief Detective-Inspector and an old friend—had gone ahead of us before the report had come up to Wharton. Now he came to meet us.

"Nothing's been touched, sir, except the body. They moved that with a fork before they saw what it was."

We went through. It was the kind of stack-bottom I'd seen hundreds of times in my Suffolk boyhood. One could visualise it as it had been before the fire: two or three feet of grey, mouldy straw not worth the carting and below it the actual bottom of hedge-cuttings and small boughs. All that was left now was a black heap with the ends of the unburnt boughs at its far edges.

"What's this?" Wharton was saying.

This was another lane, rather wider than the one that had taken us near the farm. It ran by the very edge of the burnt-out stack, and its hedge was seared and brown from the heat. "Why shouldn't we have come this way?"

"If you had, sir, you'd have had to go right to South Mimms and then turn back," Jewle told him.

"Where's it go to?"

"It's a diagonal road, sir. Connects up with the main road farther along and then goes on to St. Albans."

It was a grand sunny morning, but the east wind was keen. Wharton's shoulders were hunched, and his hands in his pockets as he went forward. He stopped by the burnt-out stack. I had a look and turned away. Wharton leaned right over for a better look. That charred thing that had the shape of a body was just a something in his line of business. I got the stench from it with a puff of wind.

The men had come nearer. Wharton spoke to the farmer. "You're Mr. Beever? . . . Let me congratulate you on having the sense to do what you did. Now tell us all about it."

"Well, sir, I came along with Fred, here, at about nine. We'd been busy till then, and what we thought was, we'd draw all this up into a heap and set alight to't again. Best way of getting rid of what bottom was left. Then we'd just spread it a bit. Then as soon as I started poking about with a fork, I came up against something. I hollered to Fred. 'Come and have a look here, Fred. Almost look like a body.' So Fred came and that's what it was. Almost scared the daylight out of me."

"Clear enough," Wharton said. "But let's go back a bit. When did you first know this had been alight?"

It was on the Tuesday morning, he said—the Tuesday which Tynworth had kept for business and shopping before the next day's flight. He pointed across at the sugar-beet field—as it had been—where we stood, to a nursery garden a good half-mile away, the sun shining on its range of glass-houses. The owner, named Rook and a friend of his, took the trouble to ring him and tell him about the fire.

It had been a night of patchy fog. Rook had been out of bed at about four o'clock in the morning and had seen a faint but peculiar glow. He put it down to a flaring up of a fire which Beever might have made of hedge-trimmings. In the course of the next morning he'd spotted the black heap and had rung Beever more out of curiosity than anything else.

"Did anything peculiar strike you when you saw it for yourself?" Wharton asked him.

"Well, yes," he said. "I did wonder why it'd burnt so well as it had. Must have been drier than I thought."

"You didn't smell anything peculiar?"

"Well, sir, now you come to mention it, I did think I smelt something like paraffin. Then I put it down to my clothes. I'd been tinkering about with that tractor."

"And what about the Monday night? Patchy fog, you say?"

Beever said the fog had been freakish. When he'd last gone out shortly after nine o'clock his buildings were clear but only an hour before there'd been a visibility of no more than twenty yards. He'd heard it was the same all round the district. There'd been best part of a week of the same sort of patchy fog, clearing in the middle of the morning and thickening again towards dusk.

"What do you say, Fred?"

Fred, a cheerful-looking chap in the early twenties, said the fog had been more like a thick mist, and all over the place, as Beever had said. He'd been out that night on his motorbike—to the pictures at St. Albans—and in some places he'd had to crawl, and then after a bit he'd been able to open the throttle.

"You wouldn't call it bad on the whole?"

Fred grinned. He said he'd been out in worse.

The third man was the camera-man who'd come with Jewle. He'd used half a dozen plates before we arrived.

"Right," said Wharton. "You got a hurdle or anything, Mr. Beever? I'd like to get this moved clear."

This was the charred body. Fred fetched the stout sack he was using as a cushion on the tractor seat and a contraption was made with some stakes from a hedge gap. They manoeuvred it under the body and drew it clear. I saw the white of flesh underneath where something had kept it from the fire. Wharton tied his handkerchief round his mouth and nose and squatted down for a close look. It was best part of five minutes before he got up. He motioned Jewle over. Both of them squatted. Jewle was nodding away as Wharton pointed something out.

I came up on the windward side as they got up.

"Ten to one this was dumped here naked," Wharton said. "You nip along to the farm, Jewle, and get the Yard. Have a fire expert here at the double. And an ambulance to take this away in. Have it come by the road here."

Fred resumed his ploughing and Beever went with Jewle to the farm. Wharton and I sat in the lee of a holly stretch in the hedge and lighted our pipes. There was nothing to do for the moment but wait.

"That bit about the body being naked," I said. "That fits in with Tynworth. X was wearing his clothes."

"How do you know?"

I told him about that whiff of the stables from the heavy tweed overcoat. Wharton was sceptical, if only to keep himself from being too optimistic. He didn't believe anyone could recognise or identify what must have been a very faint whiff. I said I'd been used to stables. My father had kept a couple of hunters. The whiff I'd caught had brought a kind of nostalgia before I'd placed it.

"No use speculating," he told me. "Murphy'll get the answer in no time. Broken ankle and collar-bones—it'll be as easy as reading a newspaper."

Jewle came back. Everything was in hand. Fred had knocked off for his meal, and he came over to us when he'd finished it. He pointed out the cottage where he lived with his mother. It was about a couple of hundred yards away and we could see it quite clearly. He hadn't gone to bed that night till nearly midnight, and if the fire had been slight then he'd have been bound to see it.

"Let's say it *is* Tynworth," Wharton said when Fred had gone back to his tractor. "He was brought here in a car—no argument about that. But why here?"

We didn't know. We'd no proof whatever that he'd been killed in town. Everything might have been planned well in advance and he might have been killed before he got there. Registration at the hotel was no proof. As Wharton said, we'd been told so many lies that he might even have been killed at Old Farm.

Soon after one o'clock Harries, the fire expert, arrived. A few minutes later the ambulance was at the road gate and the charred body was on its way to the morgue. Jewle was to go methodically through the stack-bottom with the hope of finding a clue. Wharton wanted to have a look at that back road.

I drove round to the main road and on to South Mimms, and there turned left again. The map was easy to follow, and in a mile and a half we were back at the gate. There'd been occasional houses till the last quarter of a mile, and then nothing but open farmland.

"The whole thing's crazy to me," Wharton said. "Even if it shouldn't happen to be Tynworth, it's still a body, and it was brought here. And why choose here?"

We got out for a word with Harries. He hadn't any doubt that the fire had been started with petrol, and plenty of it. Probably a two-gallon can that had been carried in the car. He and Beever were helping Jewle with the ashes and they looked like having a full afternoon. Wharton and I set off back to the Yard.

The ambulance had long since arrived but not the chief pathologist. He wasn't expected for another hour, and Wharton was fuming at the delay. I went to the flat. Bernice was out, so I made myself some tea, but somehow I wasn't hungry in spite of no midday meal. I rang Norris. Everything was under control at Broad Street.

When I got back, and after more than an hour, a ruined tea-tray was in Wharton's room but no Wharton. It was another half-hour before he came in, and I knew by the quickness of his step that something had happened.

"Tynworth all right," he said. "Couldn't be a coincidence about those fractures. And I've just checked up with Yale."

"You don't know yet what he died from?"

"Shan't know for an hour or two. It's a tricky business with the body charred like that. All I do know is that he wasn't stabbed or shot."

Jewle came in at about six and Matthews was with him. Nothing had been found in the ashes, not even a solitary button. There were no footprints of whoever had carried the body to the stack-bottom and buried it under the mouldering straw and then gone back for the can of petrol. Jewle said the site had been cordoned off, nevertheless, in case we wanted to go back to it.

The four of us sat there, talking about the case till more news came from the laboratory. Someone would suggest something and it would be talked out, or side-tracked for some new idea. Had the body been brought northwards *from* London, or southwards *to* London? Was there any special significance in the choice of that stack-bottom? Didn't the can of petrol show a crime planned well before that Monday night? Above all, who was X?

That was when I remembered that idea I'd had just before we'd been told about the discovery of the body. X, I thought, couldn't be a principal but someone specially employed. And who more likely to do that job of impersonation than an actor? An unemployed actor. One who wouldn't be missed during a week's absence.

Wharton said the trouble was we'd no description of him other than the little mole at the corner of his nose. We weren't even certain that the moustache was real. I thought it must have been. X couldn't have made that long trip under the eyes of a stewardess and through both Customs wearing in broad daylight a false moustache.

We talked that out, and the jewels came up. Who had them? Not the one who'd killed Tynworth, for that would have meant no need to employ a detective agency to find the missing wife. I noticed that George didn't take any part in that particular argument, and I was asking myself if he had something up his sleeve. We wondered what part the replicas had played. My idea was that Sally had them, and she'd convinced whoever it was—the so-called Henry Balfour—that she knew nothing about the originals.

Sandwiches and coffee came up. Wharton was getting a bit restless, but Murphy was too big a man for even Wharton to hustle. It was after eight o'clock when the ring came. The voice from the other end was too faint for us to hear, and from Wharton's end came only a series of grunts. Then there was a question.

"It couldn't have been made by a cosh?"

He wasn't pleased at the answer. He let out a breath when at last he hung up.

"Well, that's that," he said. "Killed by a blow on the right temple, and his heart wasn't in good shape. It wasn't a cosh that did it. It was something hard with a triangular edge."

Everything was consonant with death on that Monday night. Murphy was working on the stomach content.

"That heart business is queer," I said. "You'd have thought Yale would have mentioned it."

"We can check," he said. "Might as well break the news down there. Better than them reading it in the morning papers."

Yale was in the house. Wharton broke the news. Yale was to use his own judgment about passing it on to Molly Bolfray. Yale was asking questions.

"Sorry," Wharton said, "but all we're certain of is that he's dead. I'll let you have details later. But tell me something. Did he ever complain about his heart?"

Wharton was looking pleased at what he was told. He rang off with almost indecent haste.

"His heart wasn't too good," he told us. "Some strain or other when he had his last fall. The local doctor had told him to take things easy."

"Best thing now," he said, "is to get this to the Press. The more publicity the better, not that we're going to tell all we know."

That broke the meeting up. There'd be a conference in the morning with what George always called the Powers-that-be. After that, he told us cryptically, we'd have to see.

I went out early in the morning to buy extra papers. My own had what I'd call a chaste account, but the two more popular dailies had front-page banner headlines and that photograph of

Tynworth. The floods had ceased some time ago to be news and they were making the most of an undoubted sensation.

CHARRED BODY IN STRAWSTACK
OWNER-TRAINER MURDERED

That was *The Record. The Bulletin*, as I'll call it, had:

DEAD PEER'S BODY FOUND BURNT
MYSTERY OF AMERICAN TRIP

Both, as I've said, had the photograph. Both had, in spite of additional verbiage, just what Wharton had dished out and no more. Both wanted to know a whole lot of things: why that lonely stack and the concealing of identity, the motive for the actual killing, and, above all, the identity of the man who had flown to New York under Tynworth's name. Both had brief obituaries, strung together hastily from racing correspondents and probably frantic ringings of Old Farm, and rehashes from the obituaries of Baron Tynworth the first. It struck me that Old Farm and Lowman Farm would be busy places that morning.

Of the Lammerford Jewels there was never a word. When we saw Wharton—and that wasn't till after eleven o'clock—he was rather inscrutable about that, and again I wondered if he had anything up his sleeve.

It was not till well over an hour later that the three of us left with our duties assigned. Jewle would take Lowman Farm and the immediate district. Matthews would take Old Farm, and I was to concentrate on X. Wharton would sit at the end of telephones as a grand co-ordinator—till something really solid was unearthed. Asked once more if and when he was going to give the Press information about the jewels, he merely shrugged his shoulders.

"We haven't found them, have we? Why should they?"

I supposed, in a way, he was right.

In our game you never know when you'll get a square meal. I made sure of one before calling yet again on Tom Holberg, and I'd taken the precaution of making an appointment for two o'clock. I also took Miriam a big bunch of violets—long overdue.

"It's official this time, Tom," I said, though I didn't trouble to show a warrant card. "You've seen the papers?"

He'd seen them. He even had a midday *Record*, with photographs of a cordoned gateway into a field and the front of Old Farm. He also had his private curiosity. There'd been plenty of mentions of the word Tynworth on my previous calls.

There was no point in seeing him at all if I didn't take him right into my confidence. He had to know precisely what I wanted and why I wanted it.

"That moustache," he said. "That's the trouble. I know of no one with that kind of moustache. And if it was a false moustache, then what is there to go on? Just a face. Any kind of face. Everybody's got a face."

And everybody, even Tom Holberg, can advise the police. Why didn't we send out an S.O.S.?

"Wanted a man with a mole," I said. "Have a heart, Tom. And the idea may be not to warn him."

It was too big a job for him to tackle, but he gave me a list of likely agencies in town. Then I spent well over an hour in Miriam's office going through photographs. I went back twenty years with the faint hope of an infant prodigy, and there wasn't a face that had a mole near the right nostril or recalled in any way the man who'd sat in my car on a foggy Wednesday morning. It was small consolation to know that I'd recognise his voice. I'd recognised it in that bar, but they don't make photographs of voices.

I rang Wharton and told him I was making a methodical round of the agencies, but could he send a good man round the better-class bars—places like Delaney's. He said he'd see to it. I started off on Holberg's list.

By closing-down time I'd seen one place in Charing Cross Road and another in Wardour Street. The next morning I saw three more, and by that time I'd looked at a few score more photographs. There were faces that were getting quite familiar, but nothing to remind me of X. Only two more agencies were on the list and I'd finished with them by half-past four.

I went on to the Yard to report. Wharton wasn't too pleased except in so far as to take care that I knew that actor theory had been my own. That's one of the supremely irritating things about him. If a theory proves a dud, then it's mine. If it isn't wholly worthless, then it's ours. If it's a winner, then as likely as not it's his.

But nobody else had had any luck. Jewle had scoured the neighbourhood of Lowman Farm and had found no one who had seen a likely car or anything in the least suspicious. Considering that the fire hadn't been started till after midnight on a foggy night, I might have mentioned optimisms. As for Matthews, he'd got nothing from Herndown except a confirmation from Tynworth's doctor. And the news that Mrs. Drew had left Old Farm.

"According to Mrs. Bolfray," George told me, "she made a row out of nothing and then packed up and left. That was this morning. We picked her up off the train and she took a taxi to a small house about five minutes from Conn's place. Conn's housekeeper comes in by the day and she lives there. We're having it watched."

He hadn't worked out what my next assignment would be, but he said he'd ring me if there was anything urgent. That was why I didn't bother to report too early. Cooling of heels could be done just as well in the flat. It was just after nine o'clock when I gave a polite tap at George's door and walked in. He was telephoning. He screwed round to see who it was, and waved a furious hand. I stood stock-still where I was and hardly dared breathe.

"Right," George said tersely. "Right," he said again. "We'll be picking her up. . . . Much obliged. We'll let you know what happens."

Chapter XIII
RABBIT FROM THE HAT

George was having a mental struggle: he didn't know whether to tell me or not. He loves a dramatic curtain. If a rabbit is to be pulled out of the hat it has to be at the last sensational moment when he has you keyed up to a shivering anticipation. So he hated to tell me what was in the wind, and he hated still more the fact that if I were told anything it had to be everything.

"That Tynworth woman," he said. "She's just taken the nine o'clock to town."

I raised polite eyebrows.

"Don't know what's in the wind," he said, "but something had to happen when we broke the story about her husband. Her late husband."

Light was beginning to dawn on me.

"You arranged at Birmingham to have her watched?"

"That's it," he said. "It was those jewels I had in mind. One of the biggest liars I've ever come up against. You don't think I swallowed all that bilge she handed us?"

I was having to extract it by driblets.

"You think she's got the jewels?"

The old pontifical hand was raised.

"No use counting chickens before they're hatched. All the same, you don't tell me she left Herndown when and how she did if it wasn't with something?"

He waved me impatiently to the chair.

"Look," he said. "Work it out for yourself. She was a nag. Made everyone's life miserable except her husband's and she could twist him round her little finger. Then she suddenly becomes the nice little woman. Hands out some smiles and co-operation. And why? Because she wants her husband to get those jewels into the house. She wants it a family affair. Wants everybody to be in it so that when they're missing everyone'll be under suspicion except herself. What'd she tell us? She hadn't even seen 'em. She'd even handed over the replicas. Pure as the driven snow, that's what she was."

"You think she cached them somewhere in town and now she's come to collect 'em?"

"Well"—he shrugged his broad shoulders—"you can't call it beyond the bounds of possibility. That's as far as I'll go at the moment. She may be coming up for a quiet day's shopping. All I know is that when she gets here she's having us on her tail."

That was all he'd say. Matthews came in then. Wharton had evidently called him off from Herndown. Now he got his orders to have a squad car at the railway station and to pick the lady up when the eleven-thirty came in. Wharton would be there himself and would follow the squad car.

"Take whatever men you think you'll want," Wharton told him, "but don't fall down on the job. She's got a day-return, but it might be too late to pick her up then if we've lost her. All she might have done, if she's got the jewels, is change the cache."

All Wharton and I had to do was wait. We talked about X and what we could do now the actor idea had turned out a dud.

"I ought to have known," I admitted. "He wasn't all that good an actor. I suppose he didn't have to be."

"There's a rough description in the *Gazette* today," he told me. "It may bring in something. Pretty faint hope, though, with little to go on but that mole. I've also put it out to the Press."

"I can't help thinking, George, he's not all that important—" He looked horrified.

"Not important? What are you? Mad?"

"Let me finish. Not so important as finding out who Henry Balfour was. If we do get X he might lie like hell and fob us off with a yarn about some mysterious employer he never actually saw."

George's snort moved the stray papers on his desk.

"He'll talk—once we get him. And we'll know who this Balfour was."

"And who was he? I mean, what's your own idea?"

"One of four people. Rill, Conn, Bernardo or Yale." He waved impatiently. "No use guessing. Wait till we've picked up that woman. If we don't know a lot more before this day's out, then my name's Robinson."

At a quarter-past eleven I was with Wharton in another squad car in the station-yard. If traffic and the lights separated us from Matthews, then he could get in touch when the lady arrived at wherever she was going. It was a grand morning. What little mist there'd been had dispersed and it was like a day in May. The train, one of Matthews's men had reported, was running on time.

At half-past our driver started his engine. Through the rear window we could see Matthews's car. Zero hour came. Five long minutes went by and Matthews appeared and he was almost running. He was in his car and it began moving. It fell in behind a taxi and the driver of a taxi just behind it had to jam down his brakes. We swung across, but the second taxi was between us and Matthews. There'd been no chance to see who was in the first taxi, but I thought it was a woman. Traffic lights held us all up. When we moved on we cut through a street which I didn't know. The second taxi had gone on, and between Matthew's car and the vital taxi was about thirty yards. We turned left and I knew we were at the east end of Holborn. Miraculously we held together at traffic lights till we'd come out beyond St. Paul's.

"Wonder if she's making for Liverpool Street," Wharton suddenly said. "Might be going to Herndown."

That had been something he'd never envisaged, and he was leaning forward and peering like a bowler who sways his body as if some queer telepathy could make his wood move the few needed feet to the jack. In the long traffic queue at the Bank he looked out till we were on the move.

"All right, sir," the driver said. "Turning into Moorgate Street."

We turned left. The traffic lights at the bend were with us and we went through. The taxi turned left a few yards on at Cardinal Street. Halfway along its short stretch it slowed. Matthew's car stopped and we drew in behind it. What was happening we couldn't see. A couple of minutes and Matthews was reporting.

"She's just gone in there." He nodded forward. "The Consolidated Safe Deposit Company. Her taxi's waiting."

For the first time in minutes Wharton smiled. He couldn't help turning to me.

"Well, the Old Gent"—that's one of his names for himself—"wasn't so far wrong. Pay her taxi off, Matthews, and clear him out of the way." He leaned out. "Wait a minute. Find out if he was taking her anywhere in particular."

We got out. We saw the taxi move off along Cardinal Street. We went just past the door of the Safe Company.

"She wasn't going anywhere," Matthews told us. "Just told him to wait."

"Right," Wharton said. "Go inside and wait. Follow her when she comes out. Don't let her see you. We'll be here."

We waited the best part of ten minutes, then she came out. She was wearing a brown toque of a hat and that mink coat. Tight beneath her arm was an outsize in handbags. Matthews was just behind her. She hadn't noticed us. She was looking bewilderedly at where her taxi had been. Wharton stepped forward. Matthews was now at her elbow.

"Lady Tynworth? I think you know me."

The red flushed her face. She couldn't speak.

"Afraid I must ask you to come with me to Scotland Yard."

Both hands were clutching the bag.

"But why? This is an outrage!"

"Don't make a scene," Wharton told her. "Are you prepared to come or are you not?"

She suddenly went limp.

"All right, Matthews. Bring her along. And take charge of that bag."

A second man had come up. We watched her get in the car. It moved off and we came just behind it.

Wharton didn't say much till we were back at the Yard, and then he was cock-a-hoop. I wouldn't have been too surprised if he'd reared up on his toes, flapped his arms and crowed. But he pressed the buzzer and picked up the receiver.

"Keep her there, Matthews, and bring up that bag."

A couple of minutes and Matthews came in, and he was grinning all over his face.

"Nice work," Wharton told him as he undid the clasp of the bag. He was nodding to himself as he took the jewel cases out. They were of green leather, obviously old and rather worn. There was a flat, long one. That'd probably be the rivière and the earrings. A smaller, flat one would have the bracelet. The two-inch square one would probably have both rings and the much deeper, oblong one, the tiara.

"All here," he said. "Wonder what's the idea of this?"

"This" was the sealing-wax that covered the clasps. "Funny," he said. "Wonder why they were sealed up. And looks like a thumb print."

He ran the glass over the seals, and he was right. A thumb had pressed down on the still warm wax and each of the cases had been effectively sealed.

"Whoever sealed them was taking good care he'd know if they were tampered with," he said, and the cocksureness had suddenly gone. I didn't see why. What did it matter about the seals? "What about a look inside, George?"

He didn't say a word. He just stood there looking down at the cases. He pursed his lips once or twice and frowned. He nodded. The Coliseum smile was there again.

"We'll save that for the lady. Bring her in, Matthews."

He kept his gloves on while he went through the bag.

"Return-half ticket. Nothing else but the usual."

He put the bag aside and began writing something on a sheet of paper.

"Just as well to know when she deposited these," he told me, and waved at the jewel cases.

Matthews was ushering the lady through the door. Without her bag she had nothing to do with her hands and the air of bravado didn't come off. I placed a chair for her and I got a look that was haughtiness itself.

"Now," Wharton said briskly, "we're going to open these cases. Just what are they, Lady Tynworth?"

"Whatever they are, they're mine."

"That's capital," Wharton told her. I don't like him so much when he does that cat-and-mouse act. "You mean they're the replicas?"

She was moistening her lips. The hands were twitching and she was trying to find the right words. She didn't have time.

"Ah, well," said Wharton resignedly, "I suppose we can see for ourselves."

He picked up that rivière case and pushed the metal paper-knife under the clasp. The wax came away in three or four pieces. He pushed them carefully into a little heap. I could see the tiny key-hole where the wax and clasp had been.

"Locked," Wharton said. "You haven't the key, Lady Tynworth?"

"No," she said. "No."

"Probably why you didn't open them yourself." He took out his spectacle case, adjusted the old-fashioned glasses and peered at her over their tops. "You wouldn't by any chance be telling me a lie? You're aware that I can have you searched?"

"You wouldn't dare!"

"I wouldn't dare," Wharton told me amusedly. "All right, Matthews. Get someone who can open these. And attend to this at the same time."

He gave him the note. Matthews went out and the three of us just sat there. Wharton was looking at some papers on his desk. I was watching the lady. She was like a woman who'd been waiting half an hour for a belated husband.

"Smoke by all means if you feel like it," Wharton told her, and he didn't look up from his papers. His hand just pushed her bag across the desk. I gave it to her. She helped herself to a cigarette, and she wouldn't use my lighter. Then the door opened. A man—I think his name was Chapman—came in. He had a bag of keys, hundreds of them. Wharton leaned over to watch him try them out. He'd tried about twenty of the smallest when we heard the click.

"Ah!" said Wharton. He took the case and opened it. Then his mouth gaped. The lady had leaned forward and she gave a sudden gasp. *The case was empty.*

A couple of minutes and Wharton's face was grim. On it was that other Coliseum smile which wasn't a smile at all—the look on the face of the lion when the Christian has eluded the first spring. The lady's face was what they call a picture. A quick anger still lingered with the first bewilderment.

Wharton buzzed down and a stenographer came in. Another man was given the one unopened case and some quickly written instructions for Matthews. I knew later that Matthews was to check the wax print against those he'd obtained at Old Farm. Wharton cleared his throat. He cautioned the lady on a charge of being concerned with the theft of certain properties known as the Lammerford Jewels. Was she prepared to make a statement?

"And suppose I don't?"

"You'll be held in custody. You'll be brought up on the charge and remanded till you decide to talk or we get further evidence. The Press will be kept fully informed. The second sensation they'll have had in the last few days."

It was the last bit that shook her.

"All right," she said. "I don't see why I should have to take it all. Not that I've done anything wrong, because I haven't."

"Let me assure you that no one will be more pleased to know that than I," Wharton told her unctuously. "The statement, then. It'll be read over to you afterwards."

But there wasn't to be a statement, or one worth mentioning. All she said was that when she left her husband she'd decided she ought to have the replicas. No one knew it but she'd had her own key made some time before for the safe. So she just opened it and there were the replicas, which she took.

"Simple as that," Wharton said. "What about these cases? What difference is there between them and the cases of the originals?"

She said there wasn't any. As far as she knew the history of the jewels, the replicas were almost as old as the originals and their cases had been made as replicas, too. Wharton said that couldn't apply at the present moment. The originals had had infinitely less use, and therefore the replica cases ought to be far more worn. She merely shrugged her shoulders.

"Very well," Wharton told her. "What I want from you is everything you know about the originals from the moment your husband told you he was getting them out of the bank."

It was like prising out teeth with a tin-opener. Wharton had her sent out for half an hour and said she might have a meal. We were going over what we got from her when Matthews came in. The deposit box had been taken at twelve o'clock on the morning of the Tuesday she'd arrived in town. As for the finger-prints on the unopened case, *they were those of Molly Bolfray!*

Wharton raised his hands to heaven, then his look as suddenly changed.

"You're sure of it?"

"Dead sure, sir."

"My God!" Wharton said. "Face like a plaster saint and lying like hell."

If he'd had wings he'd have opened the window and been on his way down to Herndown: as it was he was shaking his head and muttering to himself as he sat down.

"Let's see what we got from the other liar."

It didn't put him in a better temper. She'd said that all of them—which meant herself, Molly and Yale—had been shown the jewels on the Sunday afternoon.

"And that makes them all liars," Wharton said. "They all swore blind they'd never seen them at all. Then she said that as far as she knew Tynworth was taking the jewels with him when he went up to town on the Monday, presumably to hand in to the cleaners. That sounds reasonable. But she hadn't any idea why he wanted the duplicates. Mean to tell me she didn't ask him?

"Then there's the mention of hole-and-corner work between Molly Bolfray and Tynworth. Something going on on the sly. What's your idea of that?"

I thought there might be something in it. After all, Molly Bolfray had been proved a liar and her prints were on the wax.

"Says she suspected some secret," George went on. "Part rings true and part doesn't. She was the one with a secret. She knew she was skipping out on the Monday night. Then there's that bit about it being everyone's idea—the same old three, that is—for him to go to America and raise the wind. That's reasonable enough."

But he looked as if he'd have liked to find some flaw in it.

"Well, there we are," he said. "I suppose you realise we can't hold her?"

Matthews looked staggered.

"You're turning her loose, sir!"

"What else can we do? She's done nothing. We know she's the world's prize liar, but we can't fake a holding charge. We can't disprove she took what she thought was her own property."

He leant back frowning as he thought it over.

"We'll have her in again," he said. "One or two questions I'd still like to ask her."

She came in and she was still a bit anxious.

"Just one or two things we'd like you to clear up," he told her mildly. "Just why did you leave your house in the dead of night when everyone was asleep? Why didn't you go out boldly as soon as your husband had gone?"

"Because I didn't want to be followed." It came so pat that she must have been thinking things out. "I was going to start my own life all over again."

"And why did you put the replicas in a safe deposit if they were your own property?"

"I was waiting to see what happened."

"But you have a bank?"

"Well, there was my husband," she said. "He'd wanted them and I didn't know why. It might have been important. I suppose really I oughtn't to have taken them. That's why I got a bit scared and deposited them." She was finding it none too easy to extemporise. "You see, when he got back from America he couldn't prove I had them."

Wharton let out a breath. He leaned forward.

"You realise what all this is involved with? You realise your husband was murdered? You know what murder means?"

"Yes," she said, and moistened her lips.

"Your husband was murdered because of the jewels. That we haven't any doubt about. You can't deny there's been considerable hanky-panky on your part and not unconnected with the same jewels." He let out another breath—a safety-valve emission for what was bottled up inside. "Now you've made a statement. I hope you realise the seriousness of that statement—and to yourself, if it isn't implicitly true in every detail. Anything you wish to correct?"

She shook her head.

"Anything you wish to add?"

"No . . . not that I can think of."

"Right," he said. "You'll be shown the statement and will sign it if you find it in order. Then you may go. Anywhere you'd like to be taken? To the railway station?"

"Yes, to the railway station."

Wharton nodded to Matthews. The stenographer got up, too.

"We may have to see you again, Lady Tynworth. I can't say, but I'd like you to remain at your Birmingham hotel till you're told otherwise."

George and I had the room to ourselves. I asked him what next.

"I'll report to Birmingham," he told me. "They might as well ask Bernardo a few questions."

It was getting on for three o'clock. He thought he'd be finished by four.

"Then Herndown," he said. The jaws clamped together. Molly Bolfray was in for a remarkably thin time.

I was feeling the loss of lunch, so I had some tea at a little place near Westminster Bridge. To me the last hours had been pretty bewildering. Every idea I'd previously had had been kicked endways. And it wasn't only that that made me disturbed. That revelation about Molly Bolfray's prints on the empty jewel cases was shattering to my assumptions of judgment. If there was one person I'd have trusted it was she. It hurt me to think she'd been mixed up in all the intrigue. And maybe more than just intrigue. As Wharton had said, a man had been murdered and because of those jewels, and instead of helping to find either the jewels or a murderer everyone had been telling us lies. Cool, suave lies—lies handed out as if they were as inconsequential as the romantic fabrications of children in a nursery.

But I was pleased to be getting into the car with Wharton and Matthews and going to Herndown and trying to worm the real truth out of Molly Bolfray. With what we knew, I didn't see how she could take refuge again in that madonna-like innocence.

"Where'd you leave the Tynworth woman?" Wharton was asking Matthews.

"At the station, sir. Over half an hour, though, before her train left."

Wharton nodded and sank back in his corner. Then he was sitting up.

"My God! Over half an hour?"

"About that, sir."

"That's torn it," he said. "Why the devil didn't I tell you to stay with her till she was on the train." He glared round at me. "You know what she'll have done? She'll have telephoned to Herndown. Told that sister of hers everything that's happened. By the time we get there everything will be nice and pat."

His face was a thundercloud. As the Frenchman once said, there's something about the misfortunes of others that's not wholly displeasing to ourselves. For once I wasn't the one who had to be blamed.

PART IV
THE SECOND BODY

CHAPTER XIV
A BRICK WALL

THE same lounge. Molly Bolfray and Yale had been waiting as Wharton had instructed before we left, but Yale had been sent out with Matthews and was standing by. But a flea had been put into two pairs of ears. *Murder*. That's what Wharton had driven home.

"Tell me a single thing that I don't know to be the truth," he'd told them, "and you'll go back with me to the Yard. The time's past for lies and shilly-shallying. I want the truth and I'm going to get it, even if I stay here all night."

So there we were with Molly Bolfray. She was looking pale and drawn, but I'd seen her more anxious.

"A bad business about your brother-in-law," Wharton began, and mildly. "It must have come as a shock."

"It was horrible. Horrible. We just couldn't believe it."

"Well, it's happened," he said. "The jewels were serious enough, but this is murder. We want all the help you can give us. And this time it's to be the truth. For instance, did your sister ring you this afternoon?"

"Yes," she said; and Wharton gave me a look as if it had been I after all who'd failed to foresee the possibility.

"And what did she tell you?"

"Abuse principally," she told us calmly. "Accused me of being a thief and emptying the jewel cases."

"And did you?"

"How could I?" she said. "I didn't know they were in the safe."

He took the empty cases from his case and laid them on the low table.

"Look at these, Mrs. Bolfray. Are they the cases belonging to the originals or the replicas?"

Her chair was so close to his that she didn't need to rise. She was frowning as she looked at them.

"The originals," she said. "The other cases are much more worn."

"You sure of that?"

"Quite sure," she told him calmly. "I've seen them often enough in Sally's room."

Wharton took out the small case with the sealing-wax intact. He showed it to her.

"Sealed with finger or thumb," he said. "Yours, Mrs. Bolfray. How do you account for that?"

What we heard was to answer two questions: the prints themselves and that hole-and-corner business which Sally had mentioned.

"It was like this," she said. "I'd suspected Sally for some time. I knew there was something behind all that act she was putting on, pretending to be nice to everyone and being so sorry about Tom's troubles and everything. And twice a man rang her when she wasn't here. Then on the Sunday I discovered that she'd begun packing. She and Tom had been occupying different rooms on account of Tom's snoring, or so she said, and I found a packed bag under her bed, so I told Tom straight. I made him believe me."

"He confronted her?"

Her lip curled.

"No. He was afraid of her. He was simply mad about her. She could never do anything wrong. I suppose he knew what she'd do if he accused her of anything. She'd just have had one of her mad fits again."

"And then?"

"Well, on the Monday morning very early, before she was up, he called me into the office upstairs. He had those cases. He said he was sealing them up in case they'd be tampered with and would I put my thumb on the wax while he did it. So I did it. What happened then I don't know. I just went out."

"He didn't say another word to you about them?"

"Nothing. Nothing at all."

He turned to me.

"Looks as if he'd emptied the cases first. But why *your* prints, Mrs. Bolfray? Doesn't it strike you now as very extraordinary? Why not do the job himself?"

"I trusted Tom," she said. "I knew he wouldn't ask me to do anything without reason. Besides, I did think he'd at last begun to see through Sally—after what I'd told him."

"But listen," he said. "I'm trying to be patient about all this. Trying to understand. Why in God's name should *you* be asked to put your thumb on the wax? How could that affect what he thought about your sister?"

"I don't know," she said. "Unless it was because he'd be away and I'd still be here."

Wharton smiled with an infinite patience.

"And yet he emptied the cases."

"If you say so—yes."

"Then what'd he do with the jewels?"

"I don't know. Why do you ask me such things? How could I know?"

Wharton's jaws clamped down—a new bottling up of what was inside. Molly was frowning slightly as she watched him—frowning as if wondering why he couldn't see things through her eyes.

"Right," Wharton suddenly said. "That's all you can tell us?"

"There's nothing else I can think of."

"Well, I want to see that nursemaid. Perhaps you'll send her down here. And stay upstairs yourself until we've seen Mr. Yale."

A couple of minutes and Daisy was coming in. She looked scared. Her round face was redder than ever and she was biting her lip. It took Wharton quite a time to put her at something like ease.

"Now, Daisy, just a simple question or two. Nothing whatever to get alarmed about. All we want to know is what happened here, as far as it concerned yourself, after Lord Tynworth had left on the Monday afternoon."

He had to drag it out of her almost word by word. Nothing had happened out of the ordinary, except that Mrs. Bolfray had gone to bed early with a bad headache. Early, it appeared, was at about eight o'clock. A little later she asked Daisy to bring in her sewing-bag.

"Curious, wasn't it?" I said. "Why should she want to sew if she had a bad headache?"

"Perhaps it was better," she said. "And she'd promised me to help with something we were doing to Master Peter's clothes. And she'd torn her nightgown and was going to mend it."

"She was still in bed when you took the bag in?"

"Oh yes, and she had only the bed light on."

Wharton asked her about Lady Tynworth. Nothing emerged but that Mrs. Bolfray had been having a glass of malted milk each night at bedtime and that night Lady Tynworth took it up to her. Asked about Yale, she said she hadn't actually seen him but she believed that he and Lady Tynworth had been out somewhere before dinner and afterwards they'd sat in the lounge. She herself slept in the small room adjoining the nursery and with the nursery door open. She'd gone to sleep that night practically at once and she hadn't woke up till just after dawn, and then it had been the boy who had woken her.

That was all, but it had taken twenty minutes to elicit. Wharton had her all smiles when she went out. He went with her to the door, but that was to go on through the hall and call in Yale.

Yale was imperturbable as ever but without that look he'd had when I'd seen him last—the sort of sitting-on-top-of-the-world-and-the-devil-take-everyone-else. Wharton waved him to a chair. There was a facer straightaway.

"Mr. Yale, why did you lie to us about not seeing those jewels? You told us you hadn't seen them, but you had. You saw them on Sunday. Everyone saw them."

"Oh, that," he said. "To tell the truth, something told me to keep my mouth shut. It looked as if something fishy had been going on and I wanted to keep well out of it."

"Fishy in what way?"

"Well, the jewels seemed to have gone. And I knew Tom oughtn't to have had them here. They should have been taken straight to that firm to be cleaned."

"Did he say anything about that when he was showing them to everybody?"

"He didn't, but we knew it. I took it for granted he'd be handing them in when he went to town the next day."

"I see. But you realise now that you can't keep out of it, as you put it?"

"I know what murder is," he told us bluntly.

"We're making progress," Wharton said dryly. "Start off now from the time Tynworth left here on the Monday and tell us everything you did."

"You'll have to give me time."

"All the time in the world provided you tell us the truth."

We couldn't discern a lie in it. He'd come in for a quick and early cup of tea and had said goodbye to his partner, whom Sally was driving to the station in her car. Then he'd gone back to the stables and was there till about six. A horse had been limping slightly after exercise and he'd seen to it among other things. He'd been in the office when Sally had come there. She'd asked about the horse and said he ought to have the vet in spite of what Tynworth had said about it. They'd sat there talking about nothing in particular and they had a sherry from a bottle he always kept there, and had smoked a cigarette or two, then they'd gone in and he'd changed for the evening meal.

Molly hadn't been well and had eaten practically nothing and had then gone up to bed. He had sat on in the lounge till about nine o'clock, with Sally—restless as ever—in and out; and then he'd had his last look as usual round the stables. He'd turned in fairly early and he'd slept like a log, maybe because Sally had brought him a hot malted milk. He hated what he called "the damn stuff", but she said he'd been looking a bit peaked and he didn't like to offend her, so he drank it. He gave his first smile as he said it hadn't been half bad.

That was all he knew. Wharton had Molly come down. I'd been taking shorthand notes and I read them over to the pair of them. Neither had anything to add or retract.

Wharton got up a bit heavily. He gave them a reminder of the seriousness of things. There was still time to withdraw or add.

"Right," he said. "We'll be going but we'll almost certainly be here again, and we'll expect to find you here. Just one last question for you, Mrs. Bolfray. That woman you had here as housekeeper-cook. I understand she forced a quarrel and left on the spot."

"Yes," she said. "It was about going into the kitchen. I've always been in and out and she'd never said anything, but then she flared up about it. She was positively rude, and when I told her so she just took off her apron and marched upstairs."

"How'd you get her here in the first place?"

For the first time she was looking a bit uneasy. Yale cut in. "Rill—I think you know him—heard we wanted someone and recommended her. I told Sally she was a fool to have her."

"Why?"

"Well, I thought it was pretty glaring. Rill had just edged his way well in here. Maybe he thought Tom was going to bolt."

"You don't mean she was a kind of spy?"

"Ask yourself," he said. "No harm in Rill asking her a few questions. I hated her. I thought her a stuck-up bitch."

"Arthur!"

"Sorry. But it's the truth, all the same."

"But she was good," she said. "She really did know her work. The best one I ever had here."

"Mr. Rill been down here recently?"

"No," Yale said. "He did ring up to say how sorry he was, and so on, about Tom."

"Kind of him," Wharton said. "And what about Mr. Conn?"

"He was here the day before yesterday. Having a look round. He was quite decent on the whole."

That seemed to be all that Wharton wanted to know. We went out alone to the car and that seemed to make a queer kind of finality. Yale had usually come out, but this time he went no farther than the hall. It made me feel as if there was a dividing line—we on one side and Old Farm on the other. Perhaps it was that that Wharton felt, too.

"Like coming up against a brick wall," he told me when we'd swung into the main road. "Here we come with those jewel cases and her prints on 'em, and what happens? Everything's explained."

He clicked his tongue annoyedly.

"When I sit there listening to that woman I know she's telling the truth. She sits there with that pathetic look of hers and you just gulp down everything she says. Then as soon as you get away you start wondering again."

Never had he had such a case, he said. Something inexplicable would turn up and then you'd find an answer to it, and the answer would be more inexplicable still.

"Why did Tynworth get her to put her prints on those cases?"

"Don't ask me, George," I said. "I'm as much in the dark as you."

"He removed the jewels," George went on, and more to himself than me. "What'd he do with them?"

"What about this for an idea?" I said. "What Molly Bolfray had told him about his wife had shaken him. He didn't trust anybody. So he went through the motions of assuring Molly that the jewels were in the cases, and then he cached them somewhere else."

"Well?"

"Then whoever killed him thought he had the jewels, but he hadn't. Hence the employment by Henry Balfour of X. Balfour knew Sally had disappeared, so it was natural to assume that she had the jewels."

"But she hadn't. She had nothing but some empty cases."

"I know," I said. "But the curious thing is that she knew very well that those cases belonged to the original jewels. She had to know that. After all, she'd seen the other cases and handled them often enough. Therefore when she took those cases from the safe, she knew she was taking, not her own replicas, but the actual jewels. You probably heard her gasp when you opened that first case."

"Yes. There's some sense in that," he said. "And that was why she cached them away in Cardinal Street. Just a little insurance for her old age."

"That leaves the replicas. What happened to them? They don't seem to fit in."

"Damn the replicas!" He'd had to let that out or burst. "Leave the whole thing. What about that Henry Balfour? Who was he?"

"Not Bernardo," I said. "If there's one thing of which I'm sure it's that he knew nothing about the original jewels being out of the bank. Sally didn't tell him. That was her private bit of scheming. That's why she deposited them as soon as the Safe Deposit Company opened that morning."

"What about Rill? Or Conn?"

"How could they have known? Mrs. Drew might have sent word that she'd overheard they were being taken from the bank; but however good a snooper she was, she couldn't have known what was being done with them. Tynworth appears to have bamboozled everybody."

"Mrs. Drew would have known about the existence of the jewels without any snooping," he said. "The Tynworth woman sometimes wore the replicas."

He tried mimicking voices.

"'How lovely you look, m'lady! What marvellous jewels!' 'That's nothing, Mrs. Drew. You ought to see the real ones.' And wouldn't the Drew woman have been told about the real ones and how they'd ultimately come to the boy? And mightn't she have suggested to Rill that Tynworth might pawn, say, some of the jewels, and pay the proceeds towards his debts?

"That's it!" he said. "I'm beginning to see daylight. Tynworth took out, say, the two rings, intending to raise money on them— the money he'd definitely promised to Rill. That surprise Rill told us about. What Tynworth hoped for was a loan in America to get the rings out again. Then he'd return the whole lot to the jewellers.

"That's it!" he told me again. "That's the business he was intending to do on the Tuesday. But someone got wise to it. We've got to find the leakage. Might do worse than start off with that Drew woman."

It was something that lulled him the rest of the way to town. I didn't disagree, if only because I had nothing better to suggest. But I could see as many holes in his theory as in so much wire-netting. It didn't explain the rest of the hocus-pocus in which Tynworth had indulged, like getting Molly to put her thumb-prints on the wax. It didn't tell us where the replicas came in or give even a hint as to where they could conceivably be. The whole theory was, as I saw it, far too tenuous—the sort of thing that Wharton would have ghoulishly demolished if I'd propounded it myself. It was an expedient, a soporific—a makeshift something that would have a certain busy-ness about it, and out of it the hope that something far more hopeful would emerge.

As soon as we got to the Yard Wharton got into touch with Birmingham. Their opinion was that Bernardo knew nothing about the original jewels. He'd asked Sally where the replicas were because he'd taken her out to dinner that first night of hers in town and she hadn't been wearing even a ring. He asked her again in Birmingham because he'd thought they might be used in the act, and she'd told him they were being polished and cleaned.

He swore he'd never seen Tynworth in his life, but he had to admit that on that Monday night he didn't have to appear at the Monterey till shortly before nine o'clock, and that his only real alibi was Sally. He owned then that he hadn't taken her out to dinner that night. She'd had sandwiches and drinks brought up to her room at that first hotel.

I could have done with sandwiches and drinks myself. It wasn't till almost ten o'clock that the day's report was down in black and white. Wharton said he'd have a conference first thing in the morning, but I might as well call on Mrs. Drew.

"Make it well after breakfast. Give her plenty of time to get up."

I went home and I was too tired to enjoy the scratch meal that was waiting for me. When I got to bed, the case began the old trick of circling in my mind and I had to get up and mix myself a stiff drink before I could get to sleep.

In the morning I took things easy. Somewhere round about half-past ten seemed the best time to turn up at Hampstead, so I read the morning papers and was actually thinking of tackling a crossword. Then the telephone bell began to shrill.

"That you, Travers? Wharton here. Get along as quick as you can."

"Something happened?"

"Yes," he said. "Looks as if we've found our friend X."

I grabbed hat and overcoat and I didn't wait for the lift. I don't think I've ever made it more quickly to the Yard. The car was there—Matthews at the wheel and Jewle with him. I got in behind Wharton. The car fairly shot away towards Trafalgar Square.

"Where is he, George?"

"At Tottendon."

I stared. Tottendon, as I call it, was an outlying suburb that always seemed to me to have the dinginess and the garish activity of stretches of the East End.

"What was he doing out there?"

"Don't know," he said, "except it was a likely place to dump him."

"He's dead?"

"Deader than a herring. Dropped over a railway bridge some time last night.

"Mind you," he said, "we're not dead sure it was X. But the mole's there. Looks to me as though it's going to fit in."

We went through streets with little shops sandwiched between the multiple ones, and past side roads of drab terraced houses, by oases of allotments and waste areas with shacks and factories. Things didn't look so dingy in the morning sunshine. When we turned off to the right you could actually see a church spire in the distance and the faint grey of the bare encircling trees. A couple of minutes and we were past the ribbon of bungalows and coming to a railway bridge. The car slowed. It drew up just beyond. Two other cars were there, and a couple of uniformed police.

We got over the railings and went sideways down the embankment. The local inspector was there and one of his men, and a foreman plate-layer who'd discovered the body. Something was lying there just clear of the track, and within three feet of the bridge. Wharton drew back the hessian wrapper.

"Have a look," he told me.

I hate corpses, but there was little to turn the stomach about this one. No train had mangled it. It was just lying there on its back. There was the mole. There was the shaved upper lip with just a glint of reddish hair.

"It's X," I said. "I haven't a shadow of a doubt."

"Right," Wharton said. "I'd like him along at the Yard. You get statements, Jewle. What'd your local doctor say, Inspector?"

"Thinks he was killed about eight o'clock last night, sir."

"Manual strangulation?"

It didn't surprise me. I'd seen the bruises on the Adam's-apple.

"That's it, sir. A blow on the back of the skull and then strangled."

"Slap-bang up to date," Wharton told him grimly. "All the best murderers are using it now. No noise, no mess. Neat little jobs."

He got down on one knee and had another good look.

"Right," he said. "I want him at the Yard inside an hour. Then the statements. You, Inspector, might get some men here and try and dig out something. Someone may have seen a car. I know it's not likely. Whoever dumped him here wouldn't have had to stop more'n a few seconds. Still, you never know."

He gave a general nod and began climbing back up the embankment. He halted and called back.

"Look round in case anything fell out of his pockets."

The car went on, reversed and headed back to town.

"Just the break we wanted," Wharton told me. "He might be almost as good to us dead as alive."

He outlined what he was going to do. X had used a washable dye for his hair and moustache for the purpose of impersonation, so as soon as the body reached the Yard it'd be given a reddish-brown moustache and photographs would be rushed for the later editions of the evening papers.

"Someone knew him," he said. "He had to earn his living somewhere. Someone will have missed him. Bet you a fiver we hear something before the day's out."

I didn't take him. Bets with George are heads he wins and tails I somehow lose.

"Why was he killed?" I said. "Because he knew too much?"

"That's it," he said. "As soon as all that stuff came out in the papers about the Tynworth murder he knew he'd been lured into something remarkably fishy. So he tried a bit of blackmail." He gave a little snort of contempt. "What he didn't do was reckon with your old friend Henry Balfour."

Chapter XV
IDENTIFICATION

There was more argument, of course, before we got back to the Yard. The method of transporting the body and dumping seemed a clear indication that both jobs had been done by the same man. But again, had the car come south *towards* London or north *from* London? Tynworth's body had been burnt so that it could never be identified, and I wondered why there'd been no attempt to do the same thing with X. Wharton said you didn't find handy stack-bottoms everywhere, and, besides, there'd been no fog.

"He wasn't wearing the same overcoat," I said. "Too dangerous, perhaps, to go on wearing Tynworth's."

There was to be something peculiar about those clothes when the body reached the Yard. Things went on at such a speed, and there were so many of them that I got most of my information at second-hand. But I did see the clothes.

Another peculiar thing, and about the contents of the pockets, was that there weren't any. Every pocket was empty and nothing had fallen from them on the embankment. As for the clothes themselves, the labels had been removed from overcoat and jacket, and the laundry tabs from the socks and vest. The shirt had never been washed and looked almost new.

"I wonder," Wharton said. "Wouldn't Tynworth have had some new things for that trip of his? He'd want to make an impression. This might be one of his shirts. Get out to Herndown with it, Matthews. Show it to Mrs. Bolfray and Yale. See what you can make out."

The rest of the clothes went to the laboratory. Word came up from the finger-print department. There was no record of the dead man's prints. Wharton wasn't too pleased. He'd been counting on a record.

The afternoon began to wear away. We had some tea sent up and the latest editions of the evening papers. A good job had been made of the photograph. It was to the very life the man who sat in my car on that Wednesday morning. There wasn't much description, of course—there couldn't be. The mole was the high-spot, and that reddish moustache.

At a quarter to five Matthews rang. Molly Bolfray thought that shirt was one of three which Tynworth had recently bought in Chelmsford. Yale knew nothing.

"Thought," Wharton said. "Doesn't she know?"

"Shirts are just shirts," he said. "She thinks this was the one she saw when she was packing his bag."

"Does she know the shop he bought it at?"

"No, sir. She remarked that the shirts were nice and he said he'd bought them in Chelmsford. Looks to me as if you'd see the same thing in hundreds of good-class shops."

"Right," he said. "If you've got a statement you might as well get back."

He hadn't hung up more than a couple of minutes when the buzzer went again. This time something had happened. Wharton was all smiles as he began writing things down.

"James Long, car salesman, corner Portland Street and Withers Street. Tell him I'll be there as fast as I can make it. Meanwhile he's to keep his mouth shut."

*

It was quite a good-class place: double windows showing cars for sale and premises going a considerable way back. Long was a shrewd-looking man of about fifty. He was on the lookout for us, and he had an evening paper in his hand. Wharton introduced himself and me.

"I think it's him all right," Long said. "Name of Fane. Ronald Fane. Been working for me about five months."

He told us about it. Fane had brought along a car for sale, a just pre-war Standard Ten, and Long had bought it. Fane said he'd bought it himself as a speculation.

"He'd a rare gift of the gab," Long told us, "and to cut a long story short, I took him on here. Purely on commission. I don't mind telling you he did pretty well. Probably spent it, though. Used to lift his elbow a bit, though that was no business of mine."

"What was he?" Wharton said. "How'd you place him?"

"According to his own account he'd been a flying officer, axed soon after the war. He'd a pretty good education, but"—he smiled—"I didn't credit everything he said. Very persuasive, if you know what I mean. That was all right for the customers, and it didn't worry me so long as he kept his hands clean."

"Well, there's one excellent test to see if he's our man," Wharton said. "Where was he on Wednesday, February the eleventh?"

"Wednesday the eleventh. Yes," he said. "On the Tuesday evening he rang me to say his mother was seriously ill and he'd have to have a few days off."

"And he was away for just over a week."

"That's right, sir." He looked a bit surprised.

"And he'd shaved off his moustache."

Long looked more surprised.

"That's all right," Wharton told him amusedly. "We're not asleep at the Yard, you know. So he came back, you say. Did he seem well heeled?"

"Couldn't say, sir. He was a bit pleased with himself. His mother had died and left him some money—that's what he said—but he didn't mention giving up his job."

He frowned as if he were remembering something.

"I told you I didn't always credit everything he said. About his mother, for instance. I'm positive he once told me he hadn't any parents."

"I know," Wharton said. "Liars should have good memories, or so they say. I suppose you don't happen to have a photograph of him?"

He didn't. But he did have the address of the place where he lived—a side street off the Marylebone Road.

"What about his friends? Did he have any?"

Long didn't know. There was what he called an indoor salesman and himself. Fane had been a kind of freelance and practically always out of doors.

"He'd a fine knowledge of cars, no denying that. He could diagnose a spot of trouble better than any of us. But about his friends." He smiled. "He'd bring prospective customers along here and you couldn't tell if they were his friends or not. You know what I mean. He was the sort of chap you'd meet in a bar, say, and before you knew it he'd be standing you a drink and hearing all your troubles—"

"And selling you a car."

"That's it, sir. He was good. I'll give him that credit."

"And about yesterday—he just didn't turn up?"

"That's right, sir. Didn't turn up or ring or anything. If I hadn't been short-handed today I'd have gone along to his place to find out what was the matter. I did ring this morning, but his landlady said he hadn't been in at all last night. Then I happened to see this paper and there he was, looking at me."

"Yes," Wharton said. "And you've no idea who could have done him in?"

Long hadn't a vestige. He did say he wouldn't put it past him to have worked a raw deal: borrowed money, for example, and bilked the lender.

"He was the sort you didn't altogether trust," he said. "I never found him out in anything, mind you. I reckon he knew I was keeping a pretty close eye on him where deals were concerned."

Wharton asked if he might use the telephone. When he came back there were the profusest of thanks. Long said he'd certainly report anything else he might remember, and with that we moved on towards Marylebone.

It was an apartment house—bed-and-breakfast but no other meals. The landlady had two rooms and a kitchen on the ground floor. She was a thin, angular woman of about sixty and quite well-spoken. When we showed our warrant cards she was very upset. She'd liked Mr. Fane and she couldn't imagine him in any trouble with the police. Wharton reminded her that he hadn't mentioned any trouble.

"The fact is, he's died suddenly under what we consider peculiar circumstances and there has to be an enquiry."

"Dead," she said. "Oh dear! And he was always so nice. Never a bit of trouble. He nearly always used to come in late, I know, but you very rarely heard him."

"How long was he with you, Mrs. Mortimer?"

"Let me see. Just over a year."

"And he didn't sleep in last night?"

"No. His bed wasn't even disturbed."

Wharton's brow furrowed in thought. I guessed he was about to put on some act.

"Now, Mrs. Mortimer, I'd say you're a woman of very good memory. I wonder if you could cast your mind back to the evening of Monday, February the ninth?"

"Do you mind if I look at the calendar?"

There was one on the wall above that sitting-room desk. It was a large one and there seemed to be notes pencilled round the squares.

"Monday, February the ninth," Wharton said. "Nothing happened to Mr. Fane that you can remember?"

"No," she said. "Nothing."

"Then the next morning. Did he go out specially early or anything peculiar?"

"He had a telephone call."

"There you are!" Wharton told me. "I knew Mrs. Mortimer would remember."

She had taken the call herself, she said, and at about half-past seven in the morning. Her help had just taken up a breakfast. A man was asking to speak to Mr. Fane. Mr. Fane was asleep but he got up and came to the telephone, and that's all she knew, except that he told her he had to go out and wouldn't want breakfast. He went off in a great hurry.

"You're sure it was as late as half-past seven?"

"Let me think," she said, and then: "Perhaps I was wrong. Gertie was getting ready to take up Mr. Wallace's breakfast. He likes it just before half-past seven. Now I come to think of it, it was at about half-past seven that Mr. Fane actually went out."

"Anything else happen that day?"

"Oh yes. Mr. Fane rang to say his mother was seriously ill and he mightn't be in for a few days. As a matter of fact he was away for just over a week." Her voice lowered. "His mother died, poor soul."

"He didn't come back here to collect any of his things? Shaving things and so on?"

"No, he didn't. He told me over the telephone there were things of his at his home which he could use."

"He didn't say where his home was?"

"I think I gathered it was Warwickshire."

"Well, you've been most helpful," Wharton told her. "Now I'd like to see his room."

It was a bed-sitter. We opened drawers and looked in the wardrobe. The first thing I noticed was that overcoat that had probably belonged to Tynworth.

"See if the car's here," Wharton told me.

The car was outside. Mrs. Mortimer was told we'd have to remove all Fane's belongings. A receipt would be given her and she'd be paid any amounts owing for the room.

"Well, so far so good," Wharton said as I moved our car on. "No doubt whatever that he's our man. The question is, how's it going to lead us to Henry Balfour?"

It must have been the so-called Balfour who'd rung Fane early on that Tuesday morning. The time-table, as we began working it out, had probably been roughly this:

Tynworth had been killed by Balfour on the Monday night and there had been the immediate question of the disposal of the body. Balfour had then almost certainly gone to Tynworth's room at the hotel and had looked through his small case and searched the room. Then had come that drive with the body. My idea was that Balfour had gone astray in the fog and that the stack-bottom had been a lucky find. He'd got to his home probably not sooner than four in the morning.

Out of his welter of thoughts had come the image of Fane, the R.A.F. type who could be made to resemble Tynworth. So he rang Fane and the rendezvous was Tynworth's room at the hotel. There Fane was told about the Tynworth, a friend of Balfour's, whose people thought he was going to America but who was really staying in England to watch his wife.

Then the telephone rang.

Balfour took the call. Molly burst out with her story. It gave Balfour time to collect his thoughts and acquire that attack of tonsilitis.

After that, or so we thought, Fane checked out of the hotel as Tynworth and the talk was carried on elsewhere. The final scheme was concocted, and it was something which, as Wharton said, would be right up Fane's alley. A bit of specious talking, a free trip to America and back, and a nice bit of pay at the end of it.

The thing now, as we knew, was to discover how Balfour had come to think of Fane at all. How had the two come into contact. Had Fane sold Balfour a car? Had they met in some bar or other? Were they distant relations? Had they both been in the R.A.F.?

We were in Wharton's room by then. Matthews came in. He had some news. He hadn't liked leaving Herndown with practically nothing, so he'd gone to that little hotel on the off chance. There he'd discovered that Fane—as he now knew him—had been at the pub on what was probably the vital Tuesday evening, and had been enquiring about Old Farm. He'd said he was a racing journalist.

"Getting a little local colour," Wharton said, and announced that he'd a score of things to do. Matthews would take anything that came through from wherever it might be about Fane. I was to see Long again.

"You've got his private address. Get him to go back to the office with you and go through the books. See if you can unearth anything about a car. I'll arrange to get the numbers of any cars at Old Farm and Bernardo's, if he has one, and Conn's and Rill's."

It was nine o'clock that night when I'd finished making notes on all of Long's deals with people with whom he hadn't been personally associated or for whom he couldn't vouch. None of the names we wanted was there. When I got back to the Yard the car numbers were in, including Sally's car. From Old Farm there was also a station wagon and a trailer outfit for horse conveyance. Bernardo hadn't a car. Conn had the Jaguar and Rill a 1939 Rolls and a 1951 Morris Twelve. None of the numbers appeared in Long's books, so something that had been promising had turned out to be a dead end. Wharton wasn't in his room, and Matthews was busy, so I went home. If I was wanted I'd be on tap.

I woke far too early in the morning, with a mind too full of things for further sleep, so I lay quietly on and began reviewing the case from the first moment I'd stumbled into it. I thought about that mole on Fane's cheek, and I thought I knew why he hadn't troubled to conceal it from me in the car, and that was because he'd never seen Tynworth for himself and was therefore unaware of its importance. And Balfour had neglected to tell him, and maybe because things had had to be done in too much of a hurry. That unnecessary mention of *valuables* showed that. Balfour had probably begun bringing them into that conference with Fane and then had changed his mind about telling more.

Two other things came to me. There was that matter of those shots at me, not that they or myself were of any consequence unless they could help in any way to solve the case, and I didn't see how they could. But there was one other thing and of far more importance, something I'd completely forgotten— that matter of Sally's eight-months child. It was something that hadn't appeared on any report and was therefore unknown to

Wharton. I wondered if I should tell him about it. Then I decided that things looked sufficiently promising without it, and I didn't see how it could concern Tynworth. He, apparently, like everyone else, had accepted the birth as merely premature.

I went out early and got some newspapers, and once more there were the banner headlines and the photograph of Fane and the clear statement that he had been the man who impersonated Tynworth for that American trip. Wharton, I thought, was relying on full publicity, and it'd be a full time job sorting the stuff that would be coming in.

When I got to the Yard Jewle was in charge of it. Matthews and Wharton hadn't left till the early hours, he told me, but Matthews was due to go to Old Farm to check up on the clothes that might have belonged to Tynworth. Wharton was somewhere downstairs. As for information about Fane, it had already been learned that he'd crashed in his pilot's final test and had spent most of the war with a maintenance crew at Halliwell. There had been some sort of scandal about sales of petrol just after the war ended, and he'd been dismissed the service. A squadron-leader who had known him was due that afternoon for an interview about it.

It was not till after nine that Wharton came in, and he had a job for me. By the time I got to Guiver Street both Rill and Conn would be there and I was to talk about alibis.

"For the night of Tynworth's death or of Fane's?"

"Fane's principally," he said. "The other by all means, but it's a bit far back. Watch out about them corroborating each other. Try and see them separately if you can. By the way, Matthews will be doing Yale's when he goes to Old Farm this morning. Tynworth's body's going out, too. The funeral'll probably be the day after tomorrow."

I had a police car and driver, and it was at half-past nine that I stepped into Rill's office. He knew only that I was coming, not what I was there for. To me he looked suave and cool as ever. He seemed to see nothing unusual in my seeing him alone and then Conn.

"By the way," I said, "what is Mr. Conn's actual position here? Does he run some special department?"

"Well, strictly between ourselves," he said, "he spends a good deal of his time interviewing unsatisfactory clients. We have no legal redress, you know, but sometimes we can bring pressure to bear."

Conn, I thought, was the very man for the job. The very bulk of him and those cold grey eyes would be quite an intimidating prospect for any welsher on bets.

"But about this visit of mine," I said, and rattled off the spiel I'd heard a hundred times from Wharton. Everybody, however faintly connected with Lord Tynworth, was being questioned. There was also the added complication of the man Fane, who seemed to have some connection. Enquiries were routine and chiefly so that those unconcerned would no longer have to be bothered.

"You, Mr. Rill"—I made it quite perfunctory—"needn't really have been bothered at all if it weren't for the records. We're tied up with red tape, you know, like everyone else. Your alibi for the night of Tynworth's death, for instance. You were in bed with influenza."

"I certainly was." He was knuckling back that silky moustache. "A particularly nasty germ, so my doctor said. Kept me in bed for well over a week."

"And the night before last?"

"Rather stupid, don't you think?" he said. "You'll be asking half London for alibis. Still—" He let out a sigh.

"You can put it on record that I was playing bridge with three golfing friends at my house from just after eight o'clock till midnight. After that, bed."

"You wouldn't mind giving me the names of, say, two of the bridge four?"

He wrote them down and I thanked him. He seemed surprised when I told him that was all.

"Now if I might have a word with Mr. Conn?"

"You'll be long?"

"Probably not so long as I've been with you," I told him. "Just something to make a show of at the Yard."

He gave a chuckle as he went out. I sat there, expecting every minute that the far door would open, but it didn't. Five minutes went by and then Rill and Conn came in together. They seemed a bit agitated.

"Morning," Conn said and held out a huge hand. "We've just made a most amazing discovery about this man Fane. He was working for us for about a year. Left us about six months ago."

He waved for me to resume my seat. I was blinking a bit: it had been so amazingly unexpected.

"What sort of work?"

"At various racecourses," he said. "When there're a lot of meetings we have to have a pretty big staff. Plenty of big coups are sprung at the small meetings. You might call him a safety-valve. Getting the feel of the market through to us here before the off of each race."

I told him I understood it and I didn't, if he knew what I meant. But had it been a paying job?

"Ten pounds a week and expenses. Not enough for Fane, though, or so I gather. He left because he thought he could make more elsewhere. Not that we were sorry. It was practically the end of the flat."

He'd been sitting on the end of Rill's desk. He spoke to Rill.

"What about getting the information typed out for Mr. Travers? I'll stay here in case there's anything he wants from me."

Rill went out. Conn took the desk seat and he gave me a smile. I wondered what he'd look like if his eyes ever smiled too.

"Now, Mr. Travers, what's all this nonsense about alibis?"

"Nonsense for you," I said, "but hard work for us."

I reeled off the same old preliminary patter.

"Tynworth's death," he said thoughtfully. "Let me see—when was that now?"

I told him.

"A goodish way back," he said, and took a small book from his breast pocket. "I don't know if there's anything here."

A moment or two and he was nodding to himself.

"Yes. Apparently I was at home all that night. Took some figures home with me to go into." The smile was regretful as he put the book back in his pocket. "Not much of an alibi, I'm afraid. My housekeeper always leaves at about six o'clock except on special occasions, so I must have been alone."

"That's all right," I told him. "Just something for our records. And the night before last?"

"Ah, that," he said. "That's easy. Let me see now. I left here at about half-past five. I'd had some tea brought in just before and I got to the Melodion just as the big picture was starting. *The Hundredth Chance.* You've seen it? You ought to. About the only racing picture I've ever enjoyed."

I must have smiled. He was giving me quite a sharp look. "Sorry," I said. "I don't want you to get annoyed about this—"

"My dear fellow, if I'd wanted to get annoyed it'd have been long ago when Howard Rill told me you were after alibis. But what was amusing you?"

"Nothing," I said. "Only that about two-thirds of the alibis we're given have to do with a cinema. Different classes of people from yourself, of course, and most of them get broken down. They don't seem to realise that such an alibi isn't one at all. What they can't produce is the one thing that makes it an alibi: someone who sat next to them all the time and would be prepared to swear they never left between certain hours. No offence, as I said."

His smile was rueful.

"Then I'm in the same boat." The smile was more ironic. "Next time you must let me know a murder's likely."

"We will," I said, and smiled too. "But you saw the whole film?"

"Couldn't take my eyes off it," he said. "I could go over every detail of it now. As a matter of fact I saw it a second time round. Didn't get out till about ten o'clock."

"Then you went home?"

"That's it." He gave a little rueful laugh. "One of the few times I've missed my dinner."

I got to my feet and put away my notebook.

"If we send you along a statement you'll sign it?"

"Why not?" he said. "Provided it's more or less what I've been saying. Now if you'll wait a minute I'll see if they've got that dope on that man Fane."

I had to wait about ten minutes, and then Rill came in and handed me an envelope. He walked with me to the lift and he was geniality itself. That was what pleased me. As I saw it, there was nothing to be genial about.

I went straight back to the Yard. Wharton was in, and like a hen trying to hatch two clutches at once. Information was still coming in about Fane.

"Here's some that'll surprise you," I said. "Fane used to work for Stalman and Company."

He gasped. A vacant look went across the room as he got up from his desk.

"You mean he was known to Rill and Conn?"

"Almost certainly. It's all in the envelope."

He had it out of my hand almost before I'd mentioned it. I left him to it. Half an hour later I'd dictated those alibis and had copies ready for signature. When I came back it was with an idea. I thought it was one that would even sound attractive to Wharton.

CHAPTER XVI
CLOSING THE GAP

I WASN'T able to leave till two o'clock: it took me all that interval to find out from Tom Holberg where Carlo Romano and his Latin Rhythm were playing. I'd been afraid they'd split up or disbanded, but they were still going strong and playing the halls. They were actually on at the Empire, Ironbridge, as I'll call it, and that wasn't more than ten miles from the Archdale Hotel and Sally de Freece. It was one of my few strokes of luck.

It was just after five o'clock when I got to Ironbridge and the taxi took me straight to the Empire. Mr. Romano, I was told, was staying at a hotel called the Warwick, on Silver Street, at the near end. It was a clean-looking, unpretentious sort of place and Romano was in his room. I was told to go up.

Bernardo had come up the hard way from Hoxton. Romano was a cockney, too, though with only a trace of accent: a short, thick-set man of about forty with side-burns that gave a somewhat romantic look, and the usual smear of a moustache. The horn-rims—he'd been working at some music scores—seemed a bit incongruous. I was to like him much better than Bernardo. He didn't throw his weight about.

"You wanted to see me?"

I gave him the warrant card. He looked at it and he looked at me.

"Scotland Yard. Not one of my boys?"

"Not a bit of it. No trouble for anyone. Just some information we think you might be able to give us. May I sit down?"

I offered him my cigarette case and held the lighter. He still wasn't too happy.

"This has to be strictly between just you and the Yard," I told him. "I'm not even taking a statement. If anything should happen to arise I guarantee here and now that your name will never be mentioned. It's to do with that Tynworth murder, and the Fane murder. We think they're connected. Maybe you've read the papers."

"Yes," he said, and then he looked up. "Do you know, I've been half expecting this. You knew Tynworth's wife used to be with my band?"

"We knew it, but it's only now that she seems important. Really important. I may tell you we've already seen her twice."

"You know she's teaming up with Bernardo? Taking her old name?"

"Yes," I said. "What was she like with you?"

"Good," he said. "She had everything. Bit of a blow to me when she suddenly sprung it on me she was marrying that Lord Tynworth."

There was no reason to spin things out, so I came straight to the point.

"When you say you were surprised, you don't mean you expected her to marry someone else?"

"Don't know about marrying," he said, "but there *was* someone else."

"You actually saw him?"

"Yes," he said slowly. "Not more than once—or twice. A big bluff sort of man. Looked about fifty."

"You didn't know his name?"

"No," he said. "That was her business. So long as she did her job her private life was her own. She wouldn't have thanked me to go poking my nose in."

"You didn't by chance guess if he was in any way connected with racing?"

"Wait a minute," he said. "You've got something there. Once or twice she gave us some damn good tips. Remember when Mayo won the Loamshire? That was one. Came in at a hundred to eight."

I smiled suggestively.

"Was that what bought her a mink coat?"

"Might have been. She couldn't have got it out of what she was getting with me, not that kind of mink."

"You ever have any suspicion this man was keeping her?"

He shrugged his shoulders.

"I can't say. You know how it is. And it was her business."

He was remembering something.

"Yes?" I said.

His smile was a bit feeble.

"Well, I wouldn't like to make any trouble. You know how it is."

I had to reassure him all over again. I even had to hint about confidences being better than evidence in a witness-box. Then he loosened up.

Where they'd been playing that particular night, Sally had had her own small dressing-room. After the first house the man turned up and there was a scene. He hadn't witnessed it himself but one of his boys had heard things. Sally had set about the man like a tigress.

"I don't know if he was exaggerating," he said, "but according to him she was calling this pal of hers all the filthiest names under the sun before she kicked him out. Mind you, she did have a temper. And she wasn't too careful about language."

"And how long after that when she left you?"

"Funny you should ask that," he said, "but it was practically at once. Sprung on me she was marrying that Lord Tynworth. Mind you, she was decent about it. Made no bones about paying up for the broken contract."

I got up. I said we were most grateful and his confidence would be respected.

"Just one last thing."

I described Rill first, and it didn't ring a bell. Then I described Conn. *That did.*

As I went downstairs I was wondering about the quickest way to get to the Archdale. I decided on a taxi. It cost a packet, but it did get me there in what I thought might be plenty of time ahead of Bernardo's show.

I went straight up to her room and knocked. I heard a movement inside. The door opened. There was a little gasp as she saw me. Then the lip drooped.

"You again?"

"Yes," I said and stepped inside.

"Where's the menagerie?"

"Just myself," I said. "The warrant card, if you like to see it?"

"What d'you want this time?"

I sat down on the hard chair. She took the easy one and helped herself to a cigarette from her bag. She was wearing a kind of house gown, and it was tight about her knees as she sat.

"I'm putting two things up to you," I said. "Either you answer a whole lot of questions or you'll be taken to the Yard to answer them there. And, believe me, I'm serious. Also I can tell you this. You give me the information I want and I'll guarantee it shall be kept strictly confidential. If not, then we'll have you in the witness-box. What that'll do for you, and your career, I don't know. I doubt if there'll be a career."

"What sort of information?"

"All sorts. Let's begin with you and Conn."

She shot me a look. She looked away and she was moistening her lips.

"You know a lot, don't you?"

"It would surprise you. Scotland Yard's a pretty big organisation. And we're dealing with a murder. Two murders. Or have you forgotten?"

"Sarcastic, eh?" She gave a little laugh. "And what about Conn?"

Then she was looking at me. I could almost see her mind working.

"Don't tell me that dirty swine has got caught out at last?"

"He's got a lot of things to explain," I said. "Maybe he won't be able to explain—if you decide otherwise."

"And suppose I do things my own way?"

"Sorry to spoil your pleasure, but there's only one way—our way. Start anything on your own and you'll be in for trouble. And I mean trouble."

Her foot was tapping the carpet. She stubbed out the cigarette and lighted another. She still didn't speak.

"Try it another way, if you like," I said. "Suppose I start telling you things?"

"Have it your own way."

"Right," I said. "I don't claim truth in every detail, but here's the broad picture. Conn was your man. I don't know yet how it began, but that's how it was. He had plenty of money and he could give you a good time. I don't think he told you too much about himself except that he was connected with racing. It was very much later you discovered he was with Stalman and Company and a partner of Howard Rill. Then it was far too late. Instead of you getting even with him, he'd got even with you. Am I right?"

"Let's hear the rest."

"It's not so good—for you. All good times come to an end. You discovered you were pregnant."

That shook her. There was no need to tap the cigarette: the hand that held it out to the ash-tray shook off the ash.

"Let's cut it short," I said. "He wouldn't marry you and you were scared of an operation. There was that scene in your dressing-room when you called him every name under the sun. But you had to do something. Tynworth had been pestering you for years. He was still handy, so you married him. Your boy was an eight-months child, but nobody suspected it was anything but a slightly premature birth. And that's why you don't like that boy of yours—because you hate his father—his real father."

It was almost a minute before she spoke, and then she didn't look at me.

"And suppose I deny it?"

"If you do, then you won't get away with it as you've done with other lies. Think of that witness-box and counsel hammering away at you. Do you think a jury won't know the truth when he's finished with you?"

She still wouldn't speak.

"Let's go back to Conn," I said. "Conn's tough. After that dressing-room scene he hated you as much as you now hate him. He set out to ruin you. I don't know the ins and outs of how it can be worked through racing and betting, but he set about doing it, and he did it pretty effectively. Then there was the money you lost yourself."

"What money?"

I was getting tired of her. I got up. I put on my hat. "Perhaps it might be better to get you to talk at the Yard. I'll arrange it with the local police. Come to think of it, I can telephone from here."

She didn't let me get that far.

"All right, then. What is it you want to know?"

"Was I right in what I told you?"

"Well—yes."

"Then take it from there," I said, and sat down again. "Let's hear about that money you lost."

At the time, she said, she'd had no idea that Conn was connected with Rill, but she'd had an introduction to Rill and had been asked to his place. She'd gone three or four times and had ended up by owing about three thousand pounds.

"You told your husband?"

"No, but Conn did. That's when I realised just the kind of fool I'd been."

"What'd your husband do?"

"He said Rill'd have to be paid."

"I see. And that's how Rill got his feet well in at Old Farm. Did Conn do any gloating over you?"

"He didn't have to," she said. "He knew it was enough for him to show his ugly face. I could have murdered him."

"But he had a hold over you in that matter of the boy."

"Yes. And all the rest of it. That was one reason why I wanted to clear out and get right away. Bernardo gave me the chance."

"Yes," I said, "and that makes something else pretty clear. It was Conn who put pressure on you to get those jewels cleaned and so on?"

"Rill," she said. "But it was the same thing."

"How'd he know about them?"

She thought it was because she'd worn the paste rings and bracelet once at Rill's house.

"Opened my big mouth too wide," she told me sneeringly. "Most of them thought they were real and I had to go and tell them about the originals. Clever—that's what I was. Look where it's got me."

She'd been talking. She'd told me far more than I'd ever hoped to get and maybe she'd tell me the rest: explain things I still didn't understand. That's why I loosened up. I could have held over her the information she'd already given me, but there was something shabby about that. I'm no plaster saint, and I don't think Wharton would have hesitated, but there it was. We're not all built the same way.

"You've had a pretty raw deal," I said, "taking it all round."

"I don't know," she said. "It was my own fault."

"Not if those games at Rill's place weren't on the square. But tell me something. Now we've got so far, you might as well get everything off your mind. And we shan't bear any malice. How do you think Rill and Conn knew your husband brought those jewels to Old Farm?"

She didn't know.

"You knew Mrs. Drew was recommended to you by Rill?"

She did know that, of course. It was before she'd tumbled to the scheme to get even with her. I told her what we knew of Mrs. Drew as Rill's spy.

"Then it was her," she said. "She could have listened to anything."

"And why did your husband do such a foolish thing as to bring those jewels home?"

"That was partly because of me. I wanted to see them. So did Molly. I thought he was going to take them to the jewellers when he got to town on the Monday."

"And that private business you spoke of between your sister and your husband—what exactly was that?"

"You know," she said. "Sort of whispering in corners. When you came into a room you knew they'd been talking about you by the way they suddenly shut up."

"And the night you left Old Farm. You went to the safe and took the cases. Surely you must have known they weren't the cases belonging to your replicas?"

"I didn't," she said. "Honestly I didn't. I daren't have a light. Only a little torch. I just saw the cases and took them and locked them in a bag. When I got to the hotel and saw them and the sealing-wax, that's when I got scared. I asked the management about a safe-deposit place and they recommended one, and that's where I put them. Then when I heard about my husband's death I was scared again and went to get them out."

"Yes," I said. "Empty cases. You were as surprised as any of us. And you've no idea where the jewels are?"

She sneered.

"You ask me that? I thought you knew."

It was Conn or Rill she meant. I didn't disillusion her.

"But what about the replicas? Your replicas."

She shrugged her shoulders.

"Why don't you ask that sister of mine? She must know something."

"Why do you hate her?" I asked the question quietly.

"Do I?" Her eyes fell. "Maybe it's because we were always different. And that smug look of hers when she disapproved of me. To hell with her." The look was bitter. "Don't suppose I'll ever see her again. Maybe she'll marry a horse."

There was no point in staying longer, but just before I left I told her I'd known her people and had heard a lot about her when she was not much more than a girl. I began talking about Kettlebourne; and then I wished I hadn't, for her mouth suddenly puckered and as I went quietly out of the room she was sobbing her heart out. I was upset, too. I felt a certain smugness about the way I'd questioned her and set myself up as a judge. I remembered the old tag about there being something good in the worst of us. Not that I'd ever come to like Sally Finder, as I thought of her. And the curious thing was that, in spite of what I'd heard, I still couldn't help liking and furtively trusting her sister.

It was a slow train and a dreary journey back to town. Before I left I'd rung Herndown and had got from Molly Bolfray an answer to a certain question. I'd also rung Wharton that I couldn't be in till eleven o'clock and that, good though my news was, details could keep till the morning. In any case he knew what I had set out to find and could form his own conclusions.

I ought to have been pleased enough myself, and yet I wasn't. I'd had that idea about the eight-months baby and had pushed it to the back of my mind. Then it had crept insidiously back and I knew it would have to be tested. And everything had turned out miraculously. And yet, as I said, I wasn't altogether happy as I began writing my notes in the train. I couldn't get away from the tragedy of Sally Finder, even if it had been of her own making: the girl I'd heard such glowing things about all those years ago at Kettlebourne, and the woman whom I couldn't get from my mind. Those days before the war and how idyllic they seemed now: Molly and Sally and the infinite possibilities of youth, and then the feeling of squalor in that hotel room and the cheapness and tawdriness, and then the time when no make-up could hide age, and the freshness—even the illusion of it—had gone from the voice and Bernardo had long since found himself yet another woman.

But there wasn't anything of that in the notes, or at least Wharton didn't make a comment. He was delighted, almost ghoulishly so, when I reported in the next morning and he even asked me what I thought we should do next. What I felt was that we shouldn't hurry things. He was inclined, I think, to have another interview with Conn and Rill and to disturb them by what we now knew, especially if they were seen at the Yard. If he were hoping to play one off against the other or that nerves would go, then I thought he was underestimating both of them.

"Jewle's got an idea about that can of petrol that was carried in the car that night Tynworth's body was burnt," he told me. "He's got men on the job now, both at Hampstead and Cockfosters."

He didn't tell me what the idea was, and I was anxious in any case to get on with my reports. They took me till midday, and when I'd finished them I knew there were more questions I ought to have put to Sally.

I couldn't have expected her to explain, even if I'd been disposed to tell her, why her sister's prints had been on the sealing-wax of those empty cases. What I might have asked her was why Tynworth was having that day—Tuesday—in town. Something about that struck me wrong and the more I thought about it the more peculiar it seemed. What possible business did Tynworth have to do? The dramatic discovery of his body and all the attendant sensationalism had produced nothing to the effect that Tynworth had been expected to see this one or that on that Tuesday but hadn't turned up. As for shopping, Molly had helped pack his bag: the bag that had been deposited at the Airport Building. And he'd bought new clothes in Chelmsford. Why, then, hadn't he left Old Farm on, say, the Tuesday afternoon and done any little thing there still remained to do before the next morning's trip?

There was another thing. I couldn't get out of my head the idea that something had been behind that huge, lower-middle-class caravanserai of a hotel. It was a place where one could hide one's self—that's what I was forced to think. The more people, the easier to hide. And Tynworth hadn't registered under his own name.

I'd actually thought of that when I was only halfway through the reports. Something made me ring Wharton.

"You haven't done anything about interviewing that Mrs. Drew?"

"Oh yes," he said. "Soon as you gave me that outline this morning I knew she had to fit in. She's being collected now. Ought to be here at any minute."

"What about Matthews at Old Farm? Any of those clothes we took from Fane's place Tynworth's?"

"Oh yes," he said, and chuckled. "Quite a few of 'em."

It was midday when I'd finished, as I'd said, and I hurried up to Wharton's room. I was just in time to see Mrs. Drew going, and she was looking as if she'd been put through a wringer. Wharton can be pretty grim when he knows there's cause.

"Everything fine," he told me. "You can see her statement later, but she blabbed everything. She's the sister of Conn's housekeeper and was out of a job when Conn got Rill to recommend her to Old Farm. She's a superior kind of woman who's had some bad luck apparently since her husband died and she was glad of the job. Conn briefed her before she went. She was to keep her ears open for everything that might be of interest and either telephone or write. You'll read the details, but she was the one who let Conn know the jewels were at Old Farm on the Sunday. It was Conn who told her to pack up and leave when she did."

"What's happening to her now?"

"When she's signed her statement she's going home and staying there. There's no telephone at her place and she'll be watched in case she attempts to communicate with either Conn or Rill."

"Be pretty awkward, won't it? Her sister'll be home this evening and she could take a message to Conn."

"Don't worry about the sister," he told me. "Soon as she leaves Conn's place tonight we're seeing Conn."

He rang Conn at Guiver Street while I was there and found him in. There wasn't much of the jocular in Wharton's voice. He told Conn he wanted to see him on certain highly important matters at seven o'clock that night and he gave him the option of being fetched to the Yard or being seen in his own house.

Conn wanted to know what matters. Wharton told him curtly certain new and serious information that had come to light. I could hear Conn still making time. Wharton cut him off.

"Sorry, but can't tell you more. Where's it to be? Here or at your place?"

Conn evidently said Hampstead. I could still hear him spluttering indignantly as Wharton rang off.

"That's fixed him," he told me. "There'll be a couple of men on his tail from now on. Hope he saves us time and tries to bolt."

"That new information you mentioned. Anything I don't know?"

"Of course you wouldn't," he said. "Jewle rang up from Hampstead. One of his men had got hold of Conn's usual garage, and what do you think?"

I had to say I didn't know. George almost drooled at the mouth.

"Conn wasn't satisfied with his petrol consumption, so he was trying things out on one of the new brands. Two gallons at a time. That's why he carried a tin in his car."

CHAPTER XVII
READ ALL ABOUT IT

IMMEDIATELY after lunch I was present at a conference that included three of Wharton's Big Wigs. It was a long-winded affair that developed into a tug-of-war between Wharton and the rest, and loyalty, if nothing else, made me pull on George's side. The Big Wigs wondered if we oughtn't to put off that inter-view with Conn till we had the completest information. Having been driven from that fox-hole, they suggested a flank attack on Rill: getting the names of some who had taken part in heavy gambling and pulling Rill in as a preliminary. Rill might then incriminate Conn still further. Wharton said he might get the names but not the information. People mightn't talk.

Then he produced his own heavy artillery. What we might get was nothing compared with what we already had. And that was enough to hold Conn for some hours. That was what would shatter Rill and make him talk. Only when he knew Conn was definitely incriminated would Rill really open his mouth to save his own skin.

George was the winner, and it was amusing to see him take the line that the Big Wigs themselves had brought him to their way of thinking and not the other way about. But everyone seemed satisfied and that was what mattered. It was why George and I left the Yard at half-past six that evening in a plain car and myself driving. By the time we were ready to ring Conn's bell it was as dark Egypt's night. Jewle's men would be in place or else the coat mightn't be long on his back.

Conn himself opened the door. His manner was quiet, but there wasn't a sign of panic. It was an old-fashioned house smelling faintly of warmth and cooking.

"In here, gentlemen."

That lounge had been modernised. Somehow we found ourselves being shepherded into chairs each side of the fire. Conn took the settee corner, his back to the door.

"Only the two of you?"

"Only the two of us," Wharton said, "and we won't waste your time. There're questions we'd like you to answer. You needn't answer them unless you like, and it's also my duty to warn you."

"Sounds a lot of fuss to me," Conn told him when the official patter was over. "Evidence against me, you say. About what?"

"A couple of murders," Wharton told him. "We're going to suggest to you that you're definitely concerned with both."

He opened his attaché-case, but he didn't put on his glasses. A moment or two and the suggestions began.

Conn was tough. That's why he held down a partnership with Rill. That's why he was obviously a good man for his job. But he wasn't tough enough. A man has to have a mental kink if he can stand Wharton's persistence and the imperturbability that is buttressed by obviously more than it chooses to divulge. And Conn wasn't a case for a psychopath. He was just a man who'd been grasping, revengeful and infinitely sure of himself, and yet had blundered into murder. At the back of his mind was the thought of eight o'clock on a certain morning and a nice walk and a long drop.

At first he absorbed plenty of punishment and he could find answers. What first shook him was the tremendous amount we knew about him and Sally de Freece, and the fact that Rill was now at the Yard and awaiting questioning. You could see him wondering just what Rill would tell. Wharton didn't let him recover. He told him about Mrs. Drew—and the two-gallon can of petrol. That was only a beginning, he said.

And then, believe it or not, Conn broke down.

"All right," he said. "I'll tell you the truth. Tynworth had promised to let us have those jewels as a guarantee till such time as he could raise some money. I didn't trust him and I had him watched when he left the train that Monday afternoon and followed to an hotel. I'd arranged for him to see me here at half-past six and he came. I was alone. He gave me what were supposed to be the jewels and wanted to go. I kept him here till I'd had a good look. He'd double-crossed me, as I'd suspected. What he'd brought were the replicas."

"And then?"

"Then I lost my temper. I got hold of him and shook the hell out of him. It was in this very room, and I smashed him away and he fell. He'd hit his head against that fender there. I thought I'd knocked him out. But he was dead."

"And that you're prepared to swear to?"

"Yes. You can't hang me for that. It was just an accident. It wasn't even manslaughter."

"Then why the body in the car? The groping about in the fog till you set fire to the body?"

"I just lost my head. I knew the story wouldn't be believed."

"Oh no," Wharton told him. "You were going to take good care there wouldn't be a story at all. And what about Fane? Was his death an accident, too? Did he knock himself out and strangle himself with his own tie?"

"Fane?" he said. He was like a man who's been under dope and is just recovering. He was realising what he'd done in confessing about Tynworth. Maybe he'd thought it would somehow buy us off.

"Yes, Fane," Wharton told him. "You killed him because he was trying to blackmail you."

"But I didn't! I've proved I didn't."

Wharton looked enquiringly at me.

"He means that alibi," I said. "Show him his statement. The last couple of pages, Mr. Conn. About your visit to the cinema. Tell us if it's accurate."

Conn glared at me from under his heavy eyebrows. He was suspecting some trick.

"That film's only been on this week. Every other night I can prove where I was to a minute."

"Read the statement," Wharton told him, and he didn't add that the Melodion had a continuous performance from half-past ten in the morning.

Conn read it. He said it was accurate.

"I just had time to see it myself this late afternoon," I said. "It was a good film, as you said. You remember it well?"

"Don't I say so?"

"Let's be sure, Mr. Conn. You still claim that you were enthralled by it? That you could go over the whole thing from beginning to end? That you didn't miss a word?"

"That's right." His look was wary. He wondered still if there were a catch and if he dared say more. He didn't.

"That seems all right, then," I told him. "You watched the performance that evening from a quarter to six till twenty-five minutes to eight and then sat on for a second showing. That being so, will you tell me this? Just when during that run of the picture did the breakdown occur. And how long did it last?"

He stared at me. Wharton stared too.

"Simple questions, Mr. Conn. Let's have the answers."

He must have sat rigid for quite a minute. Then his hand went to his pocket. When it came out a gun was in it.

"Don't be a fool," Wharton told him. "Don't you see you're putting a rope round your own neck?"

Conn was on his feet and backing towards the door. The gun wavered from Wharton to me and I felt a cold chill run down my spine. Wharton was forward in his chair. I wondered if he were going to spring, so that I could spring at the same time, but Conn was through the door. Wharton was across the room in a flash. He ripped back the curtain and lifted the window and let out a blast from a whistle. I heard a man come running up.

"He's armed! Pass the word through."

I heard the call echoing round the house. Wharton came back. He went straight on to the door.

"That's cooked his goose," he told me contemptuously. "Hope to God he doesn't use that gun. I want to see him hang."

He'd been making for the front door and I was just behind him when he heard the shot. We stepped out to the darkness beyond the hall light. A scuffle was going on somewhere to our left and we heard Jewle's voice. He came over.

"It's all right, sir. Tried to shoot himself when we collared him. Didn't hurt a thing."

"Get him away," Wharton said. "Leave a couple of men here till we can go through the house."

He went back to that lounge where he'd left his hat.

"So much for Conn," he told me. "Now let's go and have a little chat with Rill."

It was not till the following afternoon that we went to Herndown, and we didn't say we were coming. Tynworth's funeral had been in the morning and there was little reason to fear that we shouldn't find everyone at home.

Conn had been formally charged that morning and remanded. Rill had been turned loose the previous night but we'd know just where to find him when the evidence had piled up. His vehement claim was that he'd known nothing of Tynworth's death and that Conn had fooled him as he'd fooled us. Even when the body had been discovered and identified, he'd had only the vaguest of suspicions, and he'd known it just as well to keep them strictly to himself. About Fane he knew nothing. He said he'd been as surprised as anyone when Conn had worked that bluff of revealing—apparently in all good faith and innocence— that Fane had once been on the staff of Stalman and Company. As for the heavy gambling, he tried to laugh that off. Just a few friends in occasionally for a game, and we knew how it was. One wanted low stakes and then, sooner or later, the losers wanted their money back and the winners craved more excitement, and inevitably up went the stakes, and, as host, what could he do about it?

As for the jewels, they had been Conn's affair from beginning to end. That was a position from which Rill couldn't be budged.

"We'll get him," Wharton told me confidently when he'd gone. "He mightn't have known about the murder, but there's plenty we'll get him on. Conn hasn't opened his mouth yet, but he will. Rill in the witness-box! I wouldn't miss it for the coronation."

George was still in good form during that drive to Herndown, but just as we came in sight of Old Farm he thought it well to admonish me.

"You're sure you know where those jewels are?"

"I don't," I told him. "I never said I did. All I've got is a rough idea. A woman doesn't go to bed with a headache and then send for a sewing-basket just for nothing. Mending the boy's clothes couldn't have been so urgent as that. Or a torn nightgown."

He didn't seem to have much faith in me. I didn't have too much in myself.

"Ah, well—we can always squeeze it out of the Bolfray woman. Not that we needn't carry out the programme."

"You won't drop even a hint about the boy?"

"Good God, no!" he said. "Think I want to brand him for life? Aren't I a grandfather myself?"

I was drawing the car up at the porch. There'd been no sign of a soul and a Sabbatical air had been about the place, but the front door was open to the March sun. We knocked and waited. A woman appeared—the new cook, by the look of her.

"Mrs. Bolfray in?"

"No, sir. I think she's round at the stables."

"Thank you," Wharton said. "I'll see if I can find her."

He went off. Everything was working even better than schedule.

"Daisy in the nursery?" I asked her.

"Yes, sir. Least, I think she is. I believe she's just taking his little lordship out."

It quite startled me to hear that. Little Lord Tynworth, and I'd never realised it.

"I want to see her, so I'll go up," I said.

I'd given her one of my best smiles and she didn't seem to find it odd that I should be making for the stairs. On the landing I could hear Daisy talking to the boy. I tapped at the nursery door. Daisy gave a gasp as I walked in and her round face went a fiery red.

"We're just here to see Mrs. Bolfray again, Daisy, so I thought I'd have a quick look at Master Peter here. He's just going out?"

"Yes, sir. We're a bit late this afternoon."

He was a lovely boy and I could see something of his mother in him. I tried hard not to see his father. When I smiled down at him he smiled back. When I made a face, he laughed. Daisy was telling him to keep still while she buttoned his little coat and put on his gloves and I was looking round the room. It was just as I'd seen it before, and yet it wasn't. Something was missing, and for the life of me I couldn't think what.

"There now," Daisy said. "Now we're all ready."

That was as much for me as the boy. She picked him up and I closed the door behind us. At the bottom of the stairs I helped get the perambulator from its cubby-hole and push it over the step. Daisy tucked the boy in, fastened his strap and spread the rug across his knees. That was when I knew what was missing.

"Have a good walk," I said, and watched the perambulator for its first few yards. Then I nipped back up the stairs and into the nursery. I looked under both cot and low bed and in the two cupboards. I remembered Molly's room. It was unlocked and I went in. I looked under her bed. The key was in the door of the big wardrobe. I pushed frocks and coats aside and looked on the floor. I craned up to the shelf that ran above the hangers, and there it was tucked in a corner and partly covered by a scarf. There wasn't any mistaking it. It was that same teddy-bear I'd seen in the perambulator that day I'd first come to Herndown.

The joins were down the sides. At one of them, starting just under the armpit, were stitches in a silk that didn't quite match. I cut them with my knife till I could grope inside with a couple of fingers. When I'd moved the stuffing to one side I felt something hard. A couple of minutes later I was in the lounge and that teddy-bear was under my chair and I hoped my long legs would hide it.

Another minute or two and Wharton was coming in with Molly. It was the first time I'd seen her in a dress and it made her look less thin. She was looking quite cheerful as she came across to me.

"I've been telling Mrs. Bolfray about Conn and Rill," Wharton said, "and how she won't be bothered by that precious pair again. And she's had some good news of her own."

"Arthur and I think it's good," she told me. "The American cousin cabled yesterday to say he's flying over at once. We're expecting him at any time. Do you think he'll do something about Old Farm?"

"He just couldn't help it," I said. "And now Conn and Rill are out of the way you'll have more time to look round at things."

Wharton caught my eye and I signalled that all was well. He helped himself to a chair opposite Molly's.

"Well," he said, "business after pleasure. What we're really here for is to hear the truth at last about those jewels. After what you've been told, you know there's nothing now to fear."

Her face had flushed. It took her a moment or two to begin.

"I'm ashamed of myself. I don't often lie, but I had to. Honestly I had."

"There, there, there!" Wharton said consolingly. "Let's leave the apologies and get to the facts."

"That's nice of you. I didn't hope you'd take it like that. But there isn't really much to tell. Tom was going to take the jewels to the firm for cleaning when he went up on the Tuesday—"

"Wait a minute. You don't mean the Monday?"

"No, the Tuesday. He'd intended going on the Tuesday, and then Conn rang early on the Monday morning and Tom was tremendously upset. I'd already told him about Sally and he didn't know what to do. He even had an idea that she'd told Conn we had the jewels here. At any rate, Conn was insisting that the jewels should be brought to him that very day, and Tom managed to compromise on the night instead. He daren't upset Conn because he could easily get the trainer's licence taken away, and Conn said he only wanted the jewels as security." She gave a quick shake of the head. "I'm afraid I'm getting this a bit muddled."

"Not in the least."

"Well, I should have told you that no one knew Tom was going to America—no one outside the family, that is. Tom had his ticket for the Wednesday morning, but he and I—he didn't trust Sally by then—we worked out a scheme. He was to take the replicas to Conn and get out of the house before Conn discovered what they were, and then keep under cover in the hotel till the Wednesday morning. He gave me both keys of the safe and put the sealing-wax and his own thumb-marks on so that he'd know if they'd been tampered with by anyone else when he came back. We both so mistrusted Sally that we weren't even certain she didn't have a key herself."

"That American trip must have been very hush-hush if Mrs. Drew never got wind of it," Wharton said.

"It was," she told him. "Tom knew that Conn and Rill wouldn't like him to leave the country. But about the jewels. As soon as Tom had gone to town I began worrying about Sally. When she went out I locked myself in my room, removed the sealing-wax and took out the jewels and then put more wax on and my own thumb-marks and put the cases back. Later I pretended I had a bad headache and went up to bed and slit open Peter's teddy-bear and put the jewels inside. And I was glad afterwards that I did. Sally brought me my malted milk, and it wasn't like her to do anything for anybody. I wondered if she'd put anything in it. I had to sip some of it while she was there, but I did manage to get rid of the rest. I found out afterwards she brought some up to Arthur, of all people, and he was out like a log all night.

"Then later on Sally came in to see if I was asleep, and of course I was, or pretended to be. After that I heard her moving about, and then—you wouldn't believe it—but I actually did fall asleep. I didn't wake up till I heard her car. She nearly always used to clash her gears."

"And that's everything?"

"Well, I think so," she told Wharton hopefully.

"Very interesting," he said. "And what were you proposing to do with the jewels?"

"Why, see they were safe till Tom got back!"

"I see. And when you knew he would never come back?"

"Believe me or not, I was definitely going to make a parcel of them this very night and take them to Norman and Peake in the morning. I was just going to walk in and leave them and then they wouldn't know who I was. Then I was going to the nearest telephone—"

"All right, all right!" Wharton was chuckling. "A regular female conspiracy. But what about getting this famous teddy-bear?"

"I'll get it at once."

"No, don't move," I said. "I can save you the trouble."

I drew it out from under me. She stared. Her fingers went frightenedly to her mouth.

"You knew!"

My smile was a bit feeble. Pulling rabbits out of a hat is Wharton's prerogative, not mine.

And Wharton was on his feet and reaching for that teddy-bear. He didn't seem to be grudging me that preliminary curtain.

*

Just under an hour later we were going back to town—the first time, as Wharton said, with fifty thousand pounds' worth of stuff in the locker.

I wasn't feeling quite so happy as Wharton, for I was thinking I ought to have got on to Conn long before we actually did. Take that morning, for instance, when I'd first gone to Herndown. I'd seen Conn grasp Molly's wrist as he questioned her. What he'd been insisting—as she told me when I rang her that night from Birmingham—was that she knew where Sally was. So that would have qualified him for the name of Henry Balfour.

But Conn had also been to Herndown the day after Tynworth's death. That Colonel Porter had told me so in the Dog and Partridge. And why, in that same hotel, had the sight of me been such a surprise to Conn? He'd never seen me and so I must have been described to him. And by whom? Only by the man who'd called himself Lord Tynworth, ringing from the Airport Building to say that everything had gone off fine.

But it was easy, I could tell myself, to be wise after the event and rather morbid to dwell on what ought to have been done. I began thinking about the last half-hour at Herndown instead.

"What're you laughing at?" Wharton suddenly asked me.

I said I wasn't laughing—I was smiling. He answered his own question.

"No wonder," he said. "This business ought to put you in pretty solid with the insurance people."

But he was wrong. I'd been thinking of something far different.

Yale had come in and we'd stayed on for tea. Just before we were going George was talking to Yale and I was having a word with Molly as we went out to the car.

"Why don't you marry Yale?" I asked her. "I was watching during tea and he's more than got over that infatuation for Sally."

Her look was almost impudent.

"Maybe I will."

"Fine," I said. "You'll have Peter to start a family with. Sally'll never want him. I'm more than certain of that."

She didn't say anything. A shadow was on her face and I didn't want it there. That's why I went prattling on.

"Let us know and we'll scout round for a wedding present. Or would you rather like a godfather?"

"Why not both?" she told me. "Depends on what you'll give me."

"That's being mercenary," I said. "But I might kill two birds with one stone. What about giving you another couple of teddy-bears?"

THE END

Lightning Source UK Ltd.
Milton Keynes UK
UKHW011051180820
368381UK00001B/65